More . . .

"This is not a book that can be put down. It's so compelling, so dramatic, with strong suspense and mystery elements, that I had to find out what would happen. I normally don't read stories that involve stalking and crimes against women, especially involving sexual assault. They are painful and ugly. However, the women in this story take control of their lives and leave victimization behind. This book also speaks with authority about the LDS Church and especially tenets of the Church that continue to harm women. Fascinating details! It's written with a frightening intensity. I had to check the locks before I could go to sleep after finishing."

—Perri O'Shaughnessy,
New York Times bestselling author of *Unlucky in Law*

"Natalie Collins's *Wives and Sisters* is a journey through heartbreak, tragedy, and self-discovery with a courageous woman who dares to think for herself in a dogmatic society. This is a story for anyone who has ever questioned what they've been taught all their life; anyone who has ever doubted their self-worth, and everyone who loves to cheer on the underdog and watch them triumph in the end. You'll be glad you took this journey with her."

—Tina Wainscott, author of *I'll Be Watching You*

"The most astonishing thing about Natalie Collins's *Wives and Sisters* is not that it tells such a dramatic tale of betrayal, fundamentalism, denial, and abuse, but that it all rings so true. She perfectly captures the mixture of love, pain, and frustration that accompany surviving trauma in a society where victims are often silenced."

—Martha Beck, author of *Leaving the Saints: How I Lost the Mormons and Found My Faith*

"Fans will be stunned by this tense thriller that condemns extremist religions and social moral behavior at the cost of any segment of society . . . this fine tale provides food for thought when the powerful use morality as weapons of mass destruction."

—Harriet Klausner

"*Wives and Sisters* is a raw, emotional story that never gives in to sentimentality. It puts a plain, unvarnished face on the secret workings of the human soul and the price of blind faith."

—TheCelebrityCafe.com

"[An] amazing debut novel . . . There are a few things that make *Wives and Sisters* stand out. First off—though this is Collins's first novel, the tempo and pace at which the narrative is presented is that of a very seasoned author. Past and present are intricately interwoven to create a tapestry of almost palpable suspense which moves along at a pace that keeps the reader turning page after page. The writing is tight—there is no fat in this novel, and there are no long, brooding soliloquies to slow down the action. Collins tells her story with an economy of words that one rarely sees with new writers . . . *Wives and Sisters* is an amazing achievement, and . . . a just read. Natalie R. Collins is an author that we shall be seeing great things from in the future."

—ReadersRoom.com

"Well-written, fast-paced, Natalie Collins's *Wives and Sisters* is suspense-filled satisfaction with a bone-chilling, thought-provoking similarity to recent events. . . . [It] tugs at the heart and pulls at the mind. Author Natalie R. Collins, with the skill of the masters, splashes truth, and warnings against dangers of concealing truth, onto the pages of this must-read thriller."

—WritersAndReadersNetwork.com

"The author brings authentic color and gripping detail to her book which underscores the very real mentality of protecting the Church at all costs."

—*Tucson Citizen*

"Natalie R. Collins has perfected Utah's voice . . . [Readers] may also sense the attraction of this place nestled at the foot of the Wasatch Mountains and even understand at a visceral level why it is so important that religion and government be kept completely and forever separated. That, for any reader, should put *Wives and Sisters* at the top of their bedtime reading list for 2005."

—Carolyn Howard-Johnson,
author of *This Is the Place,* for BookPleasures.com

Wives

and

Sisters

Natalie R. Collins

St. Martin's Paperbacks

WIVES AND SISTERS

Copyright © 2004 by Natalie R. Collins.
Excerpt from *Behind Closed Doors* copyright © 2006 by Natalie R. Collins.

Library of Congress Catalog Card Number: 2004048387

ISBN: 0-312-93366-5
EAN: 9780312-93366-1

Printed in the United States of America

St. Martin's Press hardcover edition / October 2004
St. Martin's Paperbacks edition / March 2006

St. Martin's Paperbacks are published by St. Martin's Press, 175 Fifth Avenue, New York, NY 10010.

10 9 8 7 6 5 4 3 2 1

To my daughters, Cambre and Carissa, who proudly proclaim, "My mom writes books." Your undaunted faith and eternal optimism have been proven true. And to all of the Allis of the world: May you make peace with the past without destroying your future.

Acknowledgments

It's a little scary to list all the people who have helped and encouraged me in my writing career, because I'm afraid I will leave someone out, but I'm going to do my best. First of all, to my husband and two daughters, I realize you've never really "understood" my need to write, but have always been proud of the fact I succeeded. My partner at ReadersRoom.com, Rob Holden, has not only been a great person to do business with, but also has been the person who kicked me in the behind when needed, and the rock that allowed me to maintain faith in myself and my writing. My writing cronies Peggy Tibbetts, Calista Cates Stanturf, Mary "Dejah" Tyler, and Christine Funk are always there to answer questions, read a synopsis, bounce title ideas off of, or just listen to me complain. They are all extremely talented writers and I wish them every success in the future. Also, the incredibly talented Jennifer Apodaca, author of the Samantha Shaw Mystery Series, has offered a great supply of support and is a wonderful cheerleader. I'm incredibly thankful to my agent, Karen Solem, who saw my vision in writing this book, and offered her support and guidance, and to Jennifer Weis, my editor, for her willingness to take a chance with this book and let it have life.

Poem for a Prophet

I cannot breathe today,
stagnant air burning my lungs,
my mind mired in sorrowful yesterdays.
So
many
wasted
days and anger cemented in my mind,
spackled mud on the toes of a child
who is carefree laughing full of joy.
Not me, anyone but me.

Your dark and twisted philosophies of love and life
shadow me throughout my days and I cannot
shake
them
off
no matter the care I take
in long sandpaper showers and scrubbing
my skin raw with soap,
it bleeds between my fingers
and sticks in my mind.
The mud won't wash off.

Why I cannot rid myself of this darkness you call glory
and mockery you sing hymns about,
seems most apparent in your everyday life, when
time stands still and you dress up in
your
blue
suited
Sunday best and make your way to
a building I cannot even fathom,

to a world I will not join
and a life I cannot embrace.
I don't belong.

You cannot touch me there, anymore, that deep
abyss I reserve for truth and you
amaze me still that giving up is the last thing
you will ever do, trying once again to
swallow
me
whole
in your words and your ironies and your
twin knives of love and harmony.
Your temple is my nightmare, your endowments
the very last thing I will ever touch.

I will destroy myself first, slowly and methodically,
drink acid from a rusted cup, recite nonsensical
prose and utter foolishness, and pass it off as
bright,
glorious
praise.
I shed my clothes and revel in a naked dance
of sex and lust and bodies intertwined and only
now does my future appear before me,
possible at last.

Will you love your brothers or sisters likewise, when they have committed a sin that cannot be atoned for without the shedding of their blood? Will you love that man or woman well enough to shed their blood? . . . I could refer to plenty of instances where men have righteously slain, in order to atone for their sins. I have seen scores and hundreds of people for whom there would have been a chance (in the last resurrection if there will be) if their lives had been taken and their blood spilled on the ground . . . This is loving our neighbors as ourselves; if he needs help, help him; and if he wants salvation and it is necessary to spill his blood on the earth in order that he may be saved, spill it . . . That is the way to love mankind.

—BRIGHAM YOUNG, second president of
the Church of Jesus Christ of Latter-day Saints
(*Deseret News*, February 18, 1857)

One

I was six years old the first time I had an inkling God would not always protect me.

My parents raised their children according to the strict tenets of the Church of Jesus Christ of Latter-day Saints. What was offered to us as truth was simple: all one had to do was be baptized, pay a faithful tithe, and follow the teachings of the Lord's prophets—nothing too difficult, even for a first grader to grasp. I swallowed it dutifully, wholeheartedly, relieved that life was simple and easy. I knew the difference between right and wrong. I knew the basic truths of God's plan for us. I felt comfortable and assured that I would wake up the next day knowing exactly what to expect.

On a sunny, warm April afternoon in 1972 my friend Cindy Caldwell and I blissfully played on her property, two miles from the nearest house. Eight-year-old Cindy had picked me as her best friend in the Farmington Fifth Ward, despite our two-year age difference. I had a serious case of hero worship.

Our playground was two acres of big boulders, trees and brush, and lots of places to hide—a child's paradise. We'd received permission to go there from Cindy's mother, who was grateful for anything to distract us so she could plan her Relief Society lesson.

We knelt by the side of the shallow, ice-cold creek that flowed down from high up in the Wasatch Mountains. By the time it reached us—near the valley floor—it had divided many times, and was now no more than a small stream of water. We dipped our Barbies into the swimming hole we'd formed for them by damming up the water with rocks and twigs. The older and wiser Cindy explained to me the consequences of being baptized, something that had happened to her just a month before.

". . . And when you get baptized, you can't sin anymore, 'cause God won't automatically forgive you." She gave me a knowing look. "You don't have to worry about that yet, Alli. You still have two more years."

"What's a sin?"

"A sin is when you do something really bad, like steal something, or touch somebody's private parts. After you get baptized, if you do that stuff, you have to repent and tell the bishop."

I was quiet as I digested this information. I thought of the time several weeks before when my good friend Bernice Franklin and I had explored each other's girl parts while we played doctor. I remembered it felt really good when Bernice touched me there, and I squirmed with the memory. Feeling good was a sin? I was in deep trouble.

I also did not want to have to tell our bishop about my sins. Bishop Harwood was a big, loud, jovial man with shiny red cheeks, almost no hair on his head, and great tufts of it everywhere else we could see, including his nostrils. It sprang from the dark holes like a big unruly hair forest, hiding all types of unknown beasts and vengeful creatures. I had a hard time looking at him without fixating on his nose and all the wiry hair that came out of it.

Our neighbor, Rodney Crowell, who was in my first

grade class at school, spent the entire summer a year before trying to convince Bernice and me that the bishop was a werewolf. I told my mother, and Rodney didn't come out of his house for a week. He never brought up the werewolf theory again.

"Now, when they baptize you, they do this," Cindy prattled on, apparently not noticing my discomfort. She took her Barbie and placed her in the water. "I baptize you, Barbie Caldwell, in the name of God the Father, Jesus Christ, and the Holy Ghost."

She dipped her Barbie under the water and held her there.

"How do you keep from drowning?"

"Silly!" Cindy giggled as she pulled the doll from the water and shook it off. "They don't hold you down very long. They just dip you down and then lift you back up."

She moved from the side of the creek to the little chapel we had built a short distance away. "Now we need to confirm them . . ."

A *crrrr-aaaackkk* filled our ears, and we both jumped and screamed, as only little girls can. After our first shaken moments of terror, we looked at each other and Cindy said, "Ralph!"

Cindy's brother, Ralph, sixteen and a bully, lived to torment us. He'd gotten his first shotgun for Christmas that year and was always up at the Caldwell property looking for rabbits, squirrels, birds, and other small creatures he could torture and murder.

"Ralph!" she yelled, standing up. Her knees were covered with dirt and little red dents from the pebbles we knelt on. She had her hands on her hips, like my mother did when she scolded us. "Ralph, where are you? You're gonna get it. When I tell Mom you shot around us with your gun, you'll never see it again! You know Dad will take it."

No answer came, no snicker, no sign of Ralph. I fidgeted with uneasiness, and realized I had to pee badly and the only toilet was far away.

Cindy looked around, shrugged her shoulders, and sat back down. As she reached for her Barbie, we heard the snap of a tree branch and we both jumped again.

"Knock it off, Ralph! Dammit! Mom's gonna kill you."

"You said a bad word!"

Cindy gave me an impatient look and turned back to the trees where we believed Ralph to be hidden.

"Is swearing a sin?" I needed to know, because my devoutly religious father swore all the time.

"Alli!"

We looked over to the area across the creek where we'd heard the noise, and I saw a sight that caused my heart to jump in my chest—the barrel of a rifle pointed directly at us. We couldn't clearly see the person holding the rifle because he wore camouflage, but he sported a dark beard peppered with gray. Ralph shaved once a month at best.

Slowly it hit me. This was not Cindy's brother.

We were going to die.

"Stand up," ordered the man. His unfamiliar gruff voice caused prickles of sheer terror to run up and down my legs and arms.

I couldn't move.

Slowly, Cindy stood up.

"Stand up!" he ordered again. Cindy grabbed me by the hand and pulled me to my feet. I'd sat too long, and my feet and legs had gone to sleep. Now pins and needles ran through them as the blood began to circulate. I couldn't help it—I hopped up and down, trying to ease the pain.

"Knock it off, you little bitch!" he ordered. I couldn't stop dancing, and he lifted his rifle and aimed it directly at me. I think my heart stopped, and Cindy jumped in front of me, as though she were going to save me. He jerked the rifle up into the sky and fired a warning shot.

I peed my pants right then.

"Take off your clothes," he commanded. "Take them off now!"

We still could not see much of him besides his beard and the gun as he stayed hidden behind the tree and heavy brush.

"We won't take off our clothes!" Cindy said in a brave voice. "We won't. You'll have to kill us."

It was quiet for a moment. I imagined he was deciding whether or not he wanted to murder us. I was too young to consider any of the implications of our removing our clothes. Silently, I prayed, vowing fervently to never tattle again, never sneak cookies when I had been told no, never pick on my brother Kevin.

Please, God, please, don't let us die. Don't let the man kill us. Please save us. I promise I'll be good.

"All right," he yelled. "Little blond girl, you run. Run now. Run fast. Don't look back or I'll shoot you."

He meant me. Cindy had beautiful long brown hair that curled up at the ends. I hesitated. I wasn't going to leave my friend.

"No," I said in a squeaky voice, the loudest I could manage. "No. I won't leave her." I grabbed Cindy's hand and pulled her with me, and we ran. My shoes were loose, because Mom always bought them big so they would last. I lost them both as we ran and didn't dare stop to look back or to pick them up. Fleetingly, I thought of my mother and father. They would be mad I had lost my shoes. We didn't have much money.

I heard him crashing through the brush as he chased us. I held tightly to Cindy's hand, and I turned for just one second to see if he was close.

It was a mistake.

I tripped over a large root pushing up through the dirt, and the last thing I remembered was hitting my head on a large rock. When I woke up, cold, wet, and terrified, there was no sign of Cindy. Frozen with fear, I couldn't move, afraid the man was still there, afraid he would shoot me. I prayed silently, the same words over and over: *Dear God, please save us. Dear God, please save us.*

But there was no longer an "us." It was only me. Where was Cindy? How long I laid there I didn't know, but the cold, desperate fear that kept me unmoving gradually released its hold and I slowly, cautiously sat up. I looked around but could see no one.

"Cindy?" I whispered. "Cindy?"

She didn't answer. I moved my head slowly, and the world swayed as I sat up and looked around me.

"Cindy?" A little louder, but still no answer. The sun was setting now in the late afternoon sky, and soon it would be dark. Our mothers would be wondering where we were. Did Cindy go home without me? Was she tired of a little girl tagging along with her?

I stood, all shaky, looking around carefully, watching for the bearded man with a gun.

"Cindy? Where are you?"

I heard a slight crack from behind me, like the sound a twig makes when somebody steps on it, and I whirled around but could see nothing. I walked backward away from the noise, *Dear God, please save us,* running through my head; and I mouthed the words silently. I heard nothing more, but knew someone was out there. Someone was watching and waiting for me.

Still walking backward, I tiptoed off the pathway and into a copse of trees and bushes, heavy and scratchy. I tore my arms and legs on the brambles, and there was blood in my eyes from my earlier fall, but I didn't care. My fear numbed my pain. I settled down onto the ground in the bushes and waited, praying silently all the while, ignoring the tickles that could be bugs. I couldn't move.

I waited for Cindy to come back. I waited for God to save us. I waited.

"Cinnnnndy? Alllllliissonn?" a voice called. A voice I recognized—my father.

It was dark now, and with each deepening shade of gloom my fear had intensified, but I couldn't move. Couldn't find my own way to safety.

"Daddy? Daddy!" I tried to jump to my feet and yell, but I couldn't keep my balance and I fell over again, the bushes and brambles scratching at me more. The sound of his voice released some of my fear; and I reached up and touched my head, feeling the deep wound that no longer bled. *I'm hurt. Someone help me.* My left eye was partially glued shut, probably from dried blood, and I squinted with my right, trying to compensate for my lost vision. All this I realized now that I felt rescue was close.

"Help!" I yelled. It came out as a squeak. "Daddy!" It wasn't very loud, but it was enough.

"Hey, Richard, over here," yelled another voice. I recognized it as belonging to Brother Jacobsen, one of our neighbors. He moved toward me, and the flashlight hit my eyes, momentarily blinding me.

"Oh, shit," he muttered as he picked me up, and I heard the voices as other searchers came to us. "Call an ambulance, she's hurt."

My body went limp as I rested in the comfort of his arms. Safe. I was safe. I heard the squawk of a radio and knew our local police force must be here also, although I had a hard time discerning the shapes that surrounded me—until one stepped forward.

"Allison, where's Cindy?" It was her dad.

"I-I don't know. I think the bad man took her." I felt responsible.

It didn't matter that I prayed, or that I ran—I had turned

to look back and fallen. Now Cindy was gone. God must be terribly mad at me.

They took me to the hospital in Ogden. I screamed when the doctor came at me with the curved needle and must have passed out again. I woke up in a hospital room with my mother asleep in the chair by my bedside. The doctors and nurses were in and out of my room many times during the night, and I heard whispered words I didn't understand. Their sad faces as they exchanged mournful glances with my mother made me feel all the more guilty and responsible. Everyone was sad—sad that Cindy was missing, I guessed, and because I was not. The beautiful girl with the brown curls should have been the one saved.

All I wanted to do was sleep. When they asked me where Cindy was, I shrugged my shoulders. I didn't know where she was, and that hurt.

"It was the man. The man with the beard. He shot his gun at us. He threatened to kill us if we didn't take our clothes off."

I told that same story to the police officer standing by the side of my bed the next day. He glanced uneasily at my father and Mr. Caldwell, Cindy's dad, and I was scared. Was he getting ready to arrest me? If I hadn't turned and looked, I wouldn't have fallen. Cindy might still be safe.

Soon after the policeman left, my parents took me home and put me in bed. They moved my younger sister Corrie's pillow and books to the room that, for the time being, she was forced to share with our youngest sisters, the Little Girls. She glared at me before leaving, and I turned away and tried to bury myself under the covers. My head throbbed and the gash on my forehead, which had required twenty-four stitches, ached and itched. I kept touching it, perhaps to remind myself I was still alive.

I fell asleep, and when I woke up I could hear a hushed voice through the partially open door.

"She hasn't asked about Cindy . . . No, I think she's in shock . . . No . . . No, not yet . . . Yes, she was. She was . . ."

My mother was on the phone. Her voice went quieter, and I could no longer make out the words. I got out of bed and wobbled across the floor, still dizzy and feeling sick to my stomach. My head throbbed with each step I took, and it seemed as if I walked miles before I reached the door. I opened it a little wider and slipped through, following my mother's voice to the kitchen. I stood in the doorway and listened.

"No, there's no sign of . . . no sign of rape or abuse . . . They found footprints that led to tire tracks . . . Only one set. They think he . . ." Her voice cracked as she struggled to regain her composure. She glanced over to the doorway and gasped when she saw me standing there.

"I'll call you back," she said quickly into the phone and replaced it on the cradle. She hastily wiped away her tears and came toward me.

"Allison, honey, you need to get back in bed. You've been hurt. The doctor said you have to stay down for at least another day or two."

"Where's Cindy?"

She didn't answer. I asked again.

"Honey, we don't know," she said, her chest heaving as she spoke. My mother rarely cried, except at church services when the spirit moved her, and my heart clutched as I watched her agony. Her face was lined, her eyes deep and mournful, her dark brown hair spotted with gray. My mother looked old to me for the first time—old and very tired. The mother who had worn lipstick every day—"Always wear lipstick for your husband, Alli, even if you don't have time to do anything else"—was gone.

I remembered the boxes of Clairol hair dye on the kitchen counter next to the sink, my mother with her head under the tap, an old towel wrapped around her shoulders as she rinsed. I'd stood next to her with the ingredients, magical, mystical women things that enhanced our "beauty" and made us "alluring," at least according to the box. I'd handed each thing to her as she asked for it, including the actual dye packet—in a color called chestnut.

Now I realized I couldn't remember the last time she had colored her hair, or worn lipstick—even for church.

She was so sad, so sad for Cindy. But Cindy had just disappeared. These changes in my mother had been happening for a long time. Was this my fault? Had I disappointed her? Was Cindy's disappearance going to be the worst of all the things I had done?

No one was glad that I was safe and had not been stolen away, but I understood that. I let them down. I didn't save Cindy.

Mother reached up as if to wipe the tears again, but they were no longer there. She had become my mother again, the tired mother, and it was her job to protect me. She put on her "mother" face, the one she always wore when dealing with us children and our problems. It was her job to wipe our runny noses, to clean up the vomit and diarrhea, to bathe us and feed us.

My father went to work and came home, a hot meal on his table each morning and night. His job was to lead our household, to give us Priesthood blessings, to see we didn't stray from the teachings of the church. Should we become errant, it was also his job to see we were disciplined and led back into the fold. This often meant whippings with his belt, or any other item that was handy.

But my mother—she did the real dirty work. The cleanup. Sometimes that meant explaining why bad things happened, and convincing us that it really did hurt my father more than it hurt us. And often, that meant hiding our little indiscretions from the head of the household. In our tight-knit Mormon community, where everyone knew each other and spent hours of each week in meetings together, this often backfired on her, but she continued to do it. It was her job.

She hustled me back to bed, pulled the covers up to my chin, and stroked my cheek before she left the room. Today there was no explanation. That meant things were really bad.

I knew she couldn't protect me. If God couldn't save us, the most powerful being in the universe, what could I expect my mother to do?

Two

Farmington is a bedroom community outside Salt Lake City. it had been settled years before by Mormon pioneers, and my own father had been born in a house just a block from where we lived now. Our small house sat nestled in the foothills of the Wasatch Mountains. The old redbrick one-story home had four bedrooms, one bathroom, and no privacy. I was the oldest of five children born to my parents Under the Covenant, which meant we'd been born to parents who'd been married in the Mormon Temple.

My brother Kevin was two years younger than I, and Corrie followed closely after him. My two youngest sisters, born only thirteen months apart, were inseparable, and we called them "the Little Girls." We never called them by their given names—Christy and Cathy.

My mother stayed close by my side for the first few months after Cindy disappeared, walking me to and from school and rarely letting me out of her sight. Slowly, though, life returned to normal—for most people—and my parents began to relax, loosening the tight grip fear had brought to our household. I thought about Cindy every day, but no one ever said her name aloud, including me.

One early fall night about three months after the kidnapping, my parents hired a baby-sitter so they could attend an adults-only Elders Quorum party. I guessed that for my mother the end-of-summer barbecue offered an escape from the everyday world of messy kids, an angry husband, and laundry and cleaning that was never completely done.

While my father left to pick up our chaperone for the evening, my mother sat at the dressing table in her room applying a light coat of makeup and putting lipstick on, while I sat on her bed and watched. Catching sight of me in the mirror, she smiled brightly, giving me a glimpse of the "old mother." I should have been happy to see the woman I missed return, but I wasn't. I moved from the bed and knelt at the foot of her chair, wrapping my arms tightly around her legs, which were clad in white capris that fell modestly below her knees to cover her "garments"—the sacred Mormon underwear she wore. She allowed me to cling, and even bent over to offer me a light coating of lipstick.

I declined and buried my head in her pant leg, despite the fact I knew it wasn't going to work. She was leaving even though I was terrified the bearded man would return while she was gone and whisk me away to suffer the same unknown fate as Cindy. Even if I voiced these fears, Mom, desperate for a break from her mundane life, would go. She peeled my arms from around her leg and stood up, patting my head softly. We heard voices in the living room, and I knew my father was back with Jeannie, our thirteen-year-old baby-sitter. I trailed behind Mom closely as she left her bedroom and went to join them.

My younger brother Kevin, four years old and "full of spit and vinegar," as Grandma liked to say, was excited to have someone new to torment for a few hours, and he was already running around Jeannie in a dizzying circle. Corrie, just barely three, had a picture book clutched in her hands tightly and was wedged on the floor between the old brown sofa and a big easy chair. It was her "reading place."

She ignored all that went on around her. The two Little Girls, still just babies, had already been put to bed for the evening.

Jeannie, a nervous girl with frizzy brown hair and a face full of acne, listened carefully to my mother's instructions, nodding her head and looking very responsible and grown up. I wasn't fooled—she'd been here before. I knew the minute my parents pulled out of our driveway she would pick up the phone to call her friends, ignoring those of us who were still awake until dark spread across the Wasatch Front. Then she would put Kevin and Corrie to bed—Kevin arguing and yelling, Corrie quietly doing as she was told—and she and I would watch television. The plan was always the same. As soon as the lights from my parents' car flashed across the living room window, I would race to bed and they would be none the wiser.

The evening progressed as I knew it would, and when my scheduled bedtime—nine on a weekend night—arrived, Jeannie and I sat close together on the couch watching sitcoms. I had the feeling she was afraid of the dark, which surprised me a lot—at thirteen, she was practically a grown-up.

Following the ten o'clock news was *Nightmare Theater,* a strange choice for a girl who was very nervous and jumpy. Jeannie loved it, though, as long as she didn't have to watch it alone. I was alternately proud she wanted me with her and scared we were breaking my father's rules. In addition, I didn't much care to be scared any more. The bearded man was still too close in my mind.

That night's fare was "The Pit and the Pendulum," narrated by Vincent Price. As we sat engrossed a *thump-thump-thump* from the back stairs caused both of us to jump.

"Can you hear that? Can you?" Jeannie asked in an urgent whisper.

It sounded like footsteps. *No. Please, no. He's back. No.* Someone or something thumped up from our dark basement, headed to the room where we sat. Jeannie jumped from the couch and grabbed my mother's favorite vase off the top of the TV.

"My mom will kill you if you break that." Silly, random thoughts rushed through my six-year-old brain: my parents would know I hadn't been in bed if the bearded man took me; I would have to pay for the vase, if it broke, out of my allowance, which was meager; I forgot to lock the basement door. Terror pulsated through my veins, and I thought of Cindy.

God must really hate me.

As if my words about the vase made her realize we were no match for an intruder, Jeannie grabbed my hand and pulled me out the front door. In her terror, she didn't think of my brother and sisters, asleep in their rooms. I balked, pulling back as she dragged me.

"What about the kids? We have to get them."

She ignored me and tugged hard on my arm. We ran to the neighbor's house and pounded on the door.

When my parents drove up twenty minutes later, called home by the neighbors, the house was surrounded by police cars and the neighborhood men and ward members had formed a search party. They went through it from top to bottom and found nothing except a few small clues. The basement door which I had forgotten to lock was now firmly fastened. The side door, which I remembered to lock, was now ajar. On the fourth stair from the top a muddy footprint marred the normally clean linoleum.

Jeannie sobbed on a neighbor's shoulder as she tried to explain to my parents what happened. My father's face was tight, his thick brows knitted close together, his nose and ears bright red, his forehead wrinkled. I knew that look: he was embarrassed in front of his friends and fellow church members, and I was the cause. My mother tried to mollify him, her face a mask, her nervous fingers twisting and turning a napkin she must have brought back from the barbe-cue. Her evening out had been ruined.

Mom hastily assured everyone no one had been there, that my father must have left the footprint when he came in from the backyard earlier in the day, and we were fine. I didn't want anyone to leave. The anger emanating from my father told me that my immediate future held severe disci-pline and pain. His anger toward me was palpable.

The neighbor with the soggy shoulder offered to drive Jeannie home. The police left after my father assured them we would call if anything else appeared awry.

When we were alone, my father's anger boiled over. If only I'd gone to bed on time, I thought, as his hand clamped down on my shoulder and he led me to his room, where he pulled his belt out of the loops on his pants. But what would that have changed? Jeannie wouldn't let me go to bed. And even if she had, I knew she would have woken me up when she heard the noise—either that, or fled leav-ing me there for a monster. I firmly believed the intruder was the bearded man.

Later, when my father's anger was spent, my mother ran me a warm bath to soothe my aching, bruised backside. She wasn't gentle, though. She harshly told me I had imag-ined the noise. When I pointed out the baby-sitter heard it first, she brushed it off as one of the Little Girls thumping the wall in her sleep.

"But their room is nowhere near the stairs, Mom. I was standing right there. I heard it."

"You're tired. Your imagination is working overtime. No one was here."

"But, Mom," I protested. "What if it was him? What if he came back for me?"

"Him?"

"Him. The bearded man."

My mother blanched, her lips tightening together, her eyes wide.

"No one was here," she reiterated. "No one. And how could you just run off and leave the other kids? What if someone *had* been here? Who would have protected them?"

What did my mother want from me? I didn't understand. I was only six. How could it be I was so responsible for the people around me? If it were true, I'd done a miserable job in that respect so far. I couldn't protect Cindy nor could she protect herself, and she was older and stronger than me.

If it was true I was responsible for my brother and sisters, they were in for a rocky future. A very rocky future.

Three

Independence Day celebrations were nothing in Utah compared to the trappings surrounding Pioneer Day, a sacred Mormon holiday just three weeks later. A little more than a year after Cindy was taken, Pioneer Day, July 24, 1973, dawned hot and sunny.

The Saints were forced to flee Illinois after the Mormon founder and prophet, Joseph Smith Jr., was killed by an angry mob. Led by Brigham Young, the members of the church crossed an unforgiving and brutal wilderness, braving Indians, harsh weather, illness, and death. When they arrived in the Salt Lake Valley on July 24, local lore says a very sick Young sat up in his wagon, pointed his finger at the desert below him and said, "This is the place."

I heard the "this is the place" story many times growing up. My mother and father both came from prominent Mormon families, descended from "hardy pioneer stock"; and they were proud of the achievements of Utah's earliest residents. My father, Richard Lamont Jensen, had been born and raised in Farmington. He never left. My mother, Elise LaDell Smith, came from Logan, a city in northern Utah right next to the Idaho border. They met while they were at

Brigham Young University, the church-owned school almost all good young Mormons attended.

I hated the cold and the snow of northern Utah and cherished the too-brief summers. I wanted to live anywhere else. I dreamed of growing up in the South—chasing fireflies on hot summer nights, running barefoot for the entire summer, having lemonade and sandwiches on our veranda.

My mother always told me I had an overactive imagination.

"Those children don't run barefoot!" she exclaimed when I protested at being forced to wear my shoes. She had been reading *Where the Red Fern Grows* to Corrie and me each night after the little ones were put to bed, and I reveled in the descriptions of the life lived by those Southern children. "They have stickers and rocks and glass, just like we do. Put your shoes on or you won't be going outside. I swear, Allison, you are the strangest child . . ."

That year's celebration began early with the firing of a cannon at daybreak, shattering the peaceful calm of the morning. Rousted by the booming, we all piled out of bed and rushed to dress so we could make our way down to the city park, where the Farmington LDS Stake hosted the annual Chuckwagon Breakfast.

Following the breakfast there would be games, fishponds, carnival rides, and, at noon, the Pioneer Day Parade, the highlight of the entire day.

We piled into our old station wagon and took the five-minute ride to the park, filing obediently into the line and waiting our turn to pile our plates high with scrambled eggs, hotcakes, and, best of all, bacon and sausage—the meat a luxury our poor family rarely experienced. After my plate was filled with more food than any seven-year-old could possibly tuck away, I walked toward the table where my father already sat digging in with gusto.

"Excuse me," a gruff voice said as a man and a boy walked in front of me, and I stopped short, allowing them to pass. I looked up—and into the face of my nightmares—the man with the beard.

He stopped and stared at me, his eyes narrowing; and I dropped my plate and felt my world narrow and my heart race as my legs froze on the spot, betraying me, refusing to run.

The young boy with him suddenly tugged his hand and pulled him away, and I watched his face as they disappeared into the crowd.

My mother glanced over as several women rushed to my side to help, and she stood, a look of impatience fleetingly touching her features before the stoicism returned.

"It was an accident. Don't look so scared. They'll give you more," she admonished, taking me firmly by the shoulders and turning me back toward the food line.

I was no longer hungry. I was terrified. I shook my head and ran to our car, jumping in and locking all the side doors quickly. I curled up in the back of the wagon, oblivious to the heat of the day as it warmed up the car. I felt cold, frozen.

I screamed when the back door, which I had neglected to lock, opened and my father poked his head inside.

"Allison, what is wrong with you?" he yelled. I'd scared him when I screamed. "Come on, so you dropped your food. So what? Get out of the car. Come sit with the family."

"I saw him," I whispered; the tears that had threatened from the moment I looked into that familiar face finally choking my throat and rolling down my face. "I saw him."

"You saw who?"

"Him. I saw the man. The man that took Cindy."

My father grabbed my arm and dragged me from the car. He stopped for a moment and we stood there, me sobbing and desolate. Then he rubbed his forehead and a look of pain crossed his face.

"Look, Alli, I know you were really scared by what happened. I understand that. But that man would not be here. Okay? He wouldn't. It doesn't make sense."

"I saw him."

"Come eat with us."

"I can't."

He grabbed my arm again and dragged me to the pavilion, and I tried to still my tears so that no one would stare at me. I sat next to my mother, refusing the bits of food she tried to tempt me with. My father whispered into her ear.

Her face hardened as she looked at him; and she grabbed me by the arm, which was already sore from my father's grip. Afraid she was mad, too, I started to cry again until I realized she was taking me to the place where the town police chief sat with his wife and two teenage boys.

"She saw him, the man that took Cindy," she announced. "He was here!"

Astonished, I stared at her. She believed me, even when my father didn't.

The police chief and my mother moved me to a quiet corner of the park, and he questioned me about the man and the boy who had been with him, quietly writing in his notebook as I answered. When he was done, he gave me a sad smile and left to search the park.

I told my mother I wanted to go home. My father drove us back and then returned with the other children to the celebration, while my mother and I read stories on her bed and didn't talk about what had happened. I only half-listened to my mother's voice as she tried to distract me from the morning's terror, but it didn't work. I couldn't forget.

The bearded man was here, living in our town, had a son or relative about my age, and could reach me easily, anytime. My father did not believe me, but I knew. I would never be safe.

Four

The day before my eighth birthday celebration I woke with a great sense of despair, although at the time I had no name for what it was I felt.

That drizzly day in March, I felt as if a dark cloud circled me, threatening to swallow me up, eat me whole. Tomorrow I would be eight, and everything would change. I would be baptized a member of the Church of Jesus Christ of Latter-day Saints, and would no longer be automatically forgiven my sins. After that day, I'd be held responsible for every wrong thing I did—and I did plenty. Somehow, before the day ended, I had to find a way to kill myself.

I had only vague ideas of how to achieve my death, and no real grasp of the concept. I'd heard from kids at school that if you held your breath long enough you'd die. I told this to my mother, but she assured me it wasn't true.

"When you were little, you used to hold your breath whenever Dad and I would try to leave you with a babysitter. It was really frightening, but the doctor said to let you do it. You'd hold your breath until you'd pass out. Then you'd sleep."

If I passed out, I wouldn't be able to keep holding my

breath, so I'd probably start breathing again. This plan was flawed.

I had a deep fear of heights, so hanging, which sounded messy and painful anyway, was also out. My father, an avid hunter and outdoorsman, had numerous shotguns and rifles, but he only taught my brother how to shoot—we girls were for flushing the deer out of the woods and helping my mother clean up the camp.

Finally, an idea formed in my mind. I'd seen it on TV—medicine was dangerous. I got up on the counter of our kitchen and rummaged in the cupboard where Mom kept all the medicine. There were dangerous things in there, and I knew it. Mom always tried to keep the younger kids out of the medicine.

"It's poison! You'll get sick! You could die!"

As I searched the medicine cabinet, those dire warnings floated in my brain, and my stomach started to churn as reality hit home. I didn't want to get sick. I didn't want to die and didn't even understand death.

I just didn't want to turn eight. I didn't want to be baptized, or have my life change. I wanted to stay seven.

I'd been informed by many friends of the terrible responsibility that came with being baptized. They called it the "age of accountability." I didn't really know what baptism had to do with counting, but my friend Sandy and I had discussed this situation, as our birthdays were just several days apart, and she was as scared as I was.

"I wish I could just die," she'd whispered to me in Sunday school the week before.

Children who died before they were baptized were taken into Heaven by God. It didn't matter how much penny candy they had stolen from the five-and-dime or how many times they'd smacked their sister or brother, Heavenly Father automatically forgave them. Things changed drastically when you were baptized and became an official

Mormon. The consequences of doing wrong after that were dire.

I climbed down off the counter and went back to my room, crawling under the queen-size bed I shared with Corrie and inching my way to the back corner where a heating vent was located. I was so cold I didn't think I would ever get warm: it started in my fingers and toes, and moved inward to encompass my entire body. Familiar to me since Cindy's disappearance, the cold always accompanied my fear. I tried once to explain it to my mother, but she just bundled me up in another sweater and patted me on the head.

"Allison?"

I could see my mother's ragged, pink, fluffy house slippers as she stood on the dark blue carpet of my room. I didn't answer. I watched her thick ankles and varicose vein–lined legs move around to the closet and open it. I had earned a reputation in our family for hiding, a little tidbit my mother once discussed with the family doctor—who was also the first counselor in our Mormon ward bishopric. When she brought it up at my annual checkup, they had ushered me out of the examining room and left me to play with the broken toys in the waiting area. I never knew the outcome of their little chat, but my mother began searching me out whenever I hid. She usually tried to lure me to the family room to watch TV with the other Jensens, something I had no interest in doing. I preferred to read and daydream about a life very different from the one I lived.

Not that I had much to go on. The farthest from Utah our family had ventured was Boise, Idaho, for a family reunion. Since that part of Idaho was another Mormon mecca, the trip hadn't seemed any different than traveling to the corner grocery store.

The closet, where my mother stood, was my other customary hiding place in my room, but it had no heating vent; I needed to be warm, to fight off the chill and stop shivering.

"Allison?" Finally, she dropped to her knees and looked under the bed. I watched her face as she peered into the dark shadows. She squinted, trying to focus, and I could tell when her eyes finally adjusted and she saw me.

"Allison, I swear, you are the strangest child. What are you doing under the bed again?"

"Nothing."

"Come on out. I'm making your cake and you can help. You can lick the beaters."

"I don't want to. I don't want a birthday cake, or a birthday."

My mother laughed. She laughed at me a lot. Maybe she didn't understand me, or maybe she didn't see me as a real person, with real feelings, but she didn't do it in a mean way.

"Tomorrow is a very important day. You're so lucky to have the chance to be baptized. There are hundreds of children who never get the opportunity to join the church. You were fortunate enough to be born into this family. You chose this family in the pre-existence. Now come on out and help me with the cake."

This was my Mormon mother's equivalent of the saying used by moms all around the United States. Instead of being lucky to have food, unlike the poor starving children in China and Africa, we were fortunate to be Mormon. We were members—at least I would soon be a member—of God's One and Only True Church. So many other children didn't have the same luck. They were born to Catholic, or Baptist, or—Heaven forbid—atheist families.

Mom peered at me as I pushed my small body as close to the back wall as it could get. I heard a hiss and a roar, like some giant awakening from a long slumber, and the furnace ignited. The first few seconds after the fan kicked on were bone-chilling. The cold air from the duct fanned around my body; I gasped and held my breath until the welcome warmth crawled over me, dancing along my skin and warming up my outer parts without touching the cold despair inside. It wasn't the complete warmth I sought, but it would have to do.

"I'm cold," I finally said. "I'll come to the kitchen in a minute."

My mother laughed again. "My little Heaterella," she said.

Her head and face disappeared, and all I could see were her chubby legs again. I watched as those ankles and feet walked out of the room, and I finally prayed.

God, please forgive me, but I don't want to be lucky. I don't want to be a Mormon. I just want to be a kid.

Somehow, I knew He wasn't listening.

Five

On the night of the March baptisms, I sat in my place of honor in the front row, next to the other three eight-year-olds who would also become official members of the church that evening. On normal Sundays, the baptismal pool, set deep in the tile floor, was hidden behind an accordion curtain in the room used for Sunday school classes. I'd been here many times, and had never before seen the ominous side of this room. Today it loomed in front of us, a deep, scary ocean of water. In reality, it resembled a small tiled swimming pool, but the weight of responsibility that came with baptism made it seem huge and threatening. Behind us sat our families and ward members, an audience of onlookers in metal folding chairs.

"We're so glad all of you could join us for this wonderful event," said Bishop Hall, who presided over the baptisms. "Tonight, four of our stellar youth will become members of the Church of Jesus Christ of Latter-day Saints. It's a wonderful thing to be a part of God's true church. After an opening prayer by Brother Snow, we will proceed in this order: Michael Eliza Jeppson, Allison Marie Jensen, Sandra LaDawn Smith, and Carolyn Anderson. Brother Snow?"

For the first time in my life I wanted a long prayer. Brother Snow, however, was not known for his wordiness, and soon it was time to start. Brother Jeppson stood up and walked over to Mikey, who was oddly subdued. He was usually loud and obnoxious, teasing all the girls and getting in trouble for bringing frogs, bugs, and worms to Sunday school.

Brother Jeppson, dressed in the all-white jumpsuit worn by the Priesthood bearer during the baptism, reached out a hand to his son with a proud look on his face. Mikey took a long look at the pool, glanced over at his smiling father, quickly back at his mother, and sprinted out the door.

His mother jumped up from her seat in the middle row and took off after him while his father stood there in shock. The bishop fought back a grin. Sister Jeppson, who moved fast for a large lady, had no problem finding the missing boy. Dressed in white from head to toe, he was an easy target. We heard them head back toward the room, their voices growing louder as they neared.

"I don't wanna! No, you can't make me!"

Sister Jeppson said something in a hushed voice.

"No! I hate the water. You know I hate the water. I'm not going in there!"

More whispers from his mother.

The rest of us looked at each other with round, solemn eyes. Were they as scared as I was?

Brother Jeppson waited for Mikey to reappear. First, we saw his wife's large rear end as she tugged on her son's arm with both hands. He dug in his feet like a stubborn mule, tears streaming down his freckled face as he balked at the door. His mother had a considerable weight advantage, however, and she soon had all of his seventy pounds in the front of the room.

Finally, his father moved. He crossed over and knelt down next to his son, whispering in his ear.

"No! I'm not doing it. No!"

Brother Jeppson gave a pleading look toward the bishop, who still fought to keep the smile off his face. I knew Mikey was going to be baptized whether he liked it or not.

Bishop Hall leaned down and grabbed Mikey by the arm, and his mother finally let go of her python grip. Together the two men tugged and pulled the screaming boy toward the pool. There was a metal railing in the front, and steps on the sides leading down into the water. Brother Jeppson eased down into the water, pulling Mikey with him, while the bishop, who wore a suit and tie, pushed gingerly from behind.

With a final tug Mikey's father pulled him fully into the water, but Mikey wouldn't let go of the death grip he had on the bishop's arm; and Bishop Hall flew face first into the baptismal pool, street clothes and all.

Gasps went up from the audience, and there were some stifled giggles as the bishop finally righted himself in the four-foot-deep water. Wiping the moisture out of his eyes, he motioned to his first counselor to get him a towel. One was quickly found, and he soggily trudged up the steps, turning only to smile and wave at the audience.

Mikey, stunned silent by the fact he'd just dunked the bishop, stood with his mouth open in the water, forgetting for a moment where he was.

His father, taking advantage of Mikey's stupor, grabbed him by the back and arm and dipped him backward into the water while rapidly intoning the words "Michael Eliza Jeppson, in the name of the Holy Melchizedek Priesthood I baptize you a member of the Church of Jesus Christ of Latter-day Saints in the name of the Father, the Son and the Holy Ghost, amen."

It was probably the quickest prayer in the history of baptisms. It also shook Mikey from his stupor, and he opened his mouth to scream just as Brother Jeppson dipped him under. His father held him under the water for what seemed like an eternity, and I wondered if he meant to drown him as a punishment. I figured if I had the nerve to bolt like Mikey, my father would have a hard time restraining himself, given the opportunity. And if he didn't drown me, when we returned home, I would probably wish for death.

Mikey was finally allowed to surface. He spluttered and choked and made gagging noises, then gasped, trying to catch his breath. He made strange noises in his throat, and I could see the alarm in his father's eyes. I wondered if he'd kept his mouth open the entire time, trying to scream.

With a look of despair on his face, Mikey threw up all the holy water he'd swallowed, along with whatever he'd eaten for dinner—something that looked a lot like SpaghettiOs.

Carolyn, a pretty girl with long curly hair and a penchant for dresses, sat next to me on the right. She gasped and tears instantly rolled down her chubby cheeks. Sandy, who sat on the other side of me, came from a family of seven brothers and two sisters and was not easily shocked.

"Ewwwww. I am not going in there. That's disgusting!" she whispered into my ear.

The first counselor hastily moved to the accordion curtain and pulled it shut, blocking our view of Mikey and his mess. The second counselor stood up and announced we would take a brief break before continuing.

I heard whispers and giggles behind me, and I stood up, thinking I was off the hook. I felt my father's firm hand on my shoulder before I saw him. He exerted a strong pressure and pushed me back into my seat.

We heard noise behind the curtain—I supposed someone was cleaning up the mess. I wondered if the water drained like a bathtub. After about ten minutes, during which my father stood behind me with his hand on my shoulder, the curtain reopened with no Jeppsons in sight and clean, fresh water in the pool.

No one else tried to run, although I tried to think of excuses to get me out of what lay ahead. My father led me into the water and said the baptismal prayer, dunking me under quickly and pulling me up before I could panic.

It was over. Now I was official. Now, the guilt that would follow me for the rest of my life had been given to me like a gift. One I didn't want, that didn't fit, and I couldn't return.

Saturday's baptism was followed by a Sunday confirmation, and after a long Fast and Testimony meeting, where I steadfastly refused to be moved by the spirit and announce my firm conviction of the truthfulness of our church, we returned home to dry pot roast with mushy, overcooked carrots and potatoes. Mother always put dinner in the oven before we went to church. In honor of my birthday, baptism, and confirmation, we also had ice cream and cake.

We all gathered around the table. As the guest of honor, I sat in my father's usual place. I had gifts to open after dinner; and Grandma and Grandpa Smith, my mother's parents, drove down from Logan for the special occasion, bringing along my Aunt Carol. Baptisms and confirmations were huge celebrations in our family.

My other set of grandparents had both died years before, leaving my dad an orphan at age twelve. He'd been raised by his devoutly religious Aunt Rebecca, who was what my father called "an old maid." She had died just the year before without ever having a chance to marry. My father mourned her, and often talked about how sad it made him that she wouldn't be able to go to the Celestial Kingdom, because marriage was preordained by God.

My mother often assured him Aunt Rebecca had undoubtedly found someone and married him in Heaven, and probably had lots of children of her own, one of the most important tenets of our religion for reasons I was too young to understand. This didn't seem to ease his mind. We were his only living family now, and we were a "bunch of damn thorns in my side."

"Allison, why don't you say the prayer?" My father smiled as our raucous crew settled in at the kitchen table. "After all, this is your special day."

I shook my head quickly and dropped my eyes. I didn't want to thank God and wasn't happy I had been baptized. I was scared.

"Oh, come on now," boomed Grandpa. "Say the prayer! You're official now. You're a member of God's church."

I shook my head again and refused to look up. The God I had come to know—the one who'd ignored my prayers and threatened to rain punishment on me if I wasn't good—scared me. I wasn't happy about being one of his faithful.

"I'll say it!" piped up Kevin, the glory hog, who intended to be the good child again.

I intended to let him.

"Allison . . ." my father started.

"Don't push her, Richard," my mother said. "Let Kevin say it."

Corrie, who was only five, read *The Borrowers* while we waited to eat. She had taught herself to read the year before and always had her nose in a book. My parents pried her beloved stories out of her hands at night. She loved to read. I think it was her escape. I hid. She read.

My parents didn't seem to find it odd she could read so early, before she even started school. In fact, most of the time, they hardly noticed she was there.

"Little Girls!" My father warned the fidgety youngest

children in his booming, patriarch's voice as they poked each other and giggled. They settled down, and Mother grabbed the book out of Corrie's hands and gave her a warning look.

Kevin bowed his head and started praying without waiting for my father to urge me to do so again. He wanted the attention. He was going to say this prayer.

"Our dear Father in Heaven," he began, *"we are so thankful we could be together today as a family and we are thankful for the food before us."*

The mature words he used were common to us. We heard and said these words time and time again. We'd been hearing them since the day we were born. We knew how to pray and we prayed well. We did it at every meal, every night before we went to bed, many times during our Sunday meetings, and during Monday night Family Home Evenings. Prayer came second nature to the Jensen kids, and to all kids raised in good Mormon families.

The important thing, of course, was to be able to throw something different in, something to make your prayer stand out, earning you the praise of adult family or ward members.

"Please bless this food that it will nourish and strengthen our bodies and do us the good we need. And please bless all the sick people. Bless Mrs. Appleworth that the wart on her nose will go away and it won't be so hard to look at her," he said, referring to our fellow ward member and close neighbor.

My mother gasped aloud but didn't stop him. I figured this had to be his trump card. I couldn't have been more wrong.

"And please bless Aunt Carol that Grandpa won't find out she really likes girls because Mom says Grandpa will kill her."

The pandemonium that followed took the attention away from me, and I would have been grateful except my father's foul moods tended to explode like a bomb, ripping into everyone close enough to hear the blast. A tearful Kevin went to his room without dinner for reasons he didn't really understand. Grandma screamed loudly and had to be led to my mother's room to lie down. Grandpa used language I'd never heard before in my life.

I didn't really understand why Aunt Carol's liking girls was such a big deal. After all, I liked girls, too. My best friends were all girls.

Aunt Carol never quite forgave my brother for outing her at Sunday Fast and Testimony dinner. Of course, the family disowned her when she decided to live with her girlfriend several years later. We just stopped talking about her one day. Mom walked around with a sad expression for a while, but it seemed like if we just pretended to be normal, like all our neighbors appeared to be, then maybe it would be so.

As I grew up, however, I realized none of my friends had aunts who were lesbians. At least none I knew. My father preached long and hard to my grandfather about forgiveness, but his father-in-law wasn't listening. Of course, Dad's tune rapidly changed in 1987 when one of the Little Girls was also outed as a lesbian.

Still, an inkling as to the weight of the luggage that comes with being Mormon hit me for the first time on that Sunday, the day after my eighth birthday. It felt wrong. I liken it now to putting on ill-fitting clothes, too tight or too loose. Being Mormon was a skin I was never comfortable in, and as I grew up and became aware of all the vagaries that made up the fabric of the religion, the skin fit less and less.

Six

Although I'd dreaded my baptism, things settled back to normal quickly, and I was soon lulled into the routine of our daily Mormon lives. We rose early every morning before my father left for his job as an accountant and said a family prayer. We also read from the scriptures—those of us who could read—and my father would roundly grill us about what God was trying to tell us. I did a lot of guessing, since God and I were not on really good terms.

I asked a lot of questions about church doctrine, and for a while my father would beam proudly at me, his eldest daughter and diligent servant of the Lord. It didn't last too long. Soon my questions became deeper and required answers Dad probably did not have. He began to tell me, quoting the many church leaders who spoke to us each Sunday: "When the prophet has spoken, the thinking has been done."

"I'm not supposed to think?"

"Yes, Allison, you are supposed to think, but you are also supposed to respect the Priesthood Authority and realize that God speaks through our prophets. There are some things we cannot understand and are not to question."

As things I was not to question piled up I became strident and angry in my search for the truth. And the more questions I asked, the angrier my father became. A nimble and curious mind did not seem to be an admirable attribute, at least where I was concerned.

I felt I had good reason to ask these questions. I was haunted by Cindy, her disappearance, and my own role in what happened. If she was dead, if God had allowed her to die, I needed to know why. I needed to understand His plan. She was eight and had reached the age of accountability. If Cindy was dead where, exactly, had she ended up? Did she make it to God's highest kingdom? Or had some small sin, like stolen gum from the country store, kept her out of the Celestial Kingdom? Was she lonely? Did she get enough to eat?

These were all pressing questions to me. To my father, they were a nuisance. He was trying to teach us the "big picture." I wanted the details.

My question of a heavenly mother and where she fit into the picture finally sent him over the edge. As he tried to explain, I said "You don't really *know* the answer, do you?"

I spent a good part of my ninth and tenth years crying, tucked back under my bed, hiding from my father and the injustices of being a small Mormon girl child. My backside was often welted and sore, and the bruises on my arms ached.

The answers I sought were out there—they had to be. But my father was not going to supply them, and I would have to look elsewhere to find the real truth.

My first official meeting with our bishop, when I was twelve, did not go well. Young womanhood meant a new church program, lots of lessons on chastity, and yearly mandatory meetings with the man in charge of our ward.

We were supposed to confess to any wrongdoings while the bishop inquired about our behavior and general well-being.

Our bishop at that time was Brother Hansen, and he had only been in his position for a few short months when I was summoned for my conference. I had, however, known him all my life, as I grew up just two houses away from him. He was a tall, thin man with dark hair, bad breath, polyester clothing, bad ties, and seven daughters who all looked exactly alike, although they varied in age and height.

I entered his office on trembling legs, unsure what to expect, determined to say nothing incriminating that might make its way back to my father.

"Well, Allison," he said, steepling his hands together while he leaned back in his chair. "How are things going for you?"

"Fine."

"Nothing you want to discuss with me?"

"No."

"You're obeying your parents?"

"Yes."

"Reading your *Book of Mormon*?"

"Yes." My face reddened, since I found this particular tome dreadfully boring and usually only pretended to read it.

"Any problems with masturbation?"

"No. No problems at all." It worked just fine for me. I silently prayed that my face wasn't a vivid scarlet color that would betray me.

"You are staying away from boys?"

"As far away as I can."

The bishop stopped, apparently stumped as to where to go from there. We were at a standoff.

"Are there any questions I can answer for you?"

I thought for a minute and then blurted out, "Why won't anyone in my family talk about Cindy anymore?"

It was Bishop Hansen's turn for a red face. He didn't need to ask who Cindy was. It was a small town. Everyone knew about her disappearance.

"Because that's in the past. It's time to move on."

"But it's not in the past. Cindy is still missing."

"Cindy has been taken up to live with God, Sister Jensen."

Oh-oh. I wasn't "Allison" anymore. Now I was "Sister Jensen." This interview was taking a bad turn. But I persisted. "But you don't know that. You don't know that at all! She could still be alive somewhere."

"No, she isn't. It's time to let it go."

"What do you mean, 'no, she isn't'? How do you know that?"

"Look, Sister Jensen, I'm sure your parents explained this to you. It's over. Time to move on."

"No one has ever explained anything to me. What are you talking about? Do you know what happened to her?"

"Well, look at the time," the bishop said, glancing at his watch. "This conference is over. I have another young woman waiting so let's pray together and you can get home."

"But I want to know—"

"There's nothing to tell."

With that final word, the bishop bowed his head and folded his arms and prayed for my soul in a voice that convinced me he knew I was headed right to the Telestial Kingdom, the lowest of all God's domains. After the prayer he scooted me out of his office, and I slowly walked home, mulling over what I had—and hadn't—learned.

When I reached our house the door stood open and my father was waiting on the porch, his belt in one hand, an angry frown on his face. Evidently, the bishop had called ahead.

Later, as I cried into my pillow, punished for questioning the Priesthood Authority, I wondered why asking questions was so bad. I wondered what they knew. And most of all, I wondered if I would ever have all the answers they seemed to. I was a girl, so that was doubtful. I would never have the Priesthood.

Seven

Christmas Eve at the Jensen house was always chaotic, loud, tense, and memorable. My father's dark moods would be interrupted by periods of giddiness and glee. We reveled in those moments, precious as they were. We knew well they wouldn't last.

The subject of how to pay for Christmas started lots of fights between my parents. I knew Santa Claus was a fairy tale—it was one I'd been disabused of early in life, even before a man held me at gunpoint and my friend disappeared. My father told me shortly after I turned five that Santa Claus had been created by the department store giants as a way to sell toys and gifts. The real meaning of Christmas was about Jesus Christ and his birth.

"Great," I muttered. "More church, less presents." That comment had earned a smile from my mother and a glare from my father.

For years after that particular talk, my mother had a hard time coaxing me into JC Penney's, as I was afraid I would turn a corner and run into one of those giants, who would promptly whisk me away into his lair, butter two giant pieces of bread, stick me between them, and have lunch.

Nonetheless, I loved Christmas. The excitement of the Little Girls was palpable, and even Kevin, Corrie, and I—older and wiser about the true identity of the jolly old elf—got caught up in the mood. And the story of Jesus' birth, in all its sweetness and purity, was one part of religion I still fully embraced, without my usual questions and complaints.

The year I turned fifteen was no different. Once we put up the tree, the first Saturday in December, the whole month slowed to a crawl, leaving us to savor each delicious moment, a form of exquisite torture, waiting for Christmas Eve to arrive.

I awoke on the morning of December twenty-fourth with sheer joy pulsing through my veins. While I no longer believed in the myth of Santa Claus, I was still young enough to remember the awe and wonder surrounding his arrival.

The entire day inched by, until we gathered around the Christmas tree as a family and began our celebration. Every year we did the Christmas Pageant.

As my brother was the only boy in our family, he earned the role of Joseph by default. Because I was the oldest, I usually took the role of Mary for myself, but as my younger sisters grew older they were no longer content to wear bathrobes and towels on their heads, playing shepherds or angels. Some years, an all-out brawl occurred as we fought for the plum role of the Virgin Mother. Many a Christmas Eve ended with my father yelling and my mother sighing, and all of us girls confined to our rooms for at least an hour. On that particular night, such confinement amounted to torture.

Most years, the part of the baby Jesus was played by one of our dolls. However, that year our already-large family had been joined by a calico cat named Peaches. Peaches, we decided, was a member of this family and was going to play a central role in our play. As our parents and grand-parents sat on the couch waiting for the show to begin, we wrapped Peaches tightly in swaddling clothes and tried to place her in the manger, a doll crib my father had made when I was born.

Peaches did not want to be the baby Jesus, despite the fact that this was the most important role. She meowed furiously and hissed and spat at us. She would've had her claws out had her legs not been so tightly wrapped in the baby blanket. We'd practiced our swaddling techniques all day, and had it down to an art form. We commenced our play, trying to ignore the furious sounds issuing from the bundled cat.

"Joseph, I'm afraid I have bad news. I'm pregnant with God's child."

I'd spent all afternoon writing the dialogue for the play and was proud of the results.

"But, Mary, you're a virgin. People will talk."

My father's eyes got big, and my mother covered her mouth with her hand, like she was suppressing a giggle. She was expecting her sixth child, and her swollen belly caused her to move from side to side, trying to get comfortable on our old, hard couch. An occasional grimace of pain would shoot across her face as she moved.

"Did Kevin just say 'virgin'?" boomed my grandfather.

My grandmother hushed him, and the Christmas Pageant proceeded.

"What's a virgin?" asked one of the shepherds.

"*Reeeee-oooooweorrrrrrrrrrrrrrrr,*" howled the baby Jesus.

"I am an angel, sent by God, to tell you of the birth of his only begotten son," Corrie recited. "Follow the star in the sky and you will find a baby lying in a manger, wrapped in swaddling clothes."

The shepherds shuffled toward the manger, and as they knelt down in front of the cradle, Jesus escaped.

Worked up because of her unwilling incarceration, the confused Peaches looked for an opening to dart out of the room and into one of her many hiding places. With the shepherds, Joseph, Mary, and the angel surrounding her, she could see no exit, so she turned and ran directly into the Christmas tree. Our blue spruce tree was tall, the top reaching nearly to the ceiling, and it was as wide as our entire sofa. The living nativity scene for our play had been set up directly in front of the tree, so it could be used as a backdrop for the pictures my father took.

The cat tried to climb the base, and my father and grandfather jumped up at the same time. It was too late—Peaches, furious and frantic, toppled the tree.

The shepherds and angels, along with the cowardly Joseph, all scattered, escaping harm. I, however, as the kneeling Mary, mother of God, was directly in the tree's path. My mother, moving more quickly than I would have thought possible with her pregnant girth, reached me before anyone else and knelt down beside me as my grandfather and father pulled the tree back to an upright position.

A sharp pain in my right arm pulsed and I saw the cut and free-flowing blood as my mother lifted me up, pulling at my shoulders.

I heard a gasp, and I fell back to the floor with a heavy thunk. My mother's body fell next to mine.

The next few minutes passed in chaos as my younger brother and sisters began wailing and crying and the adults rushed to my mother, forgetting about me. I sat up shakily and wiped at the blood flowing from the deep gash in my arm. I stared at my mother, who lay unconscious on the floor with broken remnants of blue Christmas ornaments and bulbs scattered around her like a nightmare decoration. From between her legs, blood seeped and stained her old cotton dress.

An ambulance came and took her away, and we were

left with my grandparents, who were instructed by the medical technicians to drive me to the hospital for stitches.

My father went with my mother, so my grandfather had to drive me to the emergency room while my grandmother stayed and tried to calm my distraught brother and sisters. Grandpa rarely went anywhere without causing a shouting incident, and I was not thrilled to have him as my escort. I was worried about my mother, scared about getting stitches, embarrassed to be in his company, and sad that Christmas Eve, my favorite night of the year, had been ruined. I wondered once again if this religion and I were a bad mix. Was this a sign from God?

My grandparents stayed with us for several days. my father would leave early in the morning, forgoing our usual *Book of Mormon* study and prayers. His face was always pale and ashen, and he smiled even less than usual.

"Is Mom okay?" I would ask him. "Is the baby okay?"

He only stared with dull eyes and nodded. "Pray, Allison. If we have enough faith, she'll be fine."

Faith being something I was sorely lacking, I worried constantly.

In his concern and fear, my father became a different man. Normally belligerent and loud, anger emanating from his pores, he became soft-spoken and withdrawn, seemingly oblivious to all that went on around him. He'd turn on the television and watch his favorite sitcoms with vacant eyes and a still face, never laughing or even grinning. He never once picked up his beloved triple combination— *Book of Mormon,* Bible, and *Pearl of Great Price.* Family prayers, which one would assume would be so dearly needed, were abandoned.

The undercurrent running through our home became tense and dangerous, like an unseen electric charge waiting for an unsuspecting victim to reach out. I didn't trust this silent man, any more than I had his predecessor.

The deeper the current ran, the more disturbed my brothers and sisters became. They began fighting over everything. My grandparents, running the show, screamed and yelled at high decibels, but it appeared no one could hear them. They were cranky people on a good day, mean on a bad one. My gruff grandfather scared us, and he and my grandmother fought all the time. They seemed to have a great dislike for each other, despite having been married for fifty-two years. My grandfather used to joke he was going to divorce Grandma and find himself a nicer wife.

"I sure as hell don't want to be married to her for time and all eternity."

My father and grandfather would sit in opposite easy chairs in front of the television, silent, except for strange bursts of conversation.

"Don't know why you did it to her, anyway," Grandpa said.

"She wanted it, and you know it," Dad would fire back.

"You wanted it, and you know it. Can't even raise the ones you have now properly."

"We're doing just fine."

"We're doing just fine," Grandpa would mimic. "Don't see no 'we're' here at all. There's just you, fat and healthy, and my daughter clingin' to—"

"Shut up, old man." The warning in my father's voice was one I'd heard often. Grandpa, never one to heed a warning from anyone, including the church general authorities who counseled against drinking coffee and liquor, nevertheless quieted.

We weren't allowed to visit my mother in the hospital. She'd been there before, of course, having us babies; our grandparents kept reassuring us that everything would be fine. We were just anxious for her to get out and come home and rescue us from Grandpa and Grandma and their endless bickering, yelling, and spoonfuls of molasses to build up the iron in our blood.

Six days later my very tired father came home around six from his nightly visit to the hospital. His face looked gaunt and hollow, and he called us into the living room for a family meeting.

"Ow, quit poking me, Alli!"

"You started it!"

"Did not! Dad, Allison's poking me!"

"Allison, don't poke your brother."

"Dad, he started it. . . ."

"Children, I need to tell you something."

He sat before us in his chair, and we grew quiet, the fidgeting and fighting gone in an instant. Something was wrong.

"Children, I'm afraid I have some bad news. Your mother had some problems and developed some bleeding. The doctors did what they could, but unfortunately, I wasn't able to give her a blessing. She died on the operating table. The baby, a little boy, also died. They've gone to live with God."

He didn't cry. Why didn't he cry? The Little Girls burst into tears and grabbed each other, their small bodies clenched together. They sobbed loudly, despair in their voices. My brother Kevin looked to be in shock, and my father went to him and hugged him. Corrie ran from the room and out the back door. I worried that she had no coat because it was winter and freezing, but I couldn't make myself go after her. I walked slowly to my room and crawled under my bed, inching in toward the heater. It was a tight fit, as it had been quite a few years since I'd last resorted to hiding from life. The heater wasn't running and the vent was cold. My grandfather had turned the heat down "to save money."

It didn't really matter that the heat wasn't on. This chill I never got rid of. It would follow me throughout my life, as I faced all my "firsts" without my mother: first date, first kiss, first love. It colored me, changed me, so I no longer knew what was real and what was not.

Love was smoke and mirrors. You thought it was there, you reached out to touch it and it disappeared. Or your fingers met the cold, hard sting of betrayal, in the form of reflective glass. It might look like you weren't alone, but you were.

Eight

Truth is an interesting concept. it means different things to different people.

My sister Christy would probably say her truth is this: "I was born a lesbian; God made me what I am." And if you asked my brother Kevin, he undoubtedly would have said the truth could be summed up in these words—BYU Football.

If you asked my father the definition of truth, his answer would be something like this: there is only one true thing—the church.

Of course, there are many roots that branch off his truth: Joseph Smith was a prophet of God; the Mormon gospel is the restored gospel of Jesus Christ, brought back to this earth by Joseph Smith; the only good literature is written by Mormons.

At fifteen, the truth for me was this: I wanted to be a bad girl. I was tired of being good.

The year I turned fifteen was the year my mother died. I no longer believed in a just and loving God. Rather, the God I knew was vengeful and cruel, allowing children to be kidnapped and mothers to die in childbirth, leaving behind their surviving children to get by as best they could. I wanted nothing to do with the Mormon God and desired to know what else was out there. I also didn't intend to obey the rules set down by that arbitrary and fickle deity, including the canon that required me to follow my father's commands without question.

I announced to my father I didn't believe Mormonism was the only true religion, and I wanted to learn about others. The answer to this was a grounding and adamant "No."

My father sent me to see our current ward leader, Bishop Hall, who was also our dentist, after my announcement.

"Now for me," the bishop said, "it would be okay. My testimony of the truthfulness of the church is very strong. I could learn about other religions and not be swayed by them. But, Allison, right now you are unsure, and it just wouldn't be a good idea."

"But if the church is so true, what are you all so afraid of? Why can't I study other religions? If the church is true, I'll know it's right, won't I? And you and my dad have nothing to fear. I won't leave."

"It's just not a good idea, Allison. I suspect you're grieving for your mother. I understand that. I understand your anger. Why don't you come over for Sunday dinner?"

The next Sunday I refused to attend service.

"Allison, get up. Time for church."

"No, I'm not going."

I buried my face in my pillow, knowing exactly the expression he had on his face, even without looking. If I met his eyes I might cave in, fear getting the best of me, so I hid.

"Allison, you'd better mind me and get out of bed. You need to get the Little Girls ready. The potatoes need to be peeled and the roast prepared before we leave."

"I'm not going today. I'll do it while you're gone."

He grabbed me by the back of my neck and yanked me

from my bed. My head flopped forward like a rag doll's and I bit my tongue. I landed on my feet and he held me up, squeezing until I screamed in pain.

"I told you to get up and get ready. As long as you live in my house, you will live by my rules."

His foot met my backside, and I crumpled in a heap to the floor sobbing, angry I was so weak. I could taste salty blood in my mouth, and my tongue throbbed with pain where I had bitten it.

I felt Corrie's gentle hand on my hair, and I steeled myself to be quiet. I was the oldest now, and they needed me.

"Allison Marie Jensen, you had better be getting in the shower!" he yelled from the living room, where he would be settled in his chair preparing his Gospel Doctrine lesson.

"Get up, Alli, get up before he comes back," Corrie urged in a whisper.

I got up.

We ate Sunday dinner in silence. Even the Little Girls stopped their endless chatter and merely chased the food around on their plates in between furtive glances at my father and me.

"How do you suppose your poor mother feels, watching down from Heaven and knowing how disobedient you are, Allison?" my father said, breaking the silence toward the end of the meal. "She needs to be at peace, to know her family is being cared for, and raised with the right values."

"I'm not their mother."

His face tightened, and his eyes took on that dangerous light, the one that danced like devils whenever we were wayward or unruly.

My sore neck and tongue burned and stung with every bite I took. I shoved potatoes and gravy into my mouth.

The other kids stayed silent, barely nibbling at the inedible roast and lumpy potatoes. The Little Girls sat huddled close together, their chairs touching. I knew beneath the table they held hands, chubby, small fingers clasped together tightly in fear. Corrie stared at the ceiling as if reading an invisible book printed there. Kevin looked both frightened and angry. He darted accusatory glances my way, and I felt guilty, knowing I'd angered my father and everyone would pay the price.

"I expect an apology, Allison."

"Ah'm soowwwy," I said through a large mouthful of food.

My father's lips tightened, and the dancing devils did a jig. He moved quickly, slapping me with the back of his hand, and I spewed the contents of my mouth all over the table just before I hit the floor.

I looked up at him standing over me, his belt wrapped tightly in his hand. The Little Girls sobbed and hugged each other, Kevin was ghostly white, and Corrie's eyes seemed too large for her face.

Before my mother died, she'd sidetracked some of the beatings, often taking the brunt of his anger on herself. We were spanked, and spanked often, but it was easier to call it discipline when my mother's gentle voice said "Enough, Richard," and the punishment ended. Now, there was no buffer.

Without a word, he turned me over and began.

My father, who'd never been a source of comfort, became unpredictable in his own despair. Our home became a war zone, with him constantly raging and angry and we kids slipping quietly from room to room, trying not to aggravate his temper. The only kindness he showed was for my thirteen-year-old brother.

"Son, it's okay," I heard him tell Kevin one day. "God

needed your mom in Heaven. It's time for us to accept this and move on."

I could hear Kevin sobbing, and my father said, "Kevin, boys don't cry. You have to toughen up. You need to lead the girls by example. You have the Priesthood. It's an awesome responsibility. Your sisters need you now, to guide them."

The Little Girls cried themselves to sleep every night, and I began sleeping in their bed with them. That way, when they woke up screaming, I was already there.

My grandparents temporarily called a cease-fire on their fighting and came to get us every weekend, taking us out for ice cream and root beer on Saturday afternoons, giving my father time alone to wallow in his misery.

"You're responsible for them now, Allison," my grandmother told me, a pained look on her face. "You have to be the mother."

"But I'm only fifteen. I'm not ready to be a mother."

"Your great-great-grandmother married her husband, Hyrum Porter, when she was only fourteen years old. He was fifty-six, had four other wives and fifteen children. She never complained a lick. That's the stock you come from, and I expect you to take on this responsibility."

Thinking to help, she just made me feel worse.

"I've lost something, too, you know. I've lost my daughter, my only daughter," she continued.

"She wasn't your only daughter. You had two daughters, and Aunt Carol's still alive."

My grandmother's lips tightened, and she gave me a sharp look. "Don't talk about that. Stop."

"Which was worse for you? My mother dying, or Aunt Carol being a lesbian?"

She slapped my face hard. "Don't you ever say that word or *her* name again."

• • •

A magazine for Mormon teens appeared in our mailbox one day with my name on the subscription label. I threw it in the trash. That Saturday, my grandparents brought me a brightly wrapped package. While the other children eyed me enviously, I slowly unwrapped the gift. It was a romance novel, written by a famous Mormon author, just for teenage girls. With my father watching, I quietly thanked them and took it to my room, where I shoved it to the back of my underwear drawer and forgot about it.

They tried desperately to "fix" me, while I knew instinctively nothing was wrong. I'd simply realized the Mormon view of life was not the only one. In their eyes, that was blasphemy.

Sunday meant a torrent of meetings and visits and, about once a month, a youth Fireside. These meetings were geared toward teenagers, we who were fighting the rush of hormones and the desire to be bad. Church leaders believed the best way to keep us out of trouble was to keep us busy.

I usually went to these Firesides with my friends Tricia Snell and Shelly Sanders. We'd been inseparable since our twelfth year, when we discovered we'd gotten our periods all within the same week. We were young women who shared a bond. Tricia's mother had taken me under her wing and tried to care for me, making extra meals when she cooked for her own large family and sending them home with me.

"Look," Tricia said, pointing a finger to the front of the chapel.

We followed the direction of her finger and saw Tami Holt deep in conversation with four or five of the best-looking boys in our ward. Tami had a big hooked nose, a long chin, and a horsey face, which didn't seem to bother the boys. Of course, that's because they weren't looking at her face. Tami also had huge breasts, and every teenage boy wanted to touch them. Even the ones who tried hard not to masturbate, because we'd been taught it was so wrong, could not look her in the eyes. It was like hypnosis. Their eyes automatically went to her chest, and once there, weren't able to move.

Tami, knowing she was not beautiful, used her endowment to great advantage. She always preened under the attention of the boys in the ward. Behind her back, the rest of us girls talked about her. The truth in this particular instance was we were jealous. It caused us to be catty.

"I heard she went all the way," Tricia whispered.

"With who?" Shelly gasped.

"Mike Prevost." Tricia imparted this information with relish. She knew she had something over the rest of us. Mike was a "bad boy"—inactive, and a Jack-Mormon, the term for those who don't live the principles of the Gospel. His family didn't attend church, and rumor held his father kept *beer* in the fridge, something unheard-of in our little Mormon community.

I sat back and digested this information—Mike Prevost held a great deal of attraction for me. I seemed to like the "bad boys," although I didn't know for sure why. The thought of his touching Tami Holt's breasts was almost more than my young heart could take. Or course, I didn't dare admit this attraction to my two friends. They would be appalled.

I watched Tami as the boys stared at her chest and pretended to be interested in what she said. I was experiencing an emotion that seemed intangible at first, but I finally recognized it for what it was—anger. I wanted Mike Prevost to stare at *my* breasts, which were actually fairly nonexistent. Two little buds on the chest of a tiny, skinny girl with blond hair, thick glasses, and braces. No boys looked at me. They flirted with Shelly and Tricia, two of the most popular girls in our ward and our school. I was just the tag-along.

I couldn't believe I was jealous of Tami. No one really liked her. She had one or two friends, other girls who were unpopular because they were heavy or plain. I wanted to destroy her.

Mike Prevost. I wanted him for myself.

"She's a slut," I said, leaning forward and getting into the conversation. "No way would Mike Prevost touch her. No way."

"Why not? You know what kind of boy *he* is," Tricia said.

"No way. He wouldn't. I just know he wouldn't."

Slowly, the light dawned in my friends' eyes.

"You like him!" accused Shelly, a smile on her face.

"Yeah, you do, don't you?" chimed in Tricia, a little too loudly for my comfort.

"Shhhh," I told them both as the chapel grew quiet.

The bishop stepped to the podium to begin the Fireside.

"You like him." whispered Tricia, who sat on my left.

As the speaker started his talk, I traveled off into my world of daydreams. This was where I retreated whenever life became too difficult. It was also the world I ran to when I was hurt, bored, or tired.

In this world, Mike Prevost belonged to me. He gently kissed my lips and grazed my breasts with his hands. These fantasies all started out innocently enough but invariably ended with him touching me between the legs; and I felt the moisture pool as I imagined him stroking me down there, that forbidden place I wasn't allowed to even think about, let alone touch or allow a boy anywhere near. In church I had these thoughts. I felt guilty—just not guilty enough to stop.

Nine

"Children, I have great news!" My father announced one Saturday afternoon. My mother had been dead only six months, but just that morning I'd heard him whistling again. Something was definitely up.

He gathered us for a family meeting, and Sister Eileen Johnson, a widow from down the street, sat next to him on our worn couch. Her four sullen, towheaded children, who ranged in age from two to seventeen, also sat in our living room. They didn't look happy. *Neither do we,* I supposed, glancing over my sisters' and brother's morose faces. We all knew what was coming.

I missed my mother incredibly, and I was tired of being her replacement. Despite this, I was not ready for someone else to take her place.

My father and Sister Johnson were to be married two weeks later in the Salt Lake Temple. I could have forgiven his betrayal of my mother's memory, I think, if he'd acted the least bit uncomfortable, but he didn't.

"Eileen was married to a nonmember, so she'll be able to be sealed to me, too," he said, beaming as if this were excellent news.

"Sealed? What do you mean, Dad?" one of the Little Girls asked.

"That means after the Second Coming we'll all be together as a family. Isn't that wonderful?"

"What about Mom?"

"What? What do you mean, Allison? Your mother is still sealed to me. We will *all* be a family."

"What about Mom?" I said louder and with belligerence. "Did you ever think about her? Do you think she wants to live for eternity sharing you with another woman? Do you know if she even *likes* Sister Johnson? Do you even care?"

My voice had risen to close to a scream. All the other children stared at me, mortified, including the sullen-faced Johnson children.

"Allison, this is how God intended it. When God speaks, I don't ask questions. I listen. We've prayed about this, and we know it's what God wants."

"Who prayed? You and *her*?"

I'd learned enough about this religion to which I unwillingly belonged to know men could be sealed for time and all eternity to more than one woman. The subject of polygamy was a sore spot with me, and many other Mormon women. The only plus was the modern-day church no longer practiced it, having officially abolished the practice in order for Utah to become a state.

"It's not God speaking! It was Joseph Smith! And Brigham Young! They were all just dirty old men, wanting a lot of wives! It's sick. You're sick! I can't believe you're doing this to us! I hate you!"

My father rose from the couch and reached me in two steps. He opened his big-palmed hand flat and smacked me on the side of my head. The room wobbled and my eyes couldn't focus clearly, the ringing in my ear so loud I couldn't hear what he said. When my vision cleared again I saw Sister Johnson looked petrified, much to my enjoyment; her children looked scared silly. My father's temper was legendary in our family, but few outside our home ever saw it.

My outburst didn't change anything, of course, and the wedding went off as planned. As children, we weren't allowed to go into the temple for the ceremony, which was fine with me. We waited outside with our grandparents, who also could not go in. My grandfather had a great love for swear words and coffee and thus had not been given his temple recommend, a pass to go to the temple given only to faithful members. My grandmother, who bickered constantly with him, remained very loyal when it came to church matters; she refused to go back inside the temple until he could go with her.

A sealing ceremony for Sister Johnson's four children had been set up for later in the month. Nobody asked them if they wanted my father to be their patriarch for time and all eternity. Sister Johnson's husband had been a nonmember, so everyone just assumed it was the best thing.

The Salt Lake Temple is a large, ornate gray building with tall spires and a gold statue of Moroni, a *Book of Mormon* character, on the top, waiting for the Second Coming of Christ, when he would blow his horn. Both the temple and the adjoining Temple Square Visitors' Center are surrounded by large concrete pillars connected by iron bars. The temple itself cannot be accessed without going through a sentry; in this way the church kept the riffraff out.

The visitors' center is a different story; and as we waited outside the temple, a group of Japanese tourists stared over the hedges onto the temple grounds, no doubt wanting to get a glimpse of a real Mormon. I imagined they peered closely at our heads, looking for horns.

Scattered around the grounds I could see the numerous brides and grooms, most of them fresh-faced and young, who'd been married there one after another that morning. They took pictures with their entire families, framed in the huge front doors of the temple and at other picturesque places.

My father and Sister Johnson's morning wedding was followed that evening by a reception at the local ward-house. The basketball standards were raised and the cultural hall, really a gymnasium, was decorated with bright pink flowers and a fake arbor where my father and the new Mrs. Jensen stood and greeted ward members, friends, and family. The ward Relief Society, the organization for Mormon women, served green punch and small squares of frosted cake with a little nut cup on the side.

Our new family now numbered eleven—two adults and nine children. It was a little like a tongue-twister, as the former Mrs. Johnson became the new Mrs. Jensen, but her kids stayed Johnson. We were the Johnson Jensens, the other kids in the ward teased. I hated every minute of it.

With the marriage and merging of our two families came a tidal wave of change. My father, an accountant, decided his real dream and calling was to be a Seminary teacher. The Monday-through-Friday hour-long religion class, held for Mormon teens during regular school hours, was the least favorite of all my courses. I skipped it regularly. My father took a cut in pay to teach Mormon fundamentals to teenagers who could not care less; and even worse, he was teaching it to teenagers who knew me.

"Somehow, the Lord will provide," he said knowingly, as he and Eileen discussed their budget. The Lord provided by forcing us to buy our clothes and shoes at Deseret Industries, a secondhand thrift store owned by the Mormon Church, and get our groceries from the Bishop's Storehouse, an arm of the Church Welfare System.

Even so, they always faithfully gave 10 percent of their income to the church. If you didn't tithe, you lost your good standing and temple recommend. My father wasn't about to let that happen.

To my stepmother's credit, there was no favoritism shown, as my stepbrothers and stepsisters wore the same tattered clothes we did. The new Mrs. Jensen held down a job at the Church Office Building, and she continued to work despite my father's insistence that children needed a mother in the home at all times. He didn't protest too loudly, because the truth was we would soon have been homeless without the income she provided.

My oldest stepsister Sally was a senior in high school when our parents married, with almost enough credits to graduate, and she had work release from school. It was her responsibility to get the younger children dressed, fed, and to school on time. A neighbor watched my stepmother's youngest child, two-year-old Blake, for the two hours Sally had to attend high school.

Our small house seemed even smaller, now that five more people lived in it. My stepmother had been renting an apartment, and her children were used to sharing with each other, but this did not extend to us. Sally moved into the room Corrie and I shared; a small army cot pushed against the only available wall became her bed. It was probably a good thing we didn't have many clothes, because there was nowhere to put them. Blake slept on the floor of my father and stepmother's room, and ten-year-old Jeff moved in with Kevin, who had always been lucky enough to have his own room. Eleven-year-old Tiffany got a cot similar to Sally's and was assigned wall space in the room Cathy and Christy shared.

We were all expected to pitch in. We did, with the threat of my father's backhand a punishment we didn't want to receive.

"Get your hands off my ball!" Kevin screamed from his room.

"Shut up, you stupid pussy!"

Jeff's angry tones echoed through the house. Sally and I peeled potatoes in the kitchen, preparing for dinner. My stepmother had not yet returned from work; the transit bus she rode from Salt Lake City sometimes took an hour or more to make the twenty-mile trip. My father was in the living room, reading scriptures in his chair.

I froze, a tingle of fear coursing down my neck. A rustle from the living room told me my father was up and out of the chair. Sally's head dropped, her hands momentarily stilled from our tedious task. She clenched the potato peeler tightly in her right hand, the knuckles going white with the pressure she exerted.

"Jeffrey!" My father's imperious tone commanded immediate obedience. "Come into this living room."

I heard scrambling noises as all the younger kids ran through the hallway and the kitchen, headed out the back door and into our tree hut, a place they considered a refuge. I pictured them all huddled there together, scared, momentarily joined as a family by the bond of fear.

My father's temporary elation at finding a new wife had been short-lived. Once the demands of raising nine children and paying bills set in, he once again became the morose, hard-handed man we knew so well. It was usually my backside on the receiving end of his lashings. Today, it was someone else's turn.

Jeff shuffled slowly into the living room. Both Sally and I turned and watched as he passed the kitchen, his hands pushed deeply into the pockets of the hand-me-down jeans that were too big. He never looked up from the floor, and his ragged blond hair stuck out on top of his head with determination he seemed to lack.

"Did you just use a swear word in my house?"

"No."

"Excuse me? Everyone heard you. Are you lying to me now, too?"

"That's not a swear word! Shit, damn, fuck, those are swear words!"

The *smack* told us the first of his punishment had been dealt out.

"I hate you, you stupid fucker!" Jeffrey screamed, sobs tearing through his voice, already inconsistent with the onslaught of puberty.

Sally and I looked at each other in a rare moment free of any animosity, and we dropped our potato peelers and fled out the back door, heading up into the tree house where we crowded in with the rest of the kids.

Nobody spoke; we all just sat there and stared down at the floor, not making eye contact. Cathy and Christy, fighting back tears, held hands. The silence was dense, frightening, and Tiffany began to sob.

"Allison? Where are you? Sally? Get in here now and get this dinner going."

Too afraid to argue, we climbed down out of the tree house.

"What were you doing up there?"

Neither of us spoke, scurrying toward the house like frightened rats. He extended his arm and stopped us before we could pass through the door.

"I said, what were you doing up there?"

"Checking on the little kids. They were scared and ran out," I said, knowing if one of us didn't say something things would soon get much worse.

"Scared of what?"

"Not of what. Who. They're scared of you."

He dropped his arm, and we rushed into the house, Sally ahead of me. He gave me extra momentum with his foot applied sharply on my tail bone.

Even when it was someone else's turn to get a whipping, I usually got my licks, too.

For me, the next three years were a blur of fighting for bathroom time, searching for my good school clothes—which always seemed to find their way into someone else's room—and dreaming of a life very different from the one I lived. We all grew up fast, and formed an uneasy bond of siblings and step-siblings. Our common ground was my father's temper, and we learned to cover for each other.

Unlike so many of my friends, I became an adult long before I was ready, holding down a part-time job and keeping straight-A grades in school. I also toed the Mormon line, didn't drink, smoke, have sex, or party. My inner longings were afraid to manifest. I didn't want to descend into the nothingness—Outer Darkness, where God sent the wicked, those who denied His true Gospel—my father had long threatened me with.

I wish I'd understood there was no way to avoid it.

Ten

I moved the twenty-odd miles to Salt Lake City when I was eighteen for three reasons. One was to attend the University of Utah, chief rival of BYU. Another was to escape the crowded, small house. The last was that my father forced me to leave.

I could have stayed. I could have lived at his home as long as I wanted. The catch was I had to attend church every Sunday and endure beatings whenever he deemed it necessary.

"As long as you live in my home, you will live by my rules and you will go to church."

I had long before declared my intention of leaving the Mormon Church and all its entanglements behind. So I left. I discovered alcohol and drugs. I also discovered the pleasure of sex. After I lost my virginity at nineteen, college was a blur of men, each one passing through, staying a while, and then moving on. It didn't bother me. At least I didn't think it did. The skinny, four-eyed blond girl I'd been now had contacts, provocative clothing, and an attitude.

It was an act.

Depression led me to Sandra Castle's office the first time. She was my lesbian aunt's lover and live-in girl-

friend, and a therapist. I was attending the University of
Utah on scholarship and living in an apartment off campus.
Early in March 1986, several days after my twentieth
birthday, I woke up and found myself unwilling and unable
to leave my bed.

"Allison, have you been in bed all day?"

Linda, my roommate, was appalled. It was unlike me to
stay in bed, even when I was sick.

"I'm not feeling well," I said, and motioned her to go
away. She left me alone for a while. I stayed there all that
day and into the next.

Linda called my father after she forced me to get out of
bed and shower. I did, listless and without interest, then
crawled back into the sanctuary of my covers. Dad drove in
and knocked on our door. She let him in and left.

"Allison, I know what's wrong. I think you do, too."

"Really? What?" I felt sardonic and cruel. I knew by
heart the direction in which this conversation was going. I
knew him well.

"You need to come home. You need to come back to the
church. Can I give you a blessing?"

Out of his pocket he pulled his ever-present bottle of
consecrated oil. I laughed, at first quietly and then hysteri-
cally. My laughter turned to tears and I cried. He watched
me with hurt in his eyes, one of the rare times I glimpsed
his compassion. I knew he wanted to help me, using the
only tools he had. The only ones he believed in. It just
wasn't what I needed.

"Dad," I said when I could finally speak.

"Yes." He reached out his hand to pat me, the only love
he could show.

"I sent my letter to the church headquarters last week.
I've asked to have my name removed from the records."
This was a lie, but I didn't know how else to fight back
against his religious tyranny.

He recoiled, and I could see the shock in his face as he tried to digest this news. Giving up church membership meant giving up everything—a place in the Celestial Kingdom, the highest of the three kingdoms of God; a chance to live in eternity with my family; redemption and glory.

He got up without saying another word and left.

My scholarship, the only chance I had of getting my college degree, finally served as an impetus to get me back to class and to my studies. I had to keep my grades up or I would lose my funding. Without that money, I wouldn't be able to attend the university, and the extra money I received for living expenses would be gone. I'd vowed I'd never return to my father's house, and I needed a good education to make money so I could survive.

Somehow, Aunt Carol heard about my despair—I never knew how, and she didn't say. She showed up at my apartment one evening bearing a plate of homemade lasagna, fresh sourdough bread, and a business card. She put the food in front of me at the kitchen table, pointed to the chair, and waited to make sure I ate.

"I'm not hungry, Aunt Carol," I protested.

"Eat."

"But . . ."

"Eat."

I choked down about half the lasagna and a small chunk of bread.

"There, I ate."

Aunt Carol looked at me with a wistful, sad look on her broad features and handed me a card. I saw the words SANDRA CASTLE, M.S.W., LICENSED THERAPIST. I looked up, and her answering look was kind.

"I can see you're depressed, Alli. You've been through a lot in your life. But you are very smart, and you have lots of potential. I don't want to see that wasted. This is Sandra's card. She's my . . . friend. I want you to go talk to her."

"I don't need any help. I'll be okay, really."

"Alli, your father's always been a tyrant. He used to hit your mother, you know? Until her spirit was gone and she just stopped fighting."

"He hit all of us. We lived through it."

"Everyone smaller within striking range is fair game to him. But you, you've always been strong and proud, and willing to stand up for yourself. It's everything he hates in a woman. It's made you the standout, the one he's injured the most. Please, go talk to Sandra."

"Is she your lover?"

"Does it matter?"

"Not in the least."

"Go talk to her."

I found myself in Sandra Castle's office a week later, not quite sure how I mustered the courage to dial her number or make an appointment. I had no idea where to start. Sandra—she told me to call her that—began asking me questions.

A short, thin woman, Sandra Castle had long brown hair and kind brown eyes. She wore no makeup, and her face had a fresh-scrubbed, honest look to it. Her office was in a renovated mansion on South Temple. It had been turned into a professional building, as many old homes in Salt Lake City had.

There was a small outer office, decorated with a dark wood desk, four or five antique-looking chairs, dark green carpet, and large floral swags on the walls. There were two large filing cabinets behind the desk, which was manned by a kindly older woman with gray hair. After I introduced myself the woman stood up and knocked on an oak door, and then opened it, motioning me in.

The larger inner office, where Sandra waited, was decorated in soothing blues and greens. She directed me to sit in a comfortable chair next to a window. Outside, I could see a large lilac bush blooming, and immediately thought, as I always did, of my mother, who'd loved the tender purple flowers.

Sandra started the session by asking about me, and we talked for a bit about my activities, education, plans, and goals. I supposed she was trying to put me at ease, but it wasn't working.

Finally, she said, "What brought you here, Allison?"

"Well, it was my aunt—you know her." I blushed, a little flustered, and not sure what to say. "Of course, you know her, that's not what I meant." I fidgeted with the buttons on my sweater.

She smiled, and said, "I know your aunt. Why did she want you to come?"

"She hasn't told you?"

"A little bit. But I want you to tell me."

"I guess she thought I was depressed, and I *have* been a little sad, you know, since Mom died. Then my dad got re-married and he hit me a lot because I told him I didn't like it. But I'm really okay. There's nothing seriously wrong with me . . ."

I rambled. She didn't interrupt.

"I've been pretty scared ever since I was six. Life is just scary. You never know what's going to happen when you wake up, do you? I mean, the year I was six somebody broke into our house and no one believed me. And of course the whole bearded man thing happened . . ."

"Bearded man?" She interrupted my story, and I realized too late I'd let this little bit of information out, information I had intended to keep to myself. I thought by recounting the less traumatic events of my sixth year I could avoid thinking or talking about Cindy, as I'd been taught to do all my life.

"What bearded man, Allison?" Sandra prodded me.

I sat still and closed my mouth. She waited with infinite patience.

"I don't want to talk about it," I said after a moment's silence. "Not right now."

She hesitated, a look of compassion in her eyes, then nodded her head.

"All right. Tell me something else. Did your parents get you some help?"

"Help?"

"Yes, help, in dealing with the trauma of hearing an intruder in your house?"

I laughed aloud. The stair thumper was nothing compared to the bearded man. He was the boogeyman who haunted my nights and shadowed my days. I always looked over my shoulder, waiting for him to come snatch me away. If I weren't so ugly and skinny, he probably would have taken me instead of Cindy. I was thankful to be a Plain Jane.

"Well?"

"Of course not. Mormons don't go to therapy."

"They didn't do anything?"

"Well, my dad called some of the elders and they gave me a blessing. That's what they did before, too . . ." I trailed off as I realized I'd veered back into the boogeyman's territory.

"A blessing?"

"Yes, a Priesthood Blessing. Are you Mormon? I mean, were you a Mormon before you became a . . . ?"

She looked amused. "Before I became a lesbian?"

Although the Mormon question was a logical one, I felt like an idiot implying a lesbian was something someone chose to become. Although, according to my father and every other Mormon I knew, it was definitely nothing other than a choice.

"Yikes. I sound like an idiot."

"No, you don't. I moved here in college to ski. I never left. And I've always been a lesbian."

She was a Gentile, the term used by Mormons to describe people who were not members of the predominant religion.

"Can you explain the blessing to me?"

"Well, it's kind of weird." I hesitated. I'd always found the eccentricities of my faith puzzling and odd myself, and I grew up in the confines of this religion. I didn't even want to think about how different we must seem to outsiders.

In my youth, one of the General Authorities had proclaimed Mormons were "a peculiar people," a phrase taken from the Bible's New Testament: "Ye are a chosen generation, a royal priesthood, and holy nation, a peculiar people." This was something he stated with great pride. I didn't want to be peculiar, even if it meant being chosen. I wanted to belong.

"Please, tell me," Sandra urged. I hesitated, thinking I now understood why Mormons *only* seek a counselor who is also LDS. It saved a lot of time on explanations. Of course, the main reasons were that church officials did not want faithful members straying, and risking someone's introducing them to different ideas offered all sorts of temptation. It wouldn't be "faith-promoting," another favorite buzzword.

"They bless you with oil, and only men can do it. And they have to be faithful Priesthood holders. I used to think it was a really big deal, with special oil, but I found out not too long ago it's just olive oil someone has said a prayer over. Anyway, it's supposed to . . . save you, I guess. That is, if *God* wants you saved. If he decides to take you, then boom, you're gone."

"And they did this instead of seeking professional help?"

"Of course. They do it for everything. Big tests. Job interviews. Sickness. It's just a way of life."

She grew quiet, and I knew she found it puzzling. So did

I. But I also learned through study that Mormons were not as unique as they liked to think. Many Christians also used oil for anointing and blessings. And many of the "sacred— not secret" temple rituals were gleaned from Joseph Smith Jr.'s familiarity with the Masons and their secret signs.

"And this is how they approached the 'bearded man' incident?"

My finger traced a pattern on the floral-design upholstery as I took a minute to think back, nervous again as we veered once again into scary territory. Surprisingly, this piece of my patchwork memory appeared to be missing. My father continually offered his family members blessings. I assumed the trauma of Cindy's disappearance and my injury had been handled in the same way, but had no real memory of it happening.

Over and over I traced the petals of a rose. "We didn't talk about it. I don't remember if they gave me a blessing. Probably. But I don't remember."

"They never discussed it with you? Never talked to you about it?"

Sandra Castle watched me intently, and we both flinched when her phone rang. She looked at her watch and said, "Wow, it's already been an hour."

We exchanged good-byes, and she scheduled me for another session in two days.

"Allison," she said before I walked out the door, "I'll try to help you now, but it will take your cooperation. I need you to trust me. I need you to talk to me."

I left her office thinking I'd never go back. How could she help? How could she know? It was too hard to explain, and I'd been taught we didn't talk about these things with outsiders.

Months later, Sandra Castle became my only hope of salvation.

Eleven

I discovered the capacity I had for denial around the same time I discovered there was an entire world outside my sheltered Mormon one. The information about my mother's desire to stop having children before she suffered her fatal pregnancy fell into my hands quite by accident.

I rang the doorbell at Aunt Carol's house, a lovely cottage on Salt Lake City's east side. It had been three months since I first met with Sandra professionally, and although I never returned to her office, our Sunday visits had become a weekly event. Once Aunt Carol reappeared in my life and I discovered she was sharing her home with Sandra, who had been her partner for the past ten years, I found I had a new family.

"Come in, Alli. You know you don't have to ring the doorbell. Consider this your second home." Aunt Carol smiled at the laundry basket I carried under my arm.

I did my weekly wash at the house while we dined, chatted, and shared wine. I got to relax and have a pleasant evening instead of plunking down on a hard plastic chair in a dirty coin laundry. They loved to feed me, and they always cooked together, smiling at each other and laughing, although Sandra was the real chef.

As a couple, they shared an intimacy I'd never seen my parents display. It was also sorely lacking in my father's relationship with my stepmother, who stopped smiling about one week after her marriage to him. Sandra frequently patted Aunt Carol's cheek or gently slapped her butt. They weren't overtly physical, but I knew they loved each other. Somehow, it seemed natural to me.

As I stepped inside I smelled Sandra's famous homemade lasagna, and my mouth watered. I'd regained some of my appetite in the months since they'd enfolded me into their little family unit.

She shooed Aunt Carol and me out of the kitchen and into the living room.

"So, how's school, Alli?"

"Okay. I made up the assignments and tests I missed, and my favorite English teacher is allowing me to redo my paper on Romantic poets."

"Good. Glad you're back on track. You can't let this stuff bother you, you know, especially the stuff with your father. He's an authoritarian tyrant. I always hated him."

"The feeling was mutual. You were a woman who wanted to be a man and usurp a man's rightful place at the head of the family. How come it's a man's rightful place?"

"Because they have bigger fists."

"None of that!" Sandra hollered from the kitchen. "I won't have man-bashing in my house. Men are perfectly lovely creatures."

I laughed, and Aunt Carol shook her head.

"'Creatures' is right," she muttered under her breath.

"I can hear you mumbling," Sandra yelled again.

"Anyway, don't let your father get to you. Don't let him destroy you, and convince you that you should be a baby-making factory like your mother. If he'd just listened to her, and not made her get pregnant again—"

"Whoa, slow down," I interrupted her. "Listened to her?

You mean she didn't want to be pregnant? He always told us she wanted another baby."

"Hell, no, she didn't want another baby. She already had five, and no help at all from him. She busted her butt taking care of you kids, and he never did a damn thing to help her. Came home from work and sat on the couch, watching TV and asking when dinner was going to be ready."

"She didn't want another baby."

Aunt Carol gave me a funny look. "Allison?"

"He killed her."

"Well, not literally, but he sure as hell was responsible. He wanted all those damn children to populate his kingdom, like it says in the *Book of Mormon*. She had a hell of a time getting through her last two pregnancies. The doctors warned her not to try again. He pushed her into it."

This was dangerous information for me.

"Dinner's ready," hollered Sandra, and we moved into the dining room, which featured a large bay window looking out on a barren vegetable garden, lightly frosted with snow. For early January, it had been a dry year, and forecasters already predicted water restrictions in the hot summer months ahead, a not-so-subtle reminder that Utah was a big desert.

I stewed quietly, unable to enjoy the food or the company.

"Alli, please, let it go," Aunt Carol pleaded. "When am I going to learn to keep my big mouth shut?"

Sandra only watched me closely.

I begged off our regular Sunday evening ritual of videos and popcorn and said my good-byes, shivering in my thin jacket as I warmed up my car. Only half my laundry was done, but I insisted I could finish it during the week at the coin-op and study at the same time.

I was dating a man named Vincent, thirteen years older than me and totally self-involved. I usually took my bad boys home to meet my father. I suppose I did it to torture him, but it always backfired. I only succeeded in earning his contempt. I certainly had no intention of keeping any of them around for any long-term relationship. This particular one had tattoos and a pierced ear, and had been raised by a nice Catholic Italian family—the equivalent of anarchy in my father's eyes.

I drove to Vincent's apartment. I knocked on his door and he opened it slightly, giving me a wide-eyed look. His chest was bare, and I heard soft music in the background. The distinctive odor of red wine from his breath wafted toward me. He wasn't alone.

"Not a good time, Alli," he murmured, looking furtively toward his bedroom and back at me. Tears filled my eyes, but I blinked them back, and left without another word. In a fog, I got into my car and started driving, with no real idea where I was going. I was halfway to Las Vegas when I finally let the tears roll.

Damn men. Damn them all. Can't trust them. Can't trust any of them.

I cried all the way to St. George, Utah, and then became strangely dry-eyed. Gazing across the Nevada state line, I became fixated on the Joshua trees on the side of the road. They seemed to multiply the closer I came to Las Vegas. Then, at the point I could see the twinkling lights of Sin City, the trees suddenly disappeared, as though God had reached forth His powerful hand and proclaimed the land barren because of its similarity to Sodom and Gomorrah. I rolled the window down and stuck my hand out, feeling instantly that the temperature was warmer than Salt Lake City by at least fifteen or twenty degrees. Hot, very hot. Heaven.

Once in Las Vegas, I drove to the Starlight Casino and started plunking quarters into a slot machine, gratefully accepting free drinks from a short-skirted, wrinkle-faced cocktail waitress who looked to be about a hundred and two years old. A handsome man sat next to me and smiled; I returned his grin, braver than usual with four rum-and-Cokes buzzing through my veins.

The constant *ching-ching* of coins, the bright lights, buzzers ringing, and people milling around felt comfortable and homey to me, and I floated off into that space where nothing could hurt me or touch me . . .

"Hey, wanna go sit at the bar? I'll buy you a real drink instead of that watered-down shit they serve for free," my seatmate said in a Southern drawl that told me he was a transplant to the western states.

"Why not? The night is young."

I woke the next day naked, in a heart-shaped bed with a strange man. My head throbbed, my stomach threatened to spill its contents, and I quietly crawled out of the bed and hit the carpet on all fours. The room seemed to be slightly atilt. I decided trying to stand was too risky and inched my way toward a door I hoped would lead into the bathroom.

I was about halfway there when I heard a noise and the naked man was on all fours behind me, slipping inside me. I gasped a little and swayed with his rhythm. It felt good. I couldn't see his face, but he pumped gently, not trying to hurt me. In fact, I could tell he was trying to stimulate me. It worked. I felt the contraction of the orgasm seconds later, and I cried out with pleasure. He came shortly after, and we reluctantly separated and collapsed to the floor.

He smiled at me. He was beautiful. I vaguely remembered a slot machine and some quarters, with his face somewhere in the mix. At least my drunken self still had good taste. I smiled back at him, weakly, and asked, "Who are you?"

He laughed and kissed my breasts, coming up for air only long enough to say "Brett."

We climbed into the Jacuzzi tub, and he gently scrubbed me clean from top to bottom, a most thorough bath. After we emptied the tub, we dried each other off; I watched amused as he hardened at my gentle rubbing. He pushed me backward into the main room and onto the heart-shaped bed, and I watched our reflection in the mirrored ceiling. Tacky beyond words, it was also extremely erotic. Brett scooted down to my pubic region, parted my legs, and began exploring me from the waist down. He flicked me gently with his tongue and sucked, a combination that drove me wild. I came again. It was my second orgasm with a man. The first had been earlier that morning.

I decided I was in no hurry to leave. For the time being, I forgot about my anger and about my mother and just let myself feel good.

When I left Las Vegas six days later, Brett, who it turned out was an unemployed construction worker, came back to Utah with me. I could hardly wait to introduce him to my dad.

"Who's this?"

We stood on my father's doorstep, as he'd not invited us in. Brett shuffled from one foot to the other. Most of the time he was a very serene, laid-back individual. Not today.

"Dad, I want you to meet Brett. He's moved in with me."

"Moved *in* with you?"

Hovering behind my father I could see Eileen. She looked very haggard and old. He turned and gave her a glare, and she disappeared.

"Yes."

"Allison, you're such a disappointment to me."

He shut the door in my face. Brett looked relieved. I was

peeved. I'd expected more of a confrontation—at least a smack or an offer to rid me of my demons by giving me a Priesthood blessing.

My father had just barely started speaking to me again after my revelation that I'd left his church. I thought I preferred it when he ignored me, because his constant pleas for me to return to "the gospel" quickly wore thin. I knew this confrontation would end with another long silence but wanted to go out with a bang. Armed with righteous anger about my mother's death, I wanted to hurt him. I supposed it worked, although not on the grand scale I'd envisioned.

My father's disapproval of our living arrangements made Brett all the more attractive to me. My Mormon roommate moved back home, spilling all my nasty secrets to the kids we went to high school with. For the first time in my life, I officially became a bad girl.

My brother Kevin received his mission call to Argentina a week or so after I returned from Las Vegas. He would be leaving for the Provo Missionary Training Center in one week. His "farewell," the Sacrament Meeting serving as his official Mormon send-off, had been scheduled for Sunday.

Kevin would spend two years in the foreign country attempting to convert the population to God's true church, after spending several months at the training center learning the language. It was understood by Mormons everywhere that all young men would serve a mission when they turned nineteen. Wearing a white dress shirt, tie, and dress pants, he and a companion would go door-to-door and attempt to teach the Gospel of Jesus Christ—or at least the one Mormons practiced.

My father wanted me to attend Kevin's farewell, I learned, when he showed up on my doorstep speaking of family obligation and loyalty. Somehow, I persuaded Brett to put on a suit and tie, and that Sunday found me back inside the wardhouse I had so long avoided. I could see Brett's presence there made my father uncomfortable and I enjoyed it. I'd known the invitation did not include my current flame.

After the meeting, which I tuned out by daydreaming about my lovemaking the night before with Brett, we returned to the home I grew up in for an "open house." Kevin cornered me in the kitchen, next to the potato salad and ham, when Brett left to use the bathroom. He began lecturing me about my lifestyle. He'd recently been to the temple to receive his Endowments, a requirement of all missionaries; and he already acted self-righteous and important. I could see the outline of his garments showing through his white shirt. I tried to imagine him in the knee-length, short-sleeved "Jesus jammies," complete with sacred markings over the breast and genital areas, but just couldn't picture it.

"You know what you're doing is wrong, Alli. Aren't you worried about what God will think? Don't you even care you won't be with us in the Celestial Kingdom? It's not too late . . . you can repent."

This wasn't the Kevin I remembered.

"I don't have anything to repent," I said. "Don't any of you see how absolutely silly this is? To think going to the temple, and saying silly words, and wearing funny underwear makes you closer to God?"

The shock on his face foretold the earnest testimony I was about to hear, and when my lover returned to the kitchen I grabbed his arm and pulled him away. Just seconds from freedom, I was waylaid by Corrie.

"Alli, I'm getting married. See?" She held out her thin hand, and barely visible on her left ring finger was a tiny diamond.

"You're getting married to who?" I asked, in shock. I had no idea she'd been dating anyone seriously.

She motioned to a tall, thin young man chatting with my stepmother, and he excused himself and came to join us.

"Alli, this is Mark—Mark Peterson. He's a returned missionary. I met him at the singles ward. We're getting married next month."

Shocked into silence, I had no retort. I was barely twenty-one, Corrie only eighteen; I couldn't even fathom being married, let alone getting married while still a virgin, which I knew her to be.

"Well?" she demanded. "Aren't you going to say congratulations?"

"Uh, congratulations. How long have you two been dating?"

"Six weeks."

Thus far, Mark had remained mute, and I wondered whether he could speak. I examined him closely and saw nothing to command attention. He had blond hair, blue eyes, a large nose, and a tracing of pimples scattered on his forehead. His chin was weak and practically disappeared under the shadow of his nose. His eyes, small and set close together, were the only outstanding part of his face, and that only because of their rich azure color.

"Six weeks?" Strangely enough, it was Brett, who rarely spoke except in grunts and groans and one- to three-word sentences, who said it. "Isn't that kind of quick?"

Stung, Corrie hastily pulled her hand away from mine and, in her hurt, lashed out. "Not everybody has sex with a man before they even know his name!"

I regretted sharing that confidence with her in a moment of weakness, one of many regrets I carried around like a bouquet of wilted flowers. Brett just smiled, and I mumbled congratulations as we hastily made our way to the door.

I was mortified, Brett was amused, and we drove home in silence. I thought about Mark Peterson, his bland features and wordless, tight-lipped mouth. There was something oddly familiar about him, but I wasn't able to make a connection.

Corrie dreamed of marrying someone who shared her passions. She loved reading and writing—and masturbating. She was forever in the bishop's office repenting for her many sins, but couldn't seem to keep her fingers away from her private parts. This I knew, because I'd shared a room and a bed with her, and the sounds she made when she thought I slept gave her away. How could passionate Corrie, who loved Harlequin romances and sexy Mel Gibson, even think about sharing her life with Mute Mark?

I realized I wasn't being fair, since I had barely met him and never even heard his voice, but he seemed so wrong for her. I just wasn't sure why.

Twelve

My concerns about her choice of mate did not sway Corrie. After all, I was the fallen child, the one in Outer Darkness who had turned her back on God's teachings. What did I know? The marriage went off as planned in early October. I made another unwilling visit to the outside of the Salt Lake Temple to attend, and finally heard my new brother-in-law speak. I wished he'd stayed mute.

"Corrie, where are my light-blue jeans?"

He stood in the kitchen doorway, looking at us with disdain as Corrie and I chatted at their small table. I didn't visit a lot, and was surprised when she called me to come to dinner one evening after they'd been married for three months. Mark had to work the swing shift that night, so she would be alone. Corrie, who'd spent her life with her nose in a book hiding from the rest of our raucous family, suddenly seemed frightened of solitude.

"They're in the closet. Right where I put them."

"Are you being smart? I just looked. They are not in the closet."

Corrie jumped from her chair and scurried into the bedroom, Mark on her heels, while I sat at the table and looked around. The kitchen was incredibly neat, with shiny secondhand appliances and mismatched canisters decorating the countertop. It didn't mesh with my memory of Corrie, who usually dropped whatever she was carrying wherever she happened to be. Her nose constantly in a book, she was usually unaware of her surroundings, and clothing and junk could pile up for months unnoticed. Usually, it took her tripping over these piles to get her to do any straightening, something that drove me crazy when we shared a room.

I could hear muffled voices, first Corrie's quiet one, then Mark's loud and angry one.

"You know I needed those jeans! What am I supposed to wear to work? What were you doing today, anyway? Reading again? I thought I got rid of all your books. I'm warning you . . ."

Not liking the tone of things, I walked to the doorway and inserted myself into an uneasy situation.

"What are you doing?" I asked Mark.

"What do you mean, what am I doing?"

"Leave her alone. I came to visit. You shouldn't chastise her in front of other people."

"This is my marriage, Allison, stay out of it."

"No."

"You'll stay out, or I'll make sure you never come to this house again. Maybe I should tell the bishop what I know about you, sleeping around all the time and living with a nonmember. Maybe you'd think about the sinful life you lead. This is between me and Corrie. I'm the Priesthood holder here, something you've never respected. You're disgusting."

"Ooooh, big man, with the big Priesthood and the magic powers. Whatcha gonna do? Bless me that I'll die? Curse me with your holy consecrated oil?"

Corrie, cowering over by the clothes hamper holding the jeans Mark had apparently been looking for, found some strength in a desire to protect me and stood up.

"Knock it off, Mark. Leave Allison alone. Go to work. I'm sorry I didn't wash your pants. I'll put a load in now."

I walked away from the bedroom and back into the kitchen, sitting in the chair with a thump. Corrie hurried past me with a laundry basket under her arm, mumbling something about how she'd be back in a minute. She went out the front door, headed downstairs to the basement laundry room.

Mark came into the kitchen wearing a pair of neatly pressed, clean dark-blue Levi's and his red Home Depot shirt. He looked at me with a snide expression. I tried to ignore him. He wouldn't let me.

"So, Allison, how many men did you sleep with this week?"

"Oh, just twelve. Oh, wait . . . you said men. I guess you better cut that down to six, then. Women don't count, right?"

A strange expression crossed his face, and he moved in on me, invading my personal space. I felt a flush spread over my face, and a tingle of fear sparked in my brain as I saw his predatory look.

"You really don't get it, do you, Allison?"

"Get what, Markie?"

I refused to be cowed by his attempts to intimidate me, determined to hide the discomfort he was causing me.

"Don't you realize the eternal consequences of premarital sex? Of fucking every man you meet? Your father and I have discussed you, you know. He came to me for advice. I told him he should just disown you, throw you out like he should do to your sicko lesbo sister."

"Did you just say 'fucking'? That's a mouthful for you, isn't it? You seem a little fascinated with fucking lesbians, Mark. Could it be you're a little turned on by the idea?"

He took me by surprise when he reached with his right hand, a rapid jerky motion, and placed it on my left breast, first lightly and then with increasing pressure. Shocked beyond words, I smacked it away.

"Don't you *ever* touch me again. *Ever!*"

"Why not? Everyone else does."

"You sick pig . . ."

The footsteps on the stairs alerted us to Corrie's return, and he pulled away from me with a look I couldn't interpret.

"Corrie won't believe you. No one would. I suggest you just keep your slutty mouth shut."

I understood the look now—it was lust.

My downtrodden sister pushed open the door and came in with the empty laundry basket.

"Mark!" she cried, making me jump. "You're going to be late."

"Your fault, Corrie. Your fault. You better hope I don't get fired."

I was so relieved to see him out the door I almost cried. I couldn't tell Corrie about him touching me. It would kill her gentle soul—she was so meek. I decided to keep my mouth shut and just plot revenge for later.

She sat at the table and looked at me with weary eyes.

"Allison, I'm pregnant."

The words spilled out of her without a prelude, and I was aghast.

"Pregnant? But you've only been married three months."

Corrie started to cry. "Mark . . . he threw the pills out Dr. Franks gave. . . . He said the . . . the . . ."

I stood up and grabbed the roll of paper towels that sat on the counter next to the toaster, and unwound one, tearing it off and handing it to her. When she stopped sobbing, she continued, not looking me in the eye.

"Mark said birth control was against God's plan. I told

him I talked to the bishop about it, and he said it was all right, but Mark wouldn't believe me. I'm so scared, Alli. Mommy died when she was pregnant. What if I die?"

I hadn't heard her refer to our mother as "Mommy" in years. It made me understand the depths of her despair, and I took her in my arms as she cried herself out. Corrie was still a little girl in so many ways, and now she was going to be expected to take care of another human life. Since I'd seen Mark's true nature firsthand, I was very frightened for her.

"Corrie, you need to leave him. Mark's not a nice guy. He's not right for you."

"Leave?" She looked up at me with shock. "I can't leave, Allison, don't you get it? I married Mark in the Temple. I'm bound to him for time and all eternity. I can't just walk out the door, like you do when you're done sleeping with your man of the hour!"

It was back to the "Bad Allison Show," and I sighed deeply. After a few failed attempts at reasoning with her, she became tight-lipped and grim, turning her head and ignoring my attempts to communicate.

I left her behind with regret. I left her husband behind with relief.

Corrie stopped answering my phone calls. I kept calling, but her machine kicked on, or Mark answered. I didn't intend to speak to him, so I hung up.

Several weeks passed with no contact from my family, until Cathy called me one night crying. She'd always been the emotional one, sobbing over lost dogs and stray cats. Her crying always brought a painful memory with it.

I recalled my father, stopped on a quiet country road near our house on a warm summer night—I must have been nine or ten. He bent down in the headlights to see what he'd hit. He stood up holding a young kitten by the scruff of its neck, one eye squashed shut, the other open and frantic. Blood dripped from its nose as all of us kids jumped out and ran toward him.

"Oh, Dad, we've got to take it to the vet. It's hurt."

It mewled and tried to bat with its paws, but one hung limply and wouldn't move.

"No, children, this kitten is going to die. It's better we put it out of its misery."

My mother, who had reluctantly followed us as we piled out of the car, gasped and said, "Children, back in the car. Now!"

Dad turned to her and said, "No, they need to understand life. They need to understand how God works." He turned back to us, still holding the squalling feline. "Children, this young kitten didn't obey its mother. It left her guidance and care and wandered off into the world on its own. The world is not a safe place for children who leave the side of their parents."

"Dad, put it down. You're hurting it!" I insisted, knowing I risked trouble if I continued but unable to watch the suffering cat struggle helplessly in the air.

"Allison, please pay attention. There's a lesson here. Your mother and I teach you kids the right way to go. We've raised you as members of God's true church. If you ever wander away, you'll end up like this kitten."

In two strides he moved to the other side of the car set the kitten down, and picked up a rock, bashing the tiny creature soundly over the head before it could move away on its three good legs.

"Allison! Are you there?" Cathy's strident voice brought me back to reality. "Christy's leaving. She's moving to San Francisco with her . . . with her . . . How can she do this?"

The Little Girls, inseparable since they were toddlers, now faced a monumental schism. I knew Christy had a female lover. I'd met Maureen, and liked her a lot. The couple, embraced by Aunt Carol and Sandra, came often to our Sunday dinners.

Christy was very much in the closet, so she stayed at my father's house, bringing little tidbits of information to me on Sundays.

"Well, it's for the best, Cathy," I told my sobbing sister. "Dad won't allow her around once he knows, and she deserves to be happy."

"But it's wrong. God is going to punish her, Allison."

"How do you know it's wrong?"

Her sobbing stopped, and I heard her sniffle. "Well, duh! It's in the scriptures. The church leaders said it's wrong."

"Cathy, all you know is what you've been told. Have you ever asked Christy about it? Asked her why? Did it ever occur to you she was born this way?"

"Allison, don't be ridiculous! We all make choices. It's just a phase or something."

"Cathy, wake up and get a clue, and when you do, call me back."

I hung up the phone in exasperation, thinking back to the Sunday before last. Christy had confided in me after dinner about some concerns she had for Corrie.

"I don't like Mark, Alli. Dad thinks he's wonderful. Every Sunday Eileen cooks this big dinner, and everybody gathers around, and he always has Mark say the prayer. He acts so religious, but there's something off, something phony about him. Corrie pulled me aside and told me he burnt all her Harlequin Romances in the incinerator."

"Why?"

"I don't know. There's something wrong about him, but I don't know what."

Shock stabbed through my body as I remembered my exchange with Mark. He'd mentioned my "lesbo sister." I knew what he meant, but how did *he* know about Christy?

"Christy, is there any way he could know about you and Maureen?"

"She prefers Mo. Mo and Christy. Has a nice ring to it, doesn't it?"

"Christy, I'm serious. Could he know?"

"How? We've been so careful. No one knows except you and Aunt Carol and Sandra."

I told her what Mark had said, and her eyes grew wide with concern.

"If he tells Dad, I'm in so much trouble. Alli, you know what he's like when he's mad. He'll probably take the belt to me. I'm only seventeen. I can't leave home yet! As soon as I turn eighteen I'm leaving with Mo, but . . ."

I had a bad feeling in my gut, especially since Mark was involved.

"Just be careful, okay? Watch him. He's up to something."

Thirteen

I had little in common with Brett, and the only interest we shared was sex. It soon became apparent to me you can only fool yourself for so long before you accept that your relationship is empty. The fun of sex play wasn't even there for us anymore, and so it came as no real surprise when I returned home from my last class early one day and heard a female squeal and the slapping sounds bodies make when in union coming from my bedroom.

"Oh God, oh, oh, oh, don't stop. Harder, Brett, harder. Oh, God, you're so big. You fill me up so . . ."

I recognized the voice—it belonged to Melanie from across the hall. I pushed open the half-shut door and watched the two of them writhe on my sheets. When they finished and Brett climbed off, Melanie gave a little sigh that turned into a scream when she saw me standing there.

She grabbed the top sheet, hastily wrapping it around her, and sprinted from the room, throwing open the door and running to her own apartment, leaving her purse and keys behind. I shut the door and turned to face Brett, who had put on his jeans while I watched Melanie run. He was a man used to getting in and out of his jeans quickly.

We stared at each other silently, and I laughed as I heard a light knock behind me.

"Alli? Please let me in. My keys are in there. My clothes are in there. I can't stand out here naked . . ."

I ignored her. So did Brett. Our eyes were locked in combat.

The knocking grew more persistent.

"Dammit, Alli, I know you're pissed, but . . . shit . . . shit." Her voice grew muffled, and I heard the sound of heavy footsteps headed down the hall toward us. Our apartment building was old, and the walls were thin.

"Locked out?" said a male voice. "Want me to get the super?"

"No, no, Alli has a key. I know she's in there. Probably in the bathroom. Thanks."

"You can wait in my apartment." It was creepy Mr. Fanconi, who always ogled all the college girls in the building. He was at least sixty, and had propositioned everyone I knew at least once.

I smirked. Served her right.

Brett finally broke our eye contact and bent down and picked up Melanie's clothes and keys. He opened the door and threw them out into the hall, then shut the door in her face.

He was watching me again, and I finally spoke.

"How long?"

"Two weeks."

"Please go."

"I love you. She's just a fuck. You know I need sexual freedom."

"Go."

I couldn't be persuaded, not that Brett was much of a persuader. He was a man of few words, but he said good-bye in a way I never forgot. It was the same way he had said hello, with his face buried between my legs and his tongue inside me. I had my last orgasm for the next two years just before he walked out. To his credit, he did not run to Melanie.

Fourteen

Aunt Carol called me late the next night to tell me a bruised and bloodied Christy was in her spare bathroom, washing off the remains of a severe beating administered by our father. I hurried over—I knew Mark had finally revealed Christy's secret.

After Sandra let me in and told me about the severity of Christy's injuries, she led me to the door and knocked. "She won't let us call the police. Try to talk to her, okay?"

"Yes." Christy's voice sounded high and thin, and I could hear the pain resonating through the door.

"Christy? It's Alli."

"Come in."

I pushed through the unlocked door and found my younger sister in the tub, resting her head against the tile wall. Her thin naked body was covered with welts. Her hair had been chopped off haphazardly, big and little pieces missing in different areas. She resembled the Barbies we used to play beauty shop with.

"God, Christy, your hair."

"He hacked it off. With a knife. I kept thinking he was going to miss and just stab me to death, so he wouldn't have to look at me anymore. 'Want to be a boy, Christy? I'll make you a boy,' he kept saying."

She spoke in a matter-of-fact tone, hiding behind it as if it were a suit of armor. She sat up, and I gasped—the bruises on her back were already black-and-blue and swollen, the width of my father's favorite belt.

We heard voices out in the hall, and Mo arrived, rushing to Christy and shoving me aside, engulfing her in a hug.

"Ooow." Christy wilted, and Mo jumped back.

"Oh, God, baby, he did this to you? He has to pay. He has to pay."

"No, let's just go. Let's go to San Francisco, like we talked about."

I walked out of the bathroom, not wanting to intrude on their personal exchange. That they loved each other deeply was apparent in their voices and looks, something my father would refuse to see.

I knew Christy would leave, and it made me sad, yet happy for her. She'd never thrive here, in this state of patriarchal conservative men who allowed only one set of rules.

The flash of emotion that clattered through my brain registered green and vivid. Jealous they would escape, I wanted to leave with them. But I couldn't. Something held me here—something that required resolution.

I couldn't get away from my demons until I faced them down, destroyed them, and emerged victorious.

Fifteen

Cindy floated in the water face up, her beautiful long brown hair fanned out around her. Her eyes, wide open, stared sightlessly toward the sky. She was naked. I tried to reach her, but the water was thick, like quicksand, and my legs would not work. "Cindy . . . Cindy . . ." I could feel the tears running down my cheeks, but my arms weren't working either and her face dissolved, disappearing before my eyes. I let out an agonized moan.

I fought off the terrible sleep and slowly opened my eyes. I wasn't a little girl anymore.

Now wide awake, I looked around at the walls of my bedroom, trying to will myself back into slumber. I knew it wouldn't come. I threw aside the covers and padded to the kitchen, looking in my fridge for the box of wine I already knew was empty and in the garbage. I didn't know why I even wanted it. The alcohol no longer blocked my subconscious—I could remember my dreams.

I decided to go for a drive and slipped out my door and down the stairs into the night. Utah's fickle spring had been interrupted by a cold front from Canada, and frost permeated the air. The heater in my 1963 VW was not very good—I shivered until the car warmed up.

I drove through the streets of Salt Lake City, eventually ending up on the East Side bench, where I parked and looked out at the lights of the city. I thought of Cindy playing by the banks of the creek. I remembered her beautiful hair. I remembered her room, which had seemed like a toy store to me.

The tears rose to the surface and cascaded down my face. What kind of monster preyed on little girls? Why did my mother and father—everyone—ignore what had happened, refusing to speak about her again?

I had no answers. I cried until my eyes and face were raw, then drove home. At two in the morning, the streets of Salt Lake City were mostly vacant.

The same questions kept running through my head as I drove. What happened to Cindy? Why didn't anyone ever talk about her?

Her family had moved from Farmington shortly after the incident. I believed Cindy was dead, but did they ever find her body? Did they ever find the bearded man?

I drove into the parking lot and, deep in thought, locked my car and headed for the front steps. I sensed the man approach me just before he wrapped his left arm tightly around my neck and covered my mouth with his right hand. I tried to scream, but my cries were muffled under his gloved hand. He dragged me behind the Dumpster in the alleyway next to the building and warned me not to make any noise or he'd kill me.

He threw me to the ground face first, his hand breaking my fall, and then he jerked me over so I stared up into his face. My shoulder throbbed as he tore at the zipper of my jeans, fumbling with his gloved fingers.

When I focused on his face, I screamed.

It was him!

He wore a stocking mask, the kind used for skiing, and through the mouth hole I could see the bristles of a beard.

The boogeyman came back. He must have read my mind. He must have heard me wondering about Cindy. He must have . . .

He slapped my face hard when I screamed and banged my head ruthlessly onto the pavement.

Why me? Why me? I must deserve this. It's my fault. I shouldn't have been out this late.

He yanked my shirt and found my left breast, bare because I hadn't bothered to put on a bra before my impromptu drive. He pinched the nipple so hard I screamed again, and he slapped me even harder. Pain waves rolled through my head, and my terror excited him, fueled him. I could see it, and I willed myself to stay quiet.

Shut up, Alli. Just shut up and lay still. Let him do it. Then it will be over.

He raped me, shoving inside my reluctant body, tearing me with reckless abandon, throwing my jeans out of reach and ripping off my underwear that said MONDAY, pushing my naked backside into the pavement.

With my last bit of strength I reached up and yanked at the beard, trying to do some minuscule damage to him. A large, soft tuft came off in my hand, and he jumped up and ran, leaving me there on the pavement behind the Dumpster staring silently up at a sky full of brooding clouds. My lips, bloodied and bruised, throbbed, and my throat ached where he'd exerted pressure pushing me to the ground.

I knew I was still alive. I could see my breath in the frigid air. I couldn't move. I hurt, inside and out.

I heard a car pull up and looked over at the flashing lights bouncing off the shadows and the brick walls of the building. Someone must have heard me scream and called the police.

Too late. Too late for me.

I couldn't move, couldn't talk.

"Nelson, she's over here," I heard a cop say. He knelt over me, a look of concern on his boyish face.

"Oh, shit, she's hurt."

Déjà vu.

He spoke into his radio, requesting an ambulance. His partner joined him and helped the first cop pick me up and carry me to their car. A blanket appeared, almost magically, and they wrapped me in it as we waited for the ambulance to arrive.

"Can I call someone for you?"

I shook my head.

A crowd of my fellow tenants gathered on the front lawn, wearing ski parkas or wrapped in blankets.

"What's your name?" asked the cop who sat with me. I could hear the wail of the approaching ambulance and wondered how many people sat upright in their beds at the noise, automatically taking survey of all their loved ones.

"Alli. Allison," I said, almost surprised my voice worked.

"Alli, please let me call someone for you."

I looked at him for a moment before holding my hand out slowly, opening it so he could see what I held there.

"The beard. It wasn't real. He knew me. He must have known it would terrify me."

He took the small clump of hair from my hand and motioned to his partner, who brought him an evidence bag.

"Why do you think he knew you? Why would a beard terrify you?"

I shook my head. I couldn't speak, and the tears finally started to fall. I was crying for my lost childhood, my freedom of choice, which had been taken from me yet again.

"Alli, there must be someone I can call for you."

Who would I call? My father, who considered me a sinner, and who would surely blame me for what happened? My sister Corrie, whose own life was blanketed in misery?

Cathy, who offered up sincere, utter devotion and belief in my father's teachings? My lesbian aunt and her lover, who already had little use for men? There wasn't anyone else.

I shook my head again and looked up at the cop. A light, fluttering snowflake landed on his head, followed closely by another. The sky filled with white, and it soon snowed heavily, hiding the ground. In front of the building, the multicolored tulips that came up every spring drooped to the ground, their vibrant hues muted. Spring disappeared in an instant, and the discordant tunes of a Christmas song floated through my mind.

"Let it snow, let it snow, let it snow. . . ."

Sixteen

I stared at the bright overhead light of the emergency room cubicle, gritted my teeth, reminded myself to breathe slowly to avoid hyperventilating.

I wanted my mother. I ached for her gentle touch, her reassuring glance, her warmth. I missed her more right now than I could ever remember.

Transported by ambulance to the University of Utah Medical Center, I now stoically endured the indignities of the rape kit and examination, wincing at the pain as a cold speculum parted me so the doctor, a woman, could swab for semen. It hurt, the bruising I'd already endured further aggravated by the prodding.

I'd heard horror stories about the traumas inflicted on women victims after they were raped, as if being forcibly violated was not enough. I was lucky, because the doctor was gentle and compassionate.

Rape. It always happened to someone else, not to me. When someone was inside me it was because I allowed him to be there. That was forever gone. My control over my own body was gone.

It got worse.

When she was done, the doctor covered me with a thin

white blanket and walked around to the side of the bed. "Allison, I hate to bring this up, but are you on the pill, or using some form of contraception?"

Dr. Rodriguez was a short, round resident. She had long black hair and dark eyes, her brown skin like milk-chocolate cocoa. She exuded an air of confidence and gentle compassion.

"Pregnancy. You're worried about pregnancy."

"Yes, that, but also there's a possibility of a sexually transmitted disease."

I gasped and reminded myself to breathe slowly.

"It's not real likely, okay? Please don't get too upset. I know this is awful for you."

"I'm on the pill. I don't want children." I took a deep breath and looked over to the doorway to see a large woman standing there.

"Hi," she said, taking our notice of her as an invitation to enter the cubicle.

"Hi, Mary Kay." Dr. Rodriguez knew her, obviously, and she gently patted my hand before she left me with the woman.

"I'm Mary Kay French, from the Rape Crisis Center. I'm here to try and help you through this, Allison."

"How can you?"

"Well, for starters, I can let you talk. I can listen. Or I can talk, and you can listen. Whatever you need."

"Are you a doctor? Or a counselor?"

"No, but I've received training."

"You don't know me. You can't help me."

I didn't want to share this private pain, this humiliation, with a stranger. I'd allowed the boyish police officer to call Sandra. I told her not to bring Aunt Carol, not wanting to hear about the inadequacies of all men or see it in the looks the lesbian couple gave each other.

"I know this is a tough time, Allison," Mary Kay said,

reaching out to touch my arm. I pulled away like a stubborn child, not wanting to be comforted by this complete stranger.

"You don't know anything. You don't understand anything."

"Allison, do you know how we come to be volunteer counselors for Rape Crisis?"

I shook my head.

"Four years ago, on a warm summer night, I was sound asleep in my bed. I have the second-floor apartment, so I've always felt safe, and it was hot, so I left the windows open. I woke up to find a man on top of me. He raped me four times, with a gun to my head." She recounted her experience with tears in her eyes. "I remember thinking, 'What in the world would any man want with a fat old Betty like me?' Of course, rape isn't about sex. It's about power."

I watched her shiny, plump face as she spoke. I thought about my own experience that night. Rape was about power.

My attacker was someone I knew. Someone who wanted to see me destroyed.

The doctor admitted me to the hospital for observation; Mary Kay left after seeing me settled in my room. She promised to return the next day. I had suffered a slight concussion when the rapist threw me to the ground and my head hit the hard pavement, and I discovered bruises and bumps all over my body. I didn't remember much of the pain. I only remembered the terror.

A tired-looking detective interviewed me, and he kept asking me what I'd been doing out at two in the morning. His disapproving stare and the line of his Jesus jammies through his dress shirt gave away why.

The voice of my attacker had been deep and muffled, like someone trying to hide his identity.

"And this guy you had sex with a few hours before this 'rape' . . . you're sure it wasn't him?"

I glared at him, wishing I hadn't shared this information with the doctor, who had no choice but to share it with the police. From the corner of my eye, I noticed a shape in the doorway.

Sandra stood there listening to the detective's questions, and I could see the slow burn build on her face. She walked purposefully into the room as he asked me for the umpteenth time why I had been out at that time of night and announced, "I think that's enough."

He glanced at her, dismissed her with a look, and turned back to me, opening his mouth to speak again.

She didn't give him a chance. "I said that's enough!"

"Who are you?" He had a menacing look on his face.

"I'm her doctor. This woman has been raped by an unknown assailant. From what the officer who notified me said, you haven't apprehended him. She didn't know him. You have a job to do. Go catch him."

"I'm questioning the victim, Miss . . ."

"The key word here is *victim,* Detective. She was raped. It doesn't matter where she was, or who she had sex with before. She didn't ask for this. You seem to think she's responsible. That somehow she deserved it. I guarantee you, if you continue in this way, I will report you."

I couldn't believe she stood there spouting off to the detective, who reacted in the same way I knew my father would have. A deep admiration for this strong woman filled my bruised soul.

She turned her back on him and came to me. She patted my forehead and shook her head as she took in my bruises. I cried again, tears pouring out of my eyes, an involuntary action I couldn't control. Sandra encouraged my tears, told me to "get it out." I felt weak, used, humiliated. I didn't want the detective to see my weakness.

By the time the tears dried up, the spot where he once stood was empty.

Someone cleared their throat, and we both looked over at the door. The policeman who found me stood in the doorway, and Sandra's face tightened, a stern, warning expression emphasized by her eyebrows crossing her usually placid features. He looked down at his feet, then back at me shyly.

"I just . . . I wanted to know how she was. I just got off duty."

"You're Officer Jensen?" Sandra's face relaxed a little, but she looked puzzled. "I wondered when you called me—are you a relative of Allison's?"

"No, not that I know of. Pretty common name. My name's Jake."

"Well, I appreciate the call. Thank you."

"You're welcome. If this is a bad time, I could leave."

"Allison?" Sandra looked at me.

"No, it's okay. You can come in."

"I'm going to go find some coffee, and I'll be right back," Sandra said, giving Jake Jensen another stern look. He blushed under her firm glance.

After she left, he walked over to me and pulled a chair up next to my bed.

"Jake Jensen. Wonder if we *are* related?"

He laughed. In Utah, with the big families and the old-time practice of polygamy a part of our heritage, you never knew.

"Don't know. Maybe you're my half-sister. Or cousin."

Of course, Jensen was a pretty common name.

He grew serious and leaned toward me.

"Are you okay? Really, I mean? I . . . I know you're not okay, but are you . . . I mean. Shit."

"Jake Jensen. It's okay. Thanks for asking."

My heart did a funny little skip. This man, who had seen me in the worst possible light, now sat in my hospital room offering something I was unable to interpret. Was he drawn to women who were victims? In his line of work that was mostly what he saw. Victims of domestic violence, of murder, of rape.

Sandra bustled back into the room, and Jake stood up quickly.

"I'm going now. I'll check back with you tomorrow."

"I won't be here."

"Oh, I . . . oh, okay."

"Did you check out that piece of fake beard?"

"They've got it in the crime lab. I'll let you know when I hear anything. Maybe I should get your phone number."

What did he want from me? I tasted acid in my throat, swallowed painfully, ignored it.

"Do you have a piece of paper?" I asked Sandra. She pulled a small notepad out of her purse, tore out a page, and handed it to me. I scribbled my phone number on the paper and said, "If you want to check on me, you can call me. I want to know the minute you hear anything about the beard."

He smiled at me and left.

Sandra didn't comment. She pulled the chair toward the bed and sat.

"I thought you were a therapist."

She looked puzzled for a minute, then smiled as she realized I referred to her conversation with the patronizing detective.

"That type of man only appreciates authority. I needed his attention, so I got it. I adore those kinds of men."

I smiled a weak smile. "You'd love my father."

"What do you need, Alli? Talk to me, okay? Tell me what I can do. Why call me to come, instead of Carol, or your sister Corrie? Why not your family?"

I'd only had one session with her. She knew very little about me, or my past, other than what I'd told her, or Aunt Carol had shared. I thought for a moment.

"Because I'm drowning and I need help. Real help. This just capped off . . . this rape is just the . . ." The tears came back, and I hastily wiped them away and tried to dislodge the lump in my throat. "So many things happened to me when I was young, and I feel like I'm about to self-destruct. I need to stop dreaming. I need to know what happened to Cindy."

"Cindy?"

"I guess it's time I explained."

"Not now," she said gently. "There's plenty of time. Now you need to rest."

I nodded silently, and she turned off the lights and sat back down in her chair.

She didn't leave.

Seventeen

I jolted awake from an alcohol-induced sleep. My windows were open; the warm spring air, tinged with a hint of blooming flowers, wafted in and out the window, blowing the cream-colored gauze curtains gently back and forth.

I watched the curtains breathe, in and out, wondering why I had awakened so abruptly. Was it another dream? Another nightmare? Seconds later my phone rang.

"Hullo?" I glanced at the bedside clock to see it read exactly 1:00 A.M.

"Allison?"

"Uh-huh. Who's this?"

"It's Eileen."

"Eileen?"

"Your stepmother!"

I could hear the disgust in her voice.

"What's wrong?" I sat up quickly, rigid in the sudden knowledge something was amiss.

"Corrie's had her baby. She's in the hospital."

"Baby? Hospital? But she wasn't due for months! Oh, God, is the baby okay?"

"She's very sick. She's on a ventilator and has a lot of problems."

"What hospital?"

"St. Benedict's."

"I'll be there as soon as I can."

I'd only seen Corrie once since I told her to leave Mark, and I avoided her husband at all costs. She called me once in a while, leaving wistful messages on my answering machine, a hint of loneliness in her voice. But she always called when I was at school or work, and when I'd call back Mark always seemed to answer.

The thought of seeing Mark again, of looking into his eyes, terrified me.

Face up to it, Allison. Face it. Corrie needs you. If you see him, maybe you'll know for sure.

I rushed to the hospital in Ogden, and found my sister alone in her hospital room, tears streaming down her pale face.

I held her tightly in my arms and asked about the baby.

"She's so tiny, Allison, only two pounds. And she couldn't breathe when she came out. She gasped for air and her chest caved in and out, and they took her away. I never got to hold her. I have to touch her through the incubator."

"Where's Mark?" I didn't want to know. I had to know. Something had been bothering me, niggling at me, since my rape. My attacker's size, his knowledge of my whereabouts, the extreme anger he seemed to have for me, and most of all, the beard—it all pointed to someone who knew me. And someone who wanted to hurt me. The only person I could think of was Mark, for reasons I still didn't understand.

"I don't know. He . . . he wasn't here for the birth." Corrie looked at me with wide, swollen, red eyes. "Alli, I was all by myself. I was so scared. I knew it wasn't time, but my water broke at the grocery store. I drove myself here. I tried to call Mark at work, and they said he . . ."

She couldn't go on, and I put my arms around her and let her cry for a minute.

"What did they say, Corrie? What about Mark?"

"He hasn't worked there for months. He got fired before Christmas. I don't know where the hell he's been going."

I stayed with Corrie. my stepmother came and went quickly early the next morning, wearing the grim expression on her pinched face that never changed. I hadn't seen her smile in years. She brought some tiny T-shirts and baby booties for little Elise Marie, whom Corrie named after our late mother, and, surprisingly enough, me. My father also came and gave the baby a blessing, touching her tiny head through the portholes of the incubator.

He motioned me out to the hallway when the nurse came in to check Corrie and asked if she'd told me anything.

"What's going on with Mark?" I asked my father. "Corrie says he got fired from his job months ago."

"I don't know, Allison. Corrie won't talk to me, won't betray her husband. She let that information slip. But I think something's wrong. I know I can help her because I have the Priesthood, but she won't let me. She didn't even call any of us when she was having the baby. Can you talk to her?"

I was shocked. My father was asking me to help him? His lowly, bad girl, apostate daughter? Admitting he couldn't automatically solve everything with his beloved Priesthood authority?

I shook my head in disbelief and asked what he knew about Mark.

"Well, he goes to church regularly with Corrie. I tried to talk to their bishop, but he just told me he would try to help them. I know they still go to the temple together. But she's closemouthed. She's unhappy."

"And why do you think I can help?"

"Well, you certainly can't make things worse. Follow your heart, Allison. Follow the good I know is still inside you. You were given a promise by God when you were baptized. Reach into your heart of hearts, where I know you still realize the truth of the Gospel, and talk to your sister."

I turned away. It was always about one thing. Not his family, not his children, only his church. I knew he thought he was doing the right thing. He was so convinced of the purity of his actions that only Jesus himself appearing and telling him Mormonism was simply another religion would change his mind. Or maybe not. He'd probably just insist it was not Jesus but Satan in disguise.

I followed my heart.

"Corrie," I said when I returned to her bedside, "Mark is sick. There's something really wrong. The fact he lies to you, that you don't know where he is, tells me he is up to something bad. Really bad."

She just cried harder.

"Have you called his family? Asked them if they know where the hell he is?"

Corrie shook her head. "They hate me. Mark told them I was . . . he told me I was bad. He didn't want me anymore, Allison, not after I got pregnant and fat, and so I bought some lingerie and tried to . . . tried to interest him in me again. He told me I made him sick. He called his brother and mother and told them I was a whore. Now none of them will talk to me."

"Corrie, he's the bad one, not you. I *know* he's bad. Look, when I was at your house he tried to touch me. He's sick. And there's more. You need to leave him. You need to kick him out. Or just take your baby and go. Come stay with me—I have a sofa bed. You and the baby will be safe there. I'll protect you. You should have called me when you went into labor."

"What do you mean he tried to touch you?"

Corrie's eyes, which had seeped moisture nonstop since I arrived, were abruptly dry and clear.

"When I was at your house, okay? When you went to do the laundry."

"Touch you where?"

"Does it matter?"

"Of course it matters!"

"My breast, okay?"

She shook her head, a stubborn look on her face.

"It was probably an accident. He didn't mean it. Alli, I can't leave my husband. I can't. I didn't call anyone because I wanted my husband here. It was supposed to be our special time."

"You don't even know where he is, Corrie."

"I made my covenants. I married him in the Temple. I can't leave. I talked to my bishop, and he told me I have to try harder."

My throat clutched, and my heart ached for my young sister. I stood up, determined to find her asshole husband and make him pay. I was also going to find her bishop and give him a piece of my apostate mind.

Mark chose that minute to walk through the door. He sauntered up to Corrie, pushing me aside, and gave her a big bear hug. She melted.

I was hurt and confused, angry at myself. I thought I could've gotten through to Corrie, if only I'd hurried. If only Mark hadn't walked in.

A chill washed through my body as I watched him hold my sister. He turned his head to look at me once more, and I saw the truth in his small, evil eyes. I'd hoped for some sign, for a confirmation that would let me know he'd been my attacker, but when it hit me, I wasn't prepared.

With a smirk, he freed one hand and stroked his whiskerless chin.

With the growing belief Mark had been my rapist came a certain empowerment. I wasn't convinced enough to go to the police yet, not wanting to rip apart Corrie's already tattered life without real proof, but knew I must take some action.

I decided to sit down with my father and explain what I knew, to tell him about my suspicions. Surely he wouldn't be willing to let Mark do this to Corrie, and even to me. This had to be the point where he would finally accept me as his daughter, stand up for me, love me for what I was—and not what I wasn't.

I never got the chance. Three days after Corrie's baby was born, my brother Kevin was sent home early from his mission.

He came home in a coffin.

Eighteen

Phone calls in the middle of the night invariably set my heart racing. They are always harbingers of something bad—someone has died, or been in an accident, or worse.

I sat up in bed with a start—the phone ringing in my dreams was real. I reached for the receiver and put it to my ear as I switched on the lamp.

"Allison . . . Allison . . ."

I didn't recognize the male voice, and my heart started to race. It was someone who knew my name.

An obscene phone call? Mark?

Then I realized he sounded like he was crying.

"Who is this?"

There was a noise on the other end and a familiar female voice came on the line. "Allison, this is your stepmother. There's been a terrible tragedy."

Oh, no, not the baby. Not little Elise Marie.

"Kevin was working in a dangerous area of Argentina, you know, and he and his companion were coming home in the dark. They were jumped by two armed robbers who shot him in the head. He died at the hospital. They're sending his body home on a plane tomorrow."

I felt the blood drain from my face as my stepmother

coldly delivered the news of Kevin's murder. Never an expressive woman, the longer she was married to my father, the less "real" she became.

My father. The sobbing male voice belonged to my father. The man I'd never once seen shed a tear, not even when they closed the casket on my mother's lifeless, waxen body.

"I'll be there as quick as I can." I hung up and fell back onto my pillow, longing to roll over and ignore this situation. I wanted to pull the covers over my head. I needed a drink.

I forced myself to get up and dress, and my heart jumped in funny little pitter-pat motions. Kevin. Self-righteous, annoying little Kevin. The brat who delighted in tormenting me when we were children. The last words we'd exchanged had been bitter. Now, he was dead.

The leaders of the Mormon Church were fond of faith-promoting parables littered with warnings of the hazards of leaving loved ones with unkind words. One simply never knew when it might be the last time you would see them.

For once, they were right.

I drove the twenty miles to Farmington thankful the spring air was warm, as I'd forgotten my jacket. Memories of Kevin raced through my mind like a movie I couldn't stop or pause.

The time I'd accidentally slammed his hand in the car door and broken his fingers.

The time he slugged Rodney Crowell for pulling up my dress at church.

The time . . . the time he came into my room after Cindy disappeared.

I was still recuperating from the gash on my head and the confusion in my soul. He looked up at me with eyes far too serious for a four-year-old. We were so different. I had blond hair and blue eyes, and he was dark-skinned with warm brown eyes. I remember he lifted his small, grubby fingers, folded together around something he clutched tightly. He put that something on my pillow and whispered, "Don't die, Allison." Then he left.

I turned my head slowly and saw his lucky rabbit's foot, the one Aunt Carol had bought him at a garage sale. He loved the ragged, furry paw; and when life got rough or hairy, as it often did in our father's house, he would stroke it with his index finger.

Dad was forever trying to confiscate it, because he didn't like superstition. He wanted us to rely on God. Despite that, Kevin held on to the rabbit's foot and never let it out of his sight, sleeping with it under his pillow at night and shoving it into the pocket of his jeans during the day. It was a part of him.

In his four-year-old mind, it must have seemed to him that I was dying. The solemn demeanor in our house, the whispering, the unanswered questions must have seemed to carry the pall of death, an omen of the things to come.

Kevin. We were so different.

I could no longer see the road. Tears clouded my eyes and my judgment, and I pulled over in the emergency lane of I-15, sobbing in my car as I rocked back and forth, my arms twined around my torso, my screams unheard on the lonely stretch of deserted freeway. They bounced off the metal and back at me, assaulting me like the memories that came one after another.

I forgot. Oh, God, I forgot the Kevin who cried when our mother died, the Kevin who stood up tall and tried to be a man at such a young age. How did I forget him? How *could* I forget him? Was I so filled with anger that all I could see was the bad? There had been good times, too. Why couldn't I focus on them instead of always on the negative? Why weren't those gentler times the first thoughts that popped into my head instead of destructive, hurtful memories?

A sharp rap at the window brought me to reality fast. I

jumped and gasped, wiping the tears away with the back of my hand as I turned to see a young Utah Highway Patrol trooper. He rotated his finger in a circle for me to roll my window down.

"You okay, Miss?"

I tried to clear my throat and speak without any vestige of tears, but I was still choked up and my throat was raspy and sore. "My brother . . . my brother . . ."

"Allison?"

I looked closer at the officer, squinting in the dark, then reached up to flip on the domelight.

"It's me. Russell. Russell Free."

"You're Lance's brother." Kevin's best childhood friend had been Lance Free, and my brother had spent hours with Lance and his older brother, Russell, who was the same age as me. "Russell Free Ride. Free and Easy."

"Yeah, yeah, heard 'em all a million times. Hey, you said something about your brother. Is Kevin okay?" He squinted and gave me a stern look, perhaps remembering a rumor he'd heard. "Have you been drinking?"

"Kevin's dead, Russell. He died today in Argentina. He was shot."

The shock slowly transformed his face. We were young. We weren't supposed to have to cope with the deaths of our friends or family members.

He stepped back and straightened up, and I watched him swipe quickly at his eyes. Russell, Kevin, and Lance had been inseparable. The Free boys were very close for brothers, and rarely fought, instead preferring the company of each other to that of friends. But they took Kevin into their little group—they saved him really, especially after my mother died.

"Allison, come get in my car. We'll leave yours here for now, and I'll take you to your dad's house. You shouldn't be driving when you're so distraught. You haven't been drinking, have you?"

"I had some wine earlier," I admitted, refusing to lie. "But I'd already been asleep hours before I got the call."

Russell drove in silence; I admired his profile, revealed in the occasional lights from a passing vehicle.

"How come you didn't go on a mission? Haven't you been listening to the prophets?"

He jumped, as though he'd forgotten I was in the car with him. He'd probably been someplace else, wrestling with Kevin and Lance on the trampoline behind his house or catching frogs in Farmington Pond. He glanced over at me, then back to the road in front of him.

"I just didn't want to. I don't . . . It's hard to explain, okay? I just didn't think I could go out there and try to convince people to join my religion when I wasn't even sure it was the one and only true thing myself. My parents were cool with it. They didn't push me. Besides, Lance is out there serving. Oh man, he's gonna be so upset."

"I wish I'd been born into your family."

He glanced over at me one more time. "I'm sorry, Alli."

"Where is Lance?"

"St. Louis, Missouri."

We pulled into the driveway, and it was a shock to see the lights ablaze and cars lining the street at this hour. Farmington, a small, sleepy town, with one small market, no stoplights, and a five-man police force, was not the happening spot in the wee hours.

The small house brimmed with people, dancing shadows of dark and light we could see through the windows.

"I wish I hadn't come," I blurted. "Oh, why didn't I think of this? I should have known they would all be here. Now I'm going to get preached to, and warned about my lifestyle, and the eternal consequences of my apostasy."

A strong hand reached out to me and grabbed my wrist firmly. Russell pulled me toward him; and I looked at him with shock, unsure of his intentions. He enfolded me in a brotherly hug that only brought on more tears.

"Allison, the problem with you is you think too much and take everything too seriously. You always have."

I pulled away, a little offended. He'd always been "Kevin's friend," quiet and studious, although athletic and strong. For some reason, I'd never really looked at him, although we'd shared a few classes throughout elementary and high school. I looked now, but with anger in my eyes.

"You don't know me, Russell. You don't know me at all."

"I know more than you think. I've got to get back to work. Tell your dad and Eileen I'm sorry for their loss. I'll stop by when I'm off duty."

I hesitated for a moment. "I take things too seriously?"

Russell sighed and pushed me toward the door gently. "Remember, they all think they're doing and saying the right things. It's how we were all raised. Just grin and blow it off, okay?"

"I'll try."

I watched him drive away and felt very small and lonely, standing in my front yard beneath the willow tree Kevin and I had climbed—and fallen out of—many times. I turned to the house. It looked shabby and old, and the ominous shadows lurking in the unlit corners and sides held an air of disaster. Inside were people; some I wouldn't know, some I would, and all of them had unquestioned faith in Mormon tenets.

"Blow it off, Allison," I whispered to the wind, and I squared my shoulders and glanced one more time at the old tree. I could almost see Kevin's knobby, skinned knees, and hear the echoes of his child's voice floating on the warm spring wind.

I fought off the urge to climb the tree and went inside.

• • •

I was of little comfort to my father. none of us were. Kevin had been his golden child, the only boy, the one who would carry on the family name and the Priesthood.

A reporter from the local church-owned television station came to our house the next day, and asked my father to give a statement. I stood in the background with Cathy, Corrie, and my stepsisters as my father and stepmother put on a brave face for the camera. Mark stood behind them, a look of piety and solemn benevolence gracing his face. He was only twenty-one, and yet he stood there like he ruled the world. He rested his right hand on my father's shoulder in a show of Priesthood support, one I had seen often.

My father cleared his throat and spoke.

"We're all grieving right now, and we want to thank all the people who have offered their support and compassion. The outpouring of love from our community and our church has been wonderful." His voice became throaty and full as he tried to keep back the tears. A single rivulet of moisture escaped and coursed down his left cheek. "We're so grateful Kevin died honorably serving God and spreading the Gospel. It's better he came home in a pine box than to have been sent home in disgrace."

My heart started beating rapidly. Had my father just said it was preferable to die than to make a mistake?

I looked around at my relatives and at the news personnel. No one else seemed shocked. Many nodded their heads in agreement. As the small crowd dissipated and the news crew loaded up their equipment, Mark walked up to me.

I ignored him and turned to walk away. He reached out and grabbed my shoulder, a rough, firm grip that stilled the blood in my veins.

My heart sped up, my throat closed in, and I felt like Corrie's tiny baby, gasping for air as my world narrowed.

His grip implied familiarity, and made me feel lightheaded and nauseous.

I jerked away from his touch and turned to see a malicious glint in his eyes, and every muscle in my face and body tightened and strained. My teeth clenched together as pure hatred and disgust rose like bile in the back of my throat.

The look on my face must have been a beacon, a warning, for he backed away slightly, tilted his head to the right, and reached up with his right hand, stroking his chin, covered only with baby-fine skin and no hint of hair.

He smiled, a crooked, sardonic expression, and walked away.

I couldn't move, my feet cemented to the ground in fear.

No one noticed I still stood in front of our house as the crowd dissipated and my family went inside. My world had narrowed while the gulf between me and my family widened in a cataclysmic event, and no one saw it but me.

I turned and walked away.

Nineteen

On the day we buried my brother, torrents of rain poured from the sky. As we stood graveside in the Farmington City Cemetery, the raindrops pelted me, much like my father's words had pummeled me just days before. I stood at the very end of the front row, while the others—my father, his wife and her children, Cathy, my sister Corrie and her vile husband—stood under umbrellas. I'd forgotten mine, and there wasn't enough room under the family umbrellas. Several kindly ward members, including the bishop, tried to press their own on me, but I declined.

Soaked to the skin, I was miserable and cold. I kept hoping my father would *see* me instead of looking through me, and comment, maybe even yell at me to quit being so stupid and for once in my goddamned life just *listen* to the men who held the Priesthood of God. He only stared stoically ahead, wiping the occasional tear as the bishop spoke about my only brother.

He'd stood in front of news cameras for the world to see and shed tears for Kevin, who was honorable in his eyes, because he had died serving God. Apparently, my father would rather his children die than sin.

Where did that leave me? I'd always known he felt

strongly about me leaving the church, and the way I lived my life, but to realize he would rather have me dead than a sinner hurt worse than I'd ever believed possible.

And then there was Mark. I believed he had raped me. My family—father, stepmother, and the good children who hadn't strayed from my father's vision of truth—welcomed into their unit a man I now believed capable of the most despicable acts. This they did as easily as they cast me aside.

Bury this, Allison. Ignore it. Let it go.

The dedication of the grave ended quickly, the inclement weather chasing away the mourners. My father reached out and touched the mahogany casket, wiped a few more tears away, and then guided my stepmother toward the car. He walked past me without speaking, as though he didn't see me. Perhaps he didn't.

My sisters gave me quick hugs, and Mark smirked at me. I remained standing until everyone was gone except the funeral director and the bishop, who were speaking quietly at the other end of the casket. I didn't know the current leader of my father's ward, as it had been many years since I attended church, but he knew who I was. He finished his conversation and then moved around the casket to where I stood.

"Are you okay, Sister Jensen?"

"I'm fine." My lips were numb from cold, and the rain pelted my face. I didn't know if I was crying but figured it didn't matter.

"You're shivering. You need to get warm. The Relief Society has set up a luncheon for your family at the church. Can I drive you there?"

"No, thank you."

"Sister Jensen, you do realize that this is just his earthly body now, right? Kevin is not in that casket. He's with God now."

"How do you know that?" For the first time, I really

looked at the earnest man. He was small, not much taller than me, and mostly bald except for tufts of hair on the sides and back of his head. He had a prominent nose, large green eyes, and a compassionate mouth.

"I know it because God told me so."

"What, He give you a call last week? Ring you up and share some truth?"

His compassionate mouth thinned. "I've read his words, Sister Jensen, and I've prayed. God moves in mysterious ways. I'm sure you've heard that. But He speaks through our prophets. And we know that . . ."

"Look, Bishop, I'm not trying to be rude here. I'm really not. But my brother is dead, and I don't really believe the same things you do. So I have to mourn in my own way."

He frowned, and then put a hand on my shoulder. "You're Allison, right?"

"Yes." I sighed heavily. This one wasn't going away. I braced myself for his testimony.

"Allison, I'm not going to preach to you. I respect you don't feel the same way as I do, and that's okay. But I want you to know how very sorry I am for your loss. I know this hurts, and right now it doesn't seem like it's ever going to get better, but it will. You won't ever forget him, but the pain will ease. And you will always have a piece of Kevin with you. You have your memories. As long as you have those, you will always have Kevin by your side."

He nodded his head, removed his hand, and walked away.

I graduated from the University of Utah the week after Kevin's body arrived home. No one in my family attended the ceremonies. It wasn't really their fault, I supposed, since I didn't tell them the time and place. But I didn't want to give them a chance to shun me, to not show up, to *not* be proud of me. I was finally waking up to the fact I was still trying to gain my father's approval without giving him the one thing he wanted most—my return to his church.

A new face joined the nightly parade of victims marching through my dreams. It was Kevin, most often as a young boy, but with a hole in the right side of his head.

I called Sandra's office and scheduled an extra appointment. She called me back herself to confirm the time and date, and asked me why I needed to see her. Was something wrong?

When I explained, she told me to come right away. I was trying to keep my head above water, afraid if I went down under I'd meet all my demons, the ones that came to me the day I was baptized. I'd always said I wasn't bothered by my lifestyle, because I didn't believe the Mormon Church was true. But every once in a while the "what ifs" would hit me. What if I was wrong? Was God—and my mother, along with all my pioneer relatives—anxiously waiting on the other side for me, looking forward to telling me I was wrong? "Nah-nah-nah nah-nah. You should have listened!"

What if they were right?

"He said it was better Kevin was sent home in a pine box than to be sent home in disgrace."

"How did that make you feel?" Sandra's voice was tinged with emotions I couldn't identify.

"Well, it's what I've always known. But I never really heard it put into words. In his eyes, it's better to be dead than to be a sinner."

"And do you think you're a sinner?"

"Yes. No. I don't know anymore."

"You still haven't told me how it made you feel."

"Alone."

"Alone because . . . ?"

"Because I am alone. Because I don't get it, I don't understand them."

"'Them' as in your family? Or the Mormon Church?"

"Both, I guess. Most of me thinks it's utterly ridiculous, but there's this little part of me that worries, 'What if they're right? What if I have sinned and I'm exiled to Outer Darkness?'"

"Allison, I don't know what Outer Darkness is. Can you explain it?"

"It's nothing. It's a void. An eternal void."

"I think my brother-in-law Mark raped me."

The words were out before I could contain them, jumping through the doorway of my mouth like unruly children. Sandra looked momentarily surprised. She quickly covered it up.

"Why do you think it was Mark?"

"Because of who he is. Because of how he acts. Because of what he's done to me and to Corrie."

"Like what?"

"Like what? He killed her spirit. Burned her romance books. And he touched me when she left the room. He grabbed my breast. No one touches me without my permission. *They* all think he's wonderful. The returned missionary. The good guy."

"Who are 'they'?"

"The bishop. The church. My father."

"But what has he done that makes you think he could be a rapist? It's a serious charge, Allison. You must have a pretty concrete reason to believe this."

My thoughts drifted back to Mark and Corrie. To meeting Mark for the first time, and the indifference toward him I'd felt. He'd seemed so nonexistent. So nothing. I was so wrong.

"Do you feel up to talking about this now?"

I pondered this question. Would I ever feel up to that?

"You can't tell anyone what I say in here, right?"

"No, that violates patient confidentiality. And my own ethics."

"I don't think anyone will believe me."

"Allison, you need to place some confidence in our legal system. I know it's hard, but you need to tell the police your suspicions. Let them investigate. If you know who it is, you have to tell them."

"It's not that simple. If they investigate him, and don't find him guilty, or don't find any evidence, then what? I know him and he knows me. He's an upstanding member of the community. I'm just the prodigal daughter. Everyone will look at me like . . . like I just got what I deserved. No one in the Mormon Church wants to hear the truth. Not the real truth, anyway, because it's ugly and harsh.

"The real truth is being Mormon doesn't protect anyone from the bad things that happen. Mormons are always attributing everything to God and whether or not they go to church and do their temple work. Take my brother. If he hadn't died, everyone would have said it's because he was living right, serving God. When I was a kid, they used to tell us stories about Mormon Priesthood holders going to war and not being shot because they wore their garments. But Kevin died. Nothing about being Mormon protected him. So they turn it around and say God needed him."

"That's human nature, Allison. People are always looking for reasons and answers."

"Of course they are. Take me. I got raped because I sinned. I know that's what they'll think. I only got what I deserved. And part of me believes it's true."

"She didn't want to be pregnant."

"Corrie?" Sandra asked, her serious eyes squinting a little, her ever-handy pencil tapping into her palm. The first time I sat with her I thought she was impatient, tapping her pencil all the time and twirling one long strand of hair. I soon learned it was a nervous tic. It brought her down to earth a little for me, and made her human.

"Yes, Corrie. And my mother."

"Allison, I thought your mother was dead."

"Yeah, and being pregnant killed her. I had the dream again. The one where my mother is bleeding to death on the kitchen table, and my father and stepmother are laughing."

"How is your relationship with your stepmother?"

"What relationship? She just wanted someone to take her to the Celestial Kingdom. She probably thought my father was quite a catch. Boy, did she have it wrong."

"So you have a lot of anger toward her?"

"I have a lot of anger toward everyone, I guess. That's what my father always told me."

"Tell me about your mother's death, Allison."

"It was a blip on the radar, that's all. It momentarily steered my father off his course of eternal Godhood. He recovered pretty damn fast. It just wasn't the same for us kids."

"I see her face in my dreams, every night. I've been drinking a lot, trying to keep from dreaming, but it stopped working."

"Your mother's face?"

"No, Cindy's. It's like she's haunting me. Somehow I betrayed her. And my mother, too. But mostly Cindy."

"Cindy? I thought your sister's name was Corrie."

"Cindy, from my childhood."

"Oh, Cindy. Sorry, Allison, we jumped around a bit and I got a little confused. You mean your childhood playmate that disappeared? But you were only six. What could you have done? You grabbed her hand. You pulled her with you."

"He told me not to stop and look back. And I did."

Sandra didn't speak as she digested this information. She leaned forward in her chair and put her elbows on her knees, propping her chin on her hands, her pencil still clutched in her right fist.

"You were a child, Allison. You weren't responsible for her safety. You couldn't be."

"I've never listened, you know. Never just heard what someone had to say and took it at face value. Especially men. Especially my father."

"Did you ever ask your father what happened to Cindy?"

"No. I asked my mom, though, and she just hushed me. Wouldn't tell me. I think she must have been murdered."

"Do you think maybe you need to resolve this, to find out what did happen to Cindy? It seems like it would at least help you to know. Did they ever find her? Is she dead? Is she alive and well? These questions are eating you alive, Allison."

"It's not just Cindy, though, it's everything. It's my mother's death. It's the way they raised us, not allowing us to waver from their point of view."

"One thing at a time, okay? Let's start with Cindy, since the dreams are the most pressing. Cindy and the rape. Allison, you need to tell the police you believe your rapist is your brother-in-law."

Twenty

"Put your shoulder to the wheel, push along."

An old pioneer song I learned in Primary and Sunday school was the first thing on the tip of my tongue every morning when I woke up. I didn't understand why.

But I knew I did have to push along. I started a job with a small local magazine as an events reporter. I visited Aunt Carol and Sandra on Sundays, and Corrie left sad, wistful messages on my answering machine, updating me briefly on Elise Marie's progress and, more often, her setbacks. Corrie'd been sent home from the hospital without her baby, who was struggling for her life, and now spent all her spare moments at the hospital with her tiny newborn.

Other than that, I had little contact with my family. Christy sent me postcards with pictures of the San Francisco Bay and Chinatown on them. On the back she scrawled brief messages that said things like *"Get your ass out of Utah!"* or *"Get out of Happy Valley and come join the real world."*

I still wasn't sure why I didn't—couldn't—leave.

I went to work during the day and spent the evenings at a private club called Coopers with the other newsies. I'd pour myself into bed at night hoping for relief from my phantoms. It never came.

I also sat with Sandra Castle twice a week as she tried to help me wrestle my demons. It didn't appear to be enough.

"Do you think about sin a lot?"

"No, mostly I just do it."

Sandra laughed aloud at my joke, and I briefly smiled. We sat in chairs facing each other in her small office. Pictures decorated her desk, and I saw one of her with Aunt Carol. Another photograph in a gilt-edged frame showed a handsome elderly man with his arms around both Carol and Sandra, all three showing off radiant smiles.

She caught the direction of my eyes and said, "My father."

"Are you close to your father?"

"I was. He died about five years ago. It was hard to lose him."

"And he accepted Aunt Carol?"

"Loved her like a daughter-in-law. Goodness knows she needed family."

I shook my head in disbelief at her life, so different from mine. "I've never been close to my father. He's a complete stranger to me, as I probably am to him. He doesn't get me, and I sure as hell don't get him."

"Tell me about him. Did he abuse you?"

"Abuse? You mean sexually? Oh, God, no. He hit us a lot, especially me. One time I remember he knocked me out, smacked me up against the wall. He hit me so hard my head hurt for days. And his belt . . . But I was always questioning his authority. It wasn't abuse, really, you know. Just discipline."

Sandra Castle's face tightened with determination. She leaned forward in her chair. "Allison, don't ever say it wasn't abuse. If the man hit you, it was abuse. You have a right to be angry."

I was shocked into silence. No one had ever told me I had a right to my anger. They'd always told me my anger was going to be the death of me, to get over it and move on.

"I don't think I want to talk about my father anymore."

"Okay, let's talk about the dreams. Tell me about them."

"I don't know where to start. It's only dead people, like they're haunting me."

"Who's in them?"

"My mother. Cindy. Now Kevin, and . . ."

"And?"

"And me."

Twenty-one

A mottled, vividly colored bruise around Corrie's right eye convinced me to tell the police and my family my suspicions about my own rape.

She showed up on my doorstep one Sunday afternoon two weeks after Kevin's funeral. I was shocked to see her. I was appalled at the damage to her face.

"Corrie, what happened? It's Mark, isn't it?"

"He hit me. I went to the bishop, and he just told me to go back to Mark. He called him in and talked to him, but they told me not to press charges."

"The bishop told you that?"

"The bishop. And Dad. Mark has to meet with him twice a week, but it's not enough. It's not going to fix him."

Sandra had been urging me to go to the police, but I hesitated. I didn't think they would believe me. I knew my father and my family wouldn't.

"Can I stay here?"

"Of course." My shock ebbed, and I tried to cover what remained, not wanting to push Corrie away in her time of need. I opened the door wide and motioned her inside my apartment, stowed her tiny bag in my room, and told her I'd sleep on the couch.

"No, I just need a place to stay for a few weeks. Until Elise Marie gets out of the hospital. Then I'm leaving."

"Where will you go?"

"I don't know. Away. Maybe San Francisco. I can stay with Christy . . . I found something, Allison."

"You found something where?"

"Under the mattress of our bed. I found some magazines. Dirty, ugly magazines of men beating naked women and having sex with them. I found a fake beard. I found a picture of you, covered in his . . . in his semen."

"I-I . . ."

"You were right. I believed Dad, and the Church, and the bishop. I didn't tell them about the . . . the things I found, but I told them I knew he was masturbating and reading dirty magazines. I was too ashamed about the other . . . When I confronted him, he hit me. So I left."

"Oh, God, Corrie, the stuff you found. Did you bring it?"

"No! I can't touch it. It's so sick, so totally disgusting. Why?"

I put one hand on my head and pressed hard, trying to relieve the sudden throbbing. I sat on the couch with a thump and tried to think. She'd found the evidence that could connect Mark to my rape. I had to tell her. More, I had to convince her to return and get the beard and the picture.

"Corrie, I was raped. I think it was Mark. The . . . my attacker, he wore a fake beard. I tore a piece of it off and the police have it. I need that stuff."

Corrie blanched. She began to sway, and I jumped up quickly and moved her to the couch, pushing her head down between her legs so she wouldn't pass out.

"Oh, Allison. Why didn't I listen to you? Why?" she moaned, and cried.

"Because you didn't know, Corrie. Because we've been taught all our life to obey male Priesthood authority. Now, you can leave, but first we have to go back and get the magazines and the beard and—"

"It's too late. He told me he burned it. He took all that stuff and left. He said no one would believe me, and they damn sure wouldn't believe he was jerking off on a picture of you. Why you? All of our lives the boys have looked at you! I was just quiet little Corrie. Now, the one man I thought was truly mine, the only thing I've ever had that was mine alone . . . Oh, Allison, I'm so sorry. Can you forgive me? I'm not blaming you. I'm not. I'm just trying to understand."

"There's nothing to forgive. I have to call the police, though, Corrie."

"I know."

"Corrie?"

She looked up at me, her eyes rimmed in red and still full of unshed tears. The colors of her bruise seemed to deepen while I watched.

"I never encouraged this," I said in answer to her silent question. "Never. I would never do that to you."

She put her head back down and sobbed, her body wracked with anguish.

Maybe she didn't know how to believe me.

The detective investigating my rape took my information over the phone and arranged a time to meet with Corrie and me. His hard tone hadn't changed since the hospital, and I wasn't very optimistic he would pursue Mark without any evidence.

With all the trauma in my life, I lost my ability to concentrate, and my job performance began to slide. I'd spent the last semester of college serving an internship with the magazine, and had thus established a good track record as an employee, as well as a relationship with my editor.

Nonetheless, I knew what he would say when he called me into his office at work the next day.

"Allison, you've been slipping up. I'm concerned. Talk to me. What's going on?"

"I just had a personal trauma, Jack, I'm sorry. I'll do better. I haven't been sleeping well, and it's starting to affect me."

"Alli, you know I'm a friend. With your brother's death and your sister's baby being born early, you've been through a lot. Just tell me what you need."

I hesitated only a moment. I needed to confide.

"It's not just that. Jack, I was raped. They haven't found the man, but I think it was my brother-in-law. My sister told me she had found some evidence, but he destroyed it. I've reported it to the police, but I don't think they believe me."

I'd shared a lot with Jack Schroeder in the late nights we drank at Coopers. He was a sixty-year-old single man who had raised three adopted children by himself. He loved to mentor young writers and editors, and he was my confidant. He knew about my family and my past. Now, he stood up from his chair and walked around, hugging me gently.

"God, Allison, I'm so sorry. Shit, why didn't you tell me? Alli?"

"Yeah?"

"You need to keep after the cops about your suspicions. Okay? Please."

"Jack, the detective who interviewed me was a complete ass. He kept acting like I did something wrong, like I caused the rape. I did call him, and he's agreed to meet with Corrie and me, but I just don't think he'll believe me."

He walked to his desk and grabbed a Post-it note, scribbling a phone number on it.

"This is my friend, Detective Frank Kinderson. I've known him since my days working at the cop shop. Call him. I'll let him know you'll be calling. Take some time off, okay? You need a break. I'll give you two weeks, paid time off. Call it a sabbatical. Call it whatever you want. Just find the answers you need."

I agreed to call the detective. I didn't think it would do much good, but I had to find peace, and that would only come with answers to some very tough questions.

Detective Frank Kinderson was a handsome man in his mid-forties. I saw from the pictures on his desk his hair had once been jet black, but now it was gray, a fact that made him look not old but distinguished.

When I called earlier, he'd answered the phone on the first ring, and he listened to me blurt out the reason I contacted him without interrupting me.

"What was the detective's name, the one that interviewed you?"

"Castleton, I think."

"Ah. Yeah, okay. Listen, let me make a few phone calls and I'll get back to you."

Fifteen minutes later he had, and now I sat in his office at the Salt Lake City Police Department, a little unsure of why I was here, but willing to make the necessary steps to bring Mark to justice. Corrie was visiting her baby at the hospital, but I didn't want to reschedule when Detective Kinderson told me to come down, so I'd come alone.

"First off, let me apologize for Cass."

"Who's Cass?"

"Detective Castleton. I spoke with him, and he was happy to turn this case over to me. Most of these rapes belong to me anyway, but I was out of town and Cass caught this one."

It seemed strange to hear him describe a violent crime in a proprietary manner, especially one so close to me. It jarred.

"Cass's daughter was raped and murdered twelve years

ago. He hasn't been the same ever since. I think he puts on a cold exterior to shield himself from the pain."

"He acted like I was to blame."

"Well, you're not. I pulled your file and looked it over. You said on the phone you believe you know who your rapist is—please tell me."

"My brother-in-law Mark. I had an inkling, some suspicions, but my sister Corrie showed up on my doorstep yesterday with a black eye and a suitcase. She found some magazines, a fake beard and a picture of me with . . . with his . . ." I couldn't complete the sentence.

"With his semen on it?"

I nodded, grateful he'd said the words for me.

"And does Corrie believe he could be your rapist, too?"

"Well, she didn't know I'd been raped until I told her, but yes, I think she believes it. She doesn't want to. The only reason she isn't here is because her baby is in the hospital. Born too early."

"Does she have the things she found?"

"No. That's when he hit her. When she confronted him. He threw them in the incinerator."

I explained how Mark had been saying for months he was going to work when in reality he'd been fired.

"Any indication he was stalking you? Strange phone calls? Messages left on your car?"

"No, I don't think so. I get lots of strange phone calls, but they're usually from my family."

The detective gave me a funny look before he answered. "Okay, well, Allison, I'm going to have Mark picked up and I'll talk to him. You go home and don't let anyone in your house. Stay close, okay? I'll call you as soon as I know anything."

I told him I would, but I had another visit to pay. It was time to talk to my father.

Twenty-two

Conscious of the fact I wouldn't be welcome, I knocked on the wooden door of my father's house, the peeling paint and scuffed doorstop both familiar and foreign. Both he and my stepmother looked shocked to see me, but surprisingly, the door didn't shut in my face and he motioned to me to come in. He pointed to the living room and we sat. He looked old and haggard, and I realized with shock his hair had turned gray. I hadn't noticed before, because in my mind he was always the younger, crueler father of my childhood. Eileen scurried away into the kitchen, leaving us alone.

We sat in silence for a moment, and I wondered briefly if I had inherited my stubbornness from him. I spoke first.

"Dad, I need some answers. I need to know what happened to Cindy."

"Cindy? What are you talking about, Allison?"

"Cindy. Remember? Cindy Caldwell. The man with the beard? She disappeared? Come on, Dad, when I was six?"

"I don't understand why you're bringing this up now, Allison. You stay away from our house, you disobey God's word, you behave like a common floozie, and you just show up one day and ask about Cindy Caldwell? How could what happened to her possibly matter now?"

"I need to know what happened to her. And, just for the record, I didn't disobey God's word. I disobeyed your word. You must have yourself and God confused."

My father, famous for his hair-trigger temper, merely sighed, a look of consternation on his face as if he were reasoning out exactly where he had gone wrong with me. "Allison, all I ever wanted for you was the best. I wanted you to be happy. I wanted you to know the fullness of the Gospel. If I hadn't taught you the truth, it would be on my shoulders come Judgment Day." Avoidance, again. Why wouldn't he just answer me?

"I've researched it, you know, Dad? I didn't just up and decide one day that Mormonism wasn't true. I figured if I was going to say it wasn't true, I better know for sure. I looked into it, read the church history. I've read a lot. I found enough information to back up my claims."

"Where did you read it, Allison? You got it from the critics of the church. Don't you see they want to destroy us? It's Satan's work."

It was pointless. "Dad, what happened to Cindy?"

He sat silently, then blurted out, "They never found her. Nobody knows." Realization came to me in a flash of understanding—my father clung so tightly to the teachings of the church because with Mormonism there were no unknowns. Everything that happened was explained. To him, not knowing was the worst torture possible.

I sat for a moment, considering the fact that my father was human, then lashed out, wanting just once for him to take my side.

"Mark raped me. He hit Corrie. You told her to stay with him. Well, guess what? Your precious returned missionary son-in-law is going down."

His mouth fell open, and he gaped at me with bewilderment on his face.

"Rape? Mark raped . . . Allison, you can't be serious.

You've always jumped to conclusions. This is serious. Think about what this will do to Corrie. How do you know he hit her? I know he has some problems, but rape? And hitting Corrie?"

"She showed up at my doorstep with a black eye and all the proof I needed to confirm it was Mark. He waited for me outside my apartment late one night and . . . Well, I'm sure I don't need to give you the details."

The confusion and hurt on his aging face made me remorseful—a brief, quick flash of conscience. Why did I always try to hurt him? I knew he lived his life in the way he thought was right. If only he had allowed me the same opportunity.

He stood up and walked into the kitchen without saying a word. I followed him and saw my stepmother gaping at him in wonderment. I was sure she'd heard every word. He picked up the phone and dialed. Who was he calling?

"Hello, Sister Kent? Is the bishop in? This is Brother Jensen."

The bishop. I should have known.

I left without saying another word.

I pulled up in front of the redbrick house in Logan and put my car into park. The *putt-putt-putt* of the VW's motor had accompanied me on the two-hour trip to the border town, located in northern Utah next to Idaho. It lulled me into serenity, a brief respite from my overactive mind. Perhaps that's why I drove the old Bug—I found the engine noise comforting.

I sat in front of the house for a minute, scanning its black-shingled roof and heavy oak door. Newly bloomed tulips, in bright yellows, reds, and pinks, peeked through the rich-looking brown earth. The yard was immaculate, with a neatly mowed and edged lawn, rock-lined pathway, and two huge pine trees. In one of the flower beds, I could see a white statue of a small angel. Maybe Cindy.

I knew I should move but found myself frozen. What would I say to them? Would they hate me because I'd survived and become an apostate, while Cindy had died?

I'd found Cindy's parents through our old bishop and dentist, Myron Hall. He'd been surprised to find me at his doorstep, but though it had been more than five years since he last saw me, he was friendly and open.

"Oh, it's sad. They moved away because they couldn't stand the pain. I understand completely. I can't imagine how it must feel to not know where your children are. At least they have the comfort of knowing Cindy will be with them in the Celestial Kingdom after the Second Coming."

I sighed.

"Well," he said. He walked to his desk and pulled out a day planner, then scribbled an address down on a slip of notepaper that read "Remember to brush! God loves a healthy smile."

He handed me the paper and took a moment to look me in the eyes. "How are you, Allison? I know you've had some rough times lately. I'm sorry about that. I guess the Lord must have needed your mother desperately, because I know he wouldn't have taken her and left you alone unless it was of the utmost importance."

Now here I sat, in front of the Caldwell house, rehearsing lame words that stuck to the roof of my mouth like extra-thick peanut butter. My composure fled and I started the Bug, intending to follow.

From around the back of the house a woman appeared. She carried a small garden spade and a bucket. She wore the uniform of all middle-aged Mormon women in warmer weather: knee-length denim "Mormon" shorts long enough to cover her garments, a flower-print cotton short-sleeved blouse, and sandals.

At first she didn't see me; but after a glance in the direction of the noise my engine made, she stopped and stared, a quizzical expression crossing her pleasant features.

I turned off the car and exited deliberately. I needed to know what happened to Cindy.

"Mrs. Caldwell?" I called out as I neared her, and she smiled warmly. When I got closer, I watched her examine my features. Her brow wrinkled slightly, then straightened out.

"I'm Allison Jensen. I was Cindy's friend."

"Allison."

The smile left her face and pain replaced it.

"I'm sorry, I shouldn't have come."

I turned, intending to walk away; she reached out a small but strong hand and stopped me, grabbing my shoulder.

"I'm sorry, Allison. You surprised me, that's all. I knew you looked familiar. Please come inside."

Mrs. Caldwell led me inside the home, and I saw it was as nice inside as it was outside. Furnished with crafts and country designs, it reminded me of Cindy, and the warmth I had always experienced in her home. A trellis of artificial ivy ran along the top of the white pine cupboards in the kitchen, dotted here and there with sunflowers.

Cindy had loved sunflowers. A memory of her dancing and twirling in her backyard on a warm summer evening flitted through my mind. She wore a red sundress imprinted with big yellow sunflowers, and she had a real one tucked behind her left ear.

Mrs. Caldwell pointed to a chair, shaking me out of my reverie, and I sat, watching as she pulled two glasses from the cupboard and a pitcher from the fridge.

"I'm afraid I don't have any soda. Will lemonade do?"

I nodded.

She poured the lemonade and brought the glasses to the oak table, setting them on coasters before taking the chair next to me.

"So, Allison, why are you here?"

"I need to know what happened to Cindy. I dream about her all the time, and I can't forget her. Every night she's there."

I saw a tear form at the corner of her eye, and she reached up and wiped it away with the back of her hand.

"Allison, you're lucky. Sometimes I can't even remember her face. I have to pull out the pictures just to remind me what she looked like."

I reached out a hand to her and she took it, squeezing it with her fingers, roughened and calloused, perhaps from gardening.

Mrs. Caldwell regained her composure and stood up, leaving the room at a rapid pace and returning a moment later with a photo album. She plopped it down on the table and flipped it open, turning the pages until she found what she was looking for.

"There," she said, pointing to a picture of two little girls, their arms tight around each other, smiling with gap-toothed grins. Cindy and me.

"I cherish this picture. You both look so happy here."

"Mrs. Caldwell, I . . ."

"Please, call me Nancy."

"Nancy, I'm so sorry about what happened. I wish I could have saved her."

"Why, Allison, whatever could you have done? You were only six."

She didn't blame me, like I blamed myself.

"I wish I knew what happened to her, too, you know. It would make life so much easier. I still leave the porch light on every night, just in case she's still alive and finds her way home. I want her to know she's welcome here. I wouldn't move at first, you know, when LaMar wanted to. I thought, 'But she won't know where to find us.' I finally accepted in my heart that she's dead, but I've never completely given up hope. I can't."

I felt the tears sting my eyes. There were no answers here, but I felt calmer. I wasn't sure why.

"Has your husband been able to deal with it?"

"Come here, I want to show you something," Nancy said, pulling me by the hand and leading me down the narrow hallway to a closed door. She opened it, and I saw Cindy's bedroom. The same bedspread, the stuffed animals, all the childhood toys we'd played with for hours on end. As a child, I coveted Cindy's toys. She was the only girl in a family with just two children, and she had the best Troll Doll collection in town.

I walked over to the windowsill, a deep-set alcove filled with the little flighty-haired creatures with pug noses and stocky bodies. I picked up the largest one and caressed the red hair sticking out on top of its head.

"It looks just like her room in Farmington," I told Nancy, looking around in awe.

"I'm surprised you remember," she said, smiling slightly. "You were so young when . . . when it happened. You probably think I'm foolish, keeping her room like this, but it's all I have left. This, the photographs, and my memories."

"I don't think it's foolish at all."

"LaMar thought it was foolish. He wanted to have another baby. Wanted me to move on. I couldn't. We've been divorced for ten years."

I know shock registered on my face, and she gave me a sad smile. She examined me closely for a moment, and I wondered what she looked for.

"You've grown into a very beautiful woman, Allison.

I've heard about some of the troubles your family has had. I'm very sorry about your mother. And, of course, your brother. I guess you can doubly relate to my loss. Will you stay for supper?"

"You've heard about me? I guess you've heard I left the church."

"Yes, I heard that. Frankly, that's none of my concern. You'll find your way, Allison, whatever that way is. I've stayed with the church through my ordeal because it offers me comfort. It's nice to believe Cindy is in Heaven, looking down on us. I have a lot of dark moments when I wonder. But believing what I've been taught all my life is just simpler than imagining the worst. I can't stand to think a part of Cindy doesn't exist somewhere."

"But she does. She's in your heart and in your memories. And mine, too."

I politely declined her offer of dinner but thanked her for taking the time to visit with me. She pressed her phone number into my hand as I left, and I gave her mine. She made me promise to keep in touch.

"I'm glad you lived through it, Allison. I've always been glad."

I left the house wondering if I had achieved anything at all. One sentence she spoke kept running through my mind.

"Believing what I've been taught all my life is just simpler than imagining the worst."

Twenty-three

Russell Free and I sat outside on the patio of La Salsa, drinking Coronas with lime and sharing a plate of nachos. Off duty, without his formal UHP trooper uniform, he still looked young, but I found his carefree manner appealing.

He'd called me an hour earlier, asked how I was doing, and invited me out for dinner. In my shock I said yes, unable to think of a viable excuse. I'd already turned down three dates with the officer who found me after my rape. But Russell was like family, a connection to my past, one that wasn't ugly or sordid.

Now, I was glad I hadn't turned him down. I hadn't heard back from Detective Kinderson, and Corrie hadn't returned from the hospital. I felt relaxed and a little out of focus, the nice buzz from the Corona muting my inner voice and making me feel like I could float.

"You look like you're twelve without your uniform," I told him. "Are you sure you're old enough to be drinking that?" I motioned toward his beer. "And whatever would your daddy say?"

He blushed a little but mostly ignored my teasing. "Daddy would say I'm a big boy now, and I can make my own decisions."

"Man, you're lucky."

"I know I am. So, Allison, tell me what's up with you?"

Well, I've been raped, and I think my brother-in-law did it.

I waved that thought away like a pesky fly, refusing to acknowledge it right now while I was feeling so good.

"Oh, this and that. I took some time off work, so I'm just relaxing. Reading all the books I haven't had time to even open before."

"I saw you at Kevin's funeral, standing off by yourself."

Funeral. The word landed between us with a resounding thump. My high spirits followed. Guilt settled in, firmly anchoring me to the ground.

I turned away from him in the metal chair, looking out at the view of Salt Lake City. La Salsa was high on the hill just below the University of Utah; and from the patio, if the sky was clear, you could see as far as the Great Salt Lake, a massive body of water with only inlets and no outlet.

"Have you ever floated in the lake?" I asked him.

"Yeah, when I was a kid. I tipped upside down and got a mouthful of water. My dad loved to tease me that I was the only person he knew who could drown in those waters. I heard it's not true anymore, though. Too much water has filled the lake, and the salt content is down so you can't float now."

"Hmmm. I don't know. We never did, but I always wanted to do it."

"You're not missing much. I was sick for a week afterward. And the brine flies will lift you up and carry you off. I heard a baby disappeared from there just last week."

I laughed at his joke and secretly felt relief that he accepted the change of topic.

"So, why weren't you with your family at the funeral?"

"Damn, you did *not* take the hint. I don't want to talk about it, Russ, okay?"

"Okay."

We sat for a moment, and then he asked, "What happened to your boyfriend?"

"Boyfriend?"

"Yeah, you know, that Brett guy you brought to Kevin's farewell."

I didn't even remember seeing Russell there—I'd been hellbent on taunting my father with my non-Mormon boyfriend.

"He went the way of most men in my life. Adios, amigo. I'm a slut, didn't you hear?"

He flushed in embarrassment; I rubbed my temples and took a big swig of Corona, trying to make yet another memory disappear in a drunken fog.

As usual, it didn't work.

Silence followed my outburst. Then, after another twenty minutes of superficial, stilted conversation, he drove me home and parked in front of my apartment building. The momentary buzz from the beer was gone, and I'd tumbled back to earth.

"You can come up," I finally said as I let myself out the door. "Maybe Corrie is back."

"Corrie? Your sister?"

I hadn't told him anything about the rape, or Corrie's troubles. I didn't intend to elaborate now. "She's staying with me for a while. Her husband is, uh, out of town. You know her baby's in the hospital, and she doesn't want to be alone."

"Her baby's in the hospital?"

I sighed, tired of answering questions, especially the ones I was forced to lie about. "Born too early."

"Is it gonna be okay?"

"We hope so. She's on a ventilator, and is still pretty tiny."

He followed me up the stairs and stood patiently while I unlocked the door.

"Corrie?" I called as I threw my light jacket onto the sofa. "Corrie?"

She wasn't there, and I started to worry. What if she went back to her apartment? What if she ran into Mark? What if the police hadn't found him yet?

Russell followed behind me and sat on the sofa. I slipped off my shoes and sat next to him, reaching for the remote control and flipping on the television.

He put his arm around me so suddenly I didn't see it coming, and when I turned to him in surprise he bent down and kissed my lips. It felt nice, and the stirring sensation in my stomach was pleasant—at first.

As the kiss deepened, so did my anxiety; I found myself picturing another man, one with a beard, ripping at my clothes and pinching my breast, forcing himself inside me.

"No, no," I gasped, trying to pull away. He pulled me closer, put his tongue inside my mouth and I screamed.

Russell jumped away in shock, and tears flowed down my face.

"God, Allison, I'm sorry. I didn't mean . . . Did I hurt you? Shit."

I couldn't speak for a minute, and he went into the bathroom and came back with about three feet of toilet paper wrapped around his hand. He offered it to me with a grave expression; I laughed at the sight of him, carrying half a roll of toilet paper. His features were knotted together in a mixture of emotions, but mostly chagrin.

"I don't have that many tears in me, Russ."

He looked down at the toilet paper and blushed, looking back at me with questions in his eyes. "Allison, I'm sorry. I like you. I've always liked you. But I didn't mean to . . . I'm sorry."

"Stop saying you're sorry. It's my fault for not telling you. Russ, I was raped just before Kevin died. It was Mark, Corrie's husband."

I'd been holding the secret of my assault inside me for weeks, sharing only with my therapist. Now, in the space of two days I'd dumped the information on my boss Jack, Corrie, my father, a new detective, and now Russell. I felt like a blabbermouth. I also felt naked and exposed.

"What?" Shock showed on his face, and he paled. A smattering of freckles left over from childhood stood out against his wan complexion. "Have they arrested him?"

"The detective I met with today was going to have him picked up. He wore a fake beard and a mask, and I wasn't sure. Not until Corrie showed up with a black eye. She found magazines, and pictures of me under their mattress, along with the beard."

Russell turned from suitor to cop before my eyes, his features hardening, making him look older. "So they have the evidence."

"No, he burned it. But they have a piece of the beard I tore off, and Corrie's story."

"Where *is* Corrie?"

"She went to the hospital this morning and hasn't come back."

"Allison, let's go find her."

I wasn't about to argue. Every minute she was gone heightened my anxiety, and my nerves keened their agony. I needed to take action.

Please, God, don't let Corrie be hurt. Make her smart enough to stay away from him.

The phone rang as we walked out the door, and I turned back and snatched it up. "Hello?"

"Allison?"

"Yes?"

"This is Detective Kinderson. I'm afraid I have some bad news. We haven't been able to locate Mark. His family says they haven't seen him."

"Detective, my sister's been gone all day. I'm worried about her. She went to the hospital to see her baby."

"Have you called there?"

"I didn't even think of that."

I told him I'd let him know if I heard anything more and listened silently as he warned me about locking my doors and not opening them to anyone. I hung up and was reaching for the phone book when the phone's harsh peals made me jump. Russell stood in the doorway watching as I answered.

"Hello?"

"Allison, it's your father. Corrie just called from the hospital. Elise died an hour ago."

Twenty-four

Russell drove me to the hospital, the silence welcome this time. Corrie's fear of losing her life during pregnancy, as our mother had, had become reality in a grim, perverse way. Surely, I thought, it must be like suffering your own death to lose a child.

I'd known for years I didn't want children. The "whys" of that had never been apparent to me, but I understood them now. To love something that much and then lose it was more than my tortured soul could handle. It was easier to say "no" than to ever have to go through it.

As these thoughts churned through my brain, I realized it had been almost a week since I last saw Sandra Castle, and I felt needy and lost. I'd been off drinking Coronas with Russell when my sister needed me most. I felt the pangs of failure lapping at my heels.

So much had happened to our family in the past few weeks. Corrie suffered the most, losing her brother, her husband, and now her tiny baby. My anger at the callous Mormon God reared its ugly head: I clenched my fists, not wanting to lash out, not wanting to let loose the venom I'd had inside me for so long.

"Shit, I hate this. Life sucks. It's so unfair, dammit."

"I know, Alli. I'm sorry."

I knew Russell couldn't make it better, but irrationally, I wanted him to try. "Alli, I'm sorry" was a poor attempt at comfort in my bitter mind, and I couldn't stop the words that spewed from my mouth.

"Yeah, it sucks you didn't get laid tonight, huh, Russ?"

His mouth tightened and his knuckles went white on the steering wheel, and I instantly regretted my words.

"I'm sorry, Russ. You didn't deserve that, and I'm a bitch."

"You're right, you are a bitch. And I didn't deserve that."

I held my tongue, both shocked he rejected my apology and relieved to put some distance between us. He pulled into the hospital parking lot and stopped at the front door, staring straight ahead as he waited for me to exit his car.

"Russ, I really am sorry. I have so much anger inside me. I'm in therapy right now, trying to learn to deal with it."

"You've been through a lot," he said without looking at me. "Right now, I'm angry. But that doesn't mean I don't know you're hurting. I'll call you."

I watched him drive away, then entered the hospital doors, my stomach fluttering as the familiar antiseptic smell hit my nose. I forced myself to walk to the elevator, push the button for the fourth floor, where the newborn intensive care unit was.

Every step I took out of the elevator I was a little more sick, bile rising in the back of my throat as images of my dead mother, my rapist, and now Corrie's baby paraded through my mind.

I stopped at the nurse's station and asked about my sister. A solemn-faced rotund nurse led me to a room. I knocked softly and Corrie's voice, raspy and throaty, said "Come in."

I pushed through the door. She sat in a rocking chair,

moving slowly back and forth, the body of her dead baby wrapped in a blanket, cuddled in her arms. Her face went in and out of focus, and black spots appeared before my eyes. The floor moved under my feet, and my world faded to black.

Twenty-five

"They encourage the mother to hold the baby, Allison. It helps her to grieve," Sandra explained patiently.

I reached up a hand and touched the stitches on my forehead, wincing at the pain, reveling in the fact I could still feel.

"Didn't the doctor explain that to you?" she asked.

"Yes, but it seems sick. It's just a shell. A body with no soul. Elise Marie is gone, to Heaven—or wherever innocent little babies go."

"Allison, are you afraid of death?"

"I suppose so. Isn't everyone?"

"No, there are many people who aren't frightened by death. I'm not."

"Are you religious?"

"No, I was raised Catholic, but we certainly weren't devout. We were holiday Catholics. Easter Sunday, Christmas." She chuckled.

"My mother wasn't afraid, either. I think that's why she loved being Mormon. Because they answered all the questions for her. No guesswork. She knew where she was going, as long as she went to church, paid her tithing and did her temple work. And she knew only the good people would be there with her, in the Celestial Kingdom. The rest of us sinners would be in a lower kingdom, awaiting judgment."

"I think you might have an irrational fear of death, Allison. Perhaps that's why you passed out when you saw Corrie holding her dead baby. It's understandable that death means the unknown to you."

"I am scared. So many people around me, people I've loved, have died. I don't know where they are. Or if they are even anywhere. Sometimes, I wish I had the devout faith other Mormons seem to have. To be told something, and just take it at face value. I think my uncertainty is going to be the thing that ultimately kills me."

Despite my pleas, Corrie returned to her small apartment.

"He's gone, Allison," she said the day after Elise died as I drove her to the funeral home to make arrangements for the baby's tiny body to be interred. "His family has property in Wyoming, and he's probably hiding out there. They would do that. They believe just about anything he says."

"I'll be there, Corrie," I told her after we left the white brick funeral home. We'd arranged for a small graveside service with only family and close friends.

The tiny pink casket the funeral director showed us had made my eyes swim again, and I had to sit down abruptly and put my head between my knees. Corrie shed no tears, her shoulders back, her eyes round and ringed with dark circles. She had no color in her face, no emotion in her expression. She looked like death.

I wanted to be strong for her. I'd tried to be strong for everyone but myself for so long—beginning when my mother died—I now felt almost transparent and thinly drawn. My strength was sapped, while mysterious death, circling me for years like a vulture, was now so close I could almost reach out and touch it, if only I had the strength. But I didn't.

Detective Kinderson confirmed there had been no sign of Mark, and the search reached a dead end.

"We're not giving up, Allison, but right now we have nothing to go on. I called the Sweetwater County sheriff, and they're checking out the property his family owns. It's pretty remote, though. Keep your guard up."

Russell didn't call. Officer Jake Jensen, the policeman who found me after my rape, called four times. I finally accepted, just for the opportunity to leave my apartment accompanied by a man who had a gun and knew how to use it.

Jake picked me up at seven, and a wave of shock coursed through me when I opened my door, even though I peered cautiously through the peephole first. He wore a muscle shirt, tight black jeans, cowboy boots, aviator glasses, and an attitude.

"You look hot," he said, giving me the once-over with the glasses perched low on his nose, peering out over the top.

He escorted me down to the parking lot, holding tightly to my elbow as though I needed to be steered. He drove a blue 1984 Trans Am, neatly tricked out, complete with T-top. Already uncomfortable, from the time I opened the door I grew more uneasy with every passing second.

"Junior's okay?" Jake asked, referring to a popular cop hangout downtown by the police station.

"Hmm, yeah, that's fine." I'd been there before and knew it wouldn't be hard to escape if he was with his friends. I tried to put a finger on the source of my discomfort—it was unusual for me. He was the bad boy personified, everything I'd always found attractive in a man; and yet something was not quite right.

"So, you doing better?"

"I suppose. You don't heal overnight from rape. At least, not from the scars no one can see."

"I can tell you write. I like it."

"How can you tell I write? How do you know what I do?"

"You're so proper, using big words and all. I looked into you, that's all. I have the means, you know."

"You 'looked into' me? What the hell does that mean? You've been investigating me?"

"Hey, don't get pissed off. I just wanted to know more about you, that's all."

I sat stewing, wondering what in the hell I'd been thinking when I had agreed to go out with him.

"I don't think this is such a good idea. I've changed my mind. Will you please take me home?"

"What? What did I do? Shit, Allison, give me a chance. Are you always this quick to judge? I'm sorry, okay? I just asked around is all. I wanted to know more about you. You intrigue me."

I felt stupid and judgmental. "All right."

"Cool. You'll have fun, I promise. My friends are gonna be there. You'll like 'em."

The crowded, smoky club was filled to the brim with cops and cop groupies.

"Gin and tonic," I told Jake when he asked what I wanted to drink. He found me a place in a booth next to two blond women and an aging beat officer with an enormous beer belly and bloodshot eyes.

"So, you Jake's girl?" he asked.

"No, just a friend."

"Oh."

He and the blondes, who both looked to be in their forties with tanned skin the consistency of leather, exchanged knowing glances.

"Allison?"

I looked up to see Detective Frank Kinderson. Extreme relief flooded through my veins, although I wasn't sure why.

"Detective Kinderson," I said, jumping to my feet and grabbing his arm.

"Never seen you in here before. Aren't you supposed to be laying low? Or should I say I hoped you were."

"Hey, where else could I be so safe, surrounded by cops?"

Jake elbowed his way through the crowd with our drinks, half of which sloshed onto the floor when a large, burly man backed into him.

"Here, Allison. Sit down." Jake directed me to the booth again, giving Detective Kinderson an irritated look.

"You know young Officer Jensen, do you?"

"He found me . . . after the . . ."

"Allison?" said Jake, growing surlier by the minute.

"I was tired of staying home, and thought I'd be safe . . . Oh, please, get me out of here."

"With pleasure," Detective Kinderson said.

"I'm leaving, Jake. I'm sorry, but this was a mistake. I should never have said yes."

His scowl told me I was not forgiven. I was past caring.

Out in the fresh air, I gulped oxygen, slightly ashamed at dumping Jake and so relieved I could almost taste it.

"Thanks, Detective Kinderson, I kept telling him no, but he kept calling, and—"

"Frank. Please, call me Frank. Jensen isn't bad, but he's . . . busy. He gets around."

"I just couldn't stand to stay in my apartment one more day. I took some time off work, Jack pushed me to, and now I find myself twiddling my thumbs." I hesitated for a moment. "My sister's baby died."

"I heard. We've been watching the hospital, and I interviewed her there. I'm sorry. Is she okay?"

"I don't know. No. How could she be? She went back to

her apartment. She doesn't think Mark will show up. I didn't even know you'd talked to her."

"What happened to your head?" Frank asked, motioning to my wound as he directed me to his vehicle, a Ford Bronco.

"I passed out at the hospital. I walked in to find Corrie rocking her dead baby, and it just . . . It was just too much."

"Oh, God. I bet it was."

"Look, this is going to sound forward, and it's not, but would you like to have dinner with me? I don't want to go home and sit in my empty apartment."

Frank laughed and looked at me from the corner of his right eye, still paying attention to the road. "I was just going to ask if you were hungry. Market Street?"

"I love seafood."

"All right, then. Market Street, it is."

Twenty-six

"So, tell me about yourself. no deep stuff, let's keep this light."

We'd both ordered the crab and avocado sandwich, accompanied by Market Street Grill's famed clam chowder. The smell of seafood, sourdough bread, and other tempting aromas floated through the air, and I found I was ravenous, where for weeks I'd barely picked at my food.

Frank ordered a bottle of merlot and raised his eyebrows to me. "I didn't ask. You drink, Allison?"

"You're not Mormon."

"No, I'm an Ain't."

"Huh? You're a what?"

"You know, there's the Saints, as in Latter-day Saints, and then there's the Ain'ts. That's where I fit in."

I laughed, and it warmed my inner chill just a slight degree. "An Ain't—I like that. I guess I'm an Ain't, too."

"So, you'll share this wine with me?"

"I never say no to a good bottle of merlot."

"Never?"

"Never."

Our gentle camaraderie made me forget for a short time my miserable circumstances.

"Tell me about you, Mr. Ain't. Were you raised Mormon?"

"Oh, kind of. My mother was a member, my father wasn't. She had me baptized just because all the other kids in the neighborhood and school were and she didn't want me to stand out. She wanted me to belong. So I went to Primary and Mutual, and sometimes to church, but not very often because Sunday was my day with my dad. We'd go fishing, or hunting, or golfing. It didn't bother Mom. She'd go hang out with her sisters while Dad and I were out."

"Wow. I've never heard of anything like that. My family ate, breathed, and slept religion. Sundays we put our dresses on in the morning and that's the way we stayed. After dinner we'd have Bible study and read our scriptures. My father gave us pop quizzes on the *Book of Mormon*. If we didn't pass, we earned a trip to our rooms to read up for the next time."

"God, I would have gone fucking nuts. Oh, sorry. Didn't mean to swear. Comes from working around cops."

"You don't owe me any apology. I'm a journalist, remember?"

Frank laughed, a warm, rich sound that started in his chest and gurgled upward, spilling out his mouth. "Well, good, because I definitely have a hard time around little old ladies. One of these days I'm going to give my mother a heart attack with my language."

"Your folks are still alive?"

"Yeah, they live down in St. George. Suits them both. Mom likes the warm weather and the bingo games at the rec center, and Dad likes the forty-minute drive to Mesquite, Nevada, where he can gamble and smoke the cigars my mother forbids in her house."

"They sound lovely."

"Oh, they are. I gather you didn't have as much luck with your family."

"No. My mother died when I was fifteen. My father re-married shortly afterward."

"I'm sorry about your mother. If my daughter has troubles, the first person she turns to is her mom. It's sad you didn't have that luxury."

"You have a daughter? Oh, my God, I didn't even ask if you were married, and I—" I felt a flush start at my throat and move slowly upward, the warmth an indicator I had reddened noticeably. "I'm sorry. I mean, I know this isn't a date and all, but I still should have . . . Oh, God."

"Relax, Allison, I'm divorced. Have been for ten years now. She couldn't handle being the wife of a cop. I understand that. We're good friends, and we share custody of Melissa."

"Oh, what a relief. Boy, did I feel like an idiot. You must wonder about me, about what kind of girl would ask a man to dinner without even knowing if he's married or not."

My thoughts darkened as I thought of Jake Jensen and his persistence in calling me after I was raped. I briefly wondered if Frank Kinderson made it a habit to court the women he met in his line of work. Then I shut the thoughts down, not willing to explore the dark recesses of my mind when I finally felt a little bit good.

"Allison? You look a million miles away."

"I feel like I don't know myself anymore. I'm so different since the rape. The man who attacked me took everything I thought I knew about me away. I'll never be the same. I suppose, in some ways, that's good. Some of my behavior has been self-destructive. I'm just rambling. It probably makes no sense at all to you."

"No, it does. You had a life-threatening event happen to you. That always causes us to take stock of our lives, and if possible, to set about righting our wrongs. Mine happened to me when my daughter was sick. Anne—that's my ex—and I had been separated for about six months when she called me one night, frantic. Missy's fever was a hundred and five, and she was throwing up and crying. They told us she had meningitis, and they did a spinal tap to see if it was viral or bacterial. The twenty-four hours we waited were the longest of my life. What a relief when we found out it was viral, which is much less serious than bacterial."

"That must have been hard, seeing her like that."

"Yeah, it was. And I was bitter and angry at Anne, because she threw me out. I was also stupid, because I cheated on her and that's why she did it. About then I decided to change my life. Of course, I still fuck up. But I'm only human."

Frank grinned, and I realized how incredibly handsome he was. His dark blue eyes were surrounded with generous laugh lines, and his nose was slightly crooked, which gave him a dangerous but attractive look.

"What?"

"What do you mean?"

"You're staring at me like there's something on my teeth. Should I go to the bathroom and check?"

I blushed again, and giggled, a high, nervous, female sound. I had spent the last four years honing my femme fatale act, and I rarely let a man get the upper hand. This man seemed to be able to see through the core to the real Allison, and I wasn't sure whether that was good or bad.

He drove me home in the warm spring night, and I could smell the lilacs blooming, which always brought back memories of my mother.

"I miss her."

"Who?"

"My mother. I wish she hadn't died, but I'm not sure things would have been different. She always let my father control our family, never stopped him from forcing us to bend to his will and his definition of right and wrong. It's easy for me to blame him and the church, and think everything would have been all right if she hadn't died. But the truth is, it might not have been different at all."

"Anger will eat you alive, Allison. It's best to come to terms with it."

"I'm working on it."

We reached my apartment building and he walked me up the stairs to my door, pausing for a moment to make sure I was safely inside.

"Do me a favor and let me check the rooms, okay?"

"Okay."

He did a quick sweep of my small apartment, checking the closets and under the bed, and then he walked to the door, leaned down and kissed me gently on the forehead and said, "Good night, Allison."

I smiled as he left and set about getting ready for bed, applying makeup remover to my face and gently rubbing as I replayed the evening in my head. A nice guy. Frank Kinderson was a nice guy.

I jumped when the phone rang and I ran to answer it, still holding a washcloth in my hand.

"H'lo?"

"Allison, it's Frank."

"Hey, you missed me already, huh?"

"Allison, when I came down here, I noticed a truck sitting in the back of your parking lot, and someone inside it. It made me suspicious, so I called the plates in."

My stomach did a somersault, and fear began to tighten at my throat.

"Mark?"

"No, Allison. It wasn't Mark."

"I don't understand. Was it someone I should be worried about?"

"Allison, it's your father."

Twenty-seven

Why, I wondered, would my father be watching my apartment? What was he looking for? Did he suspect me of setting Mark up, of betraying my sister?

Frank offered to go talk to him, but I said no. I needed to think this through, and to try to understand what intentions my father had.

I finally decided confronting him was the only way to get answers, and I quickly washed my face and ran downstairs, only to find a parking lot empty of all cars except those belonging to tenants. I scanned the area one more time but saw no sign of my father's small Toyota truck.

I returned to my apartment and quickly dialed his number, getting only an insistent ringing on the other end. I walked into my bedroom without turning the light on and took the few steps to the window.

The moon was full, just rising over the Wasatch Mountains, and I shivered as I looked down at the big blue Dumpster, the place where my rapist left me, like the garbage from yesterday's dinner. A storm was building in the east above the mountains, one that would cause the warm spring temperatures to drop abruptly. The telltale signs were apparent in the thin layer of clouds that sat on top of the ridges and crevices, an extra dollop of icing on a cake. The east wind would uproot hundred-year-old trees and tear signs off buildings, like a large angry child who didn't get his way.

Unbidden memories of the violence played again in my head, and I was helpless to stop them. I remembered the half moon that night, sitting low in the black sky, its luminous glow casting shadows as wispy clouds moved across its surface. I remembered watching a moth throwing itself at the one dim light illuminating the carport. Over and over again it batted against the light.

I could sympathize—I'd been trying to find the light for all of my twenty-two years.

Kevin used to pull the wings off flying creatures when we were little, at first because he was curious, but then because it made me cry. Now he was dead, and I felt as though the wings were ripped off my body.

"It can't get worse than this. It can't. This must be Outer Darkness," I mumbled, pulling the curtains together in an abrupt motion and rushing across to turn on the light and dispel the gloom and my depression.

I was no longer afraid of Outer Darkness. I'd been there, to the place of exile, the land of nothingness.

It was my home.

Twenty-eight

The phone rang and I wrestled with sleep, fighting to surface from the place where I'd just rescued both Cindy and Corrie from a ten-foot-tall Mark Peterson.

I squinted as my eyes came open, and I looked at the clock. Four A.M. What now?

"Hello?"

There was no answer.

"Hello? Who's there?"

I could hear someone breathing heavily on the other end of the line, and goose bumps rose along my arms as all the last vestiges of sleep cleared from my mind. Alert and cautious, I was also terribly afraid.

I slammed the receiver down and glared at it, turning on the bedside lamp and making sure the curtains were still closed. I knew sleep was impossible, so I rose and wandered into the living room. The only other window in my apartment was in the kitchen, just four steps from where I stood; I stopped, frozen with fear, as I saw the open blinds. I'd flipped on the light as I walked into the living room and now felt like a target, exposed to anyone who might be watching from the parking lot or any of the surrounding buildings.

With one sudden spurt of courage I ran to the kitchen and pulled the cord so the wooden blinds clattered down, clicking and clacking against the windowpane. I gasped, then forced myself to breathe slowly. The fear slowly faded, and I was left only with a slight sense of apprehension.

Another frightened thought streamed into my mind, and I raced to the front door to ensure both the door lock and the safety chain were securely fastened. The chain rested on the door unused, and I chastised myself as my fingers fumbled to engage it.

Stupid, stupid, stupid.

I turned and rested my back against the door, my heart beating in my chest like I'd just run a marathon.

The phone rang.

I stood frozen, staring at the instrument. My answering machine clicked on, and the caller disconnected. It rang again.

Corrie. The thought came to me with sudden clarity. How could I not answer? What if it was Corrie, and Mark was there? What if she was trying to send me a message, and needed help?

I moved quickly to the extension next to the sofa and answered. "Hello? Who is this?"

No answer. Breathing.

"Who the fuck is this? Is that you, Mark, you sick fuck? You're going down, you know. We know what you did. It's over for you."

A sharp click told me the caller had disconnected.

The world began to spin, and I sat with a plop onto my sofa. What should I do now?

The phone rang again, and I snatched it up, and screamed, "What?"

"I'm going to kill you," he said.

"This phone is tapped. You are so busted."

He hung up abruptly; I sat there for the next hour, glaring at the phone, willing it to ring, my fear almost gone, my anger ripe and ready to burst.

It didn't ring.

At five-thirty I remembered the card Frank Kinderson had given me with his home phone number scrawled on the back, his work number and name printed on the front. I fetched it from my purse and dialed quickly, hoping he answered, praying I didn't hear a female voice.

"Hello?"

He sounded wide awake. I didn't know if this was because his line of work required constant alertness, or because he didn't sleep much.

"Frank, it's me, Allison."

"Allison, what's wrong?"

"He called me. He kept calling me, until I told him the phone was tapped. I guess I shouldn't have done that, because now we can't tap the phone, and even if we did, he won't call back. I'm sure he'll be afraid you'll track him down and now I've ruined the only chance—"

"Allison, slow down. Are you all right? I'll be right over."

"Okay."

"Don't answer the door until I tell you it's me."

"Okay."

"I'll be there in a few minutes."

"He said he was going to kill me."

There was silence for a minute before he said, "I'm sending a cruiser by for now. I'm sure someone is closer than me. Make sure it's the cops before you open the door."

"Okay. Frank?"

"Yeah?"

"Thank you."

I stared through the peephole of my door to see Officer Jake Jensen and his partner standing in the hallway. I groaned aloud before opening the door.

"Allison," Jake said, nodding his head, a frosty look gracing his young, handsome features. I stood aside so they could come in.

"So, tell us what happened," Officer Barlow said, taking the lead. Jake just watched me, his silence making me squirm.

I explained about the calls, and what Mark had said.

"How do you know it was Mark? Mark's your brother-in-law, right?"

It was obvious Jake had kept up on the developments in my case.

"I recognized his voice. At least I think it was . . . Oh, who else would it be?"

"Maybe somebody you rejected?" Officer Jensen asked.

I searched his tone for sarcasm but found none. Nonetheless, his implication irritated me.

"You mean like you?"

He sighed, and his features transformed from the hard mask of a seasoned police officer to that of an unsure boy and rejected suitor.

"Look, I'm sorry about that, Jake, okay? I really am. I should never have said yes. I'm just getting back on my feet after the . . . after it happened."

He smiled slightly.

Officer Barlow looked away and reddened, as if embarrassed to be included in this personal exchange, and he crossed to the window to survey the landscape below.

"Look, you showed up at my doorstep and I barely recognized you. You didn't look anything like the man who took care of me after I was raped."

"That wasn't the real me," Jake said.

"Which one wasn't the real you? The nice guy, or the player? Oh, I know, it was your evil twin Rake, right?"

His lips twitched as he fought back a smile.

"Why'd you leave with Kinderson?"

The smile was gone.

"He's investigating my case. You know that, I'm sure. All the people and the smoke, it all just got to me and when I saw him—"

"He's a ladies' man, Allison."

"He said the same about you."

"Sounds like we're competing, doesn't it?"

"I don't want to be the object of your competition. I just need this over with. I need Mark behind bars, and I need everyone around me to stop dying and . . ."

"Dying?" Jake looked puzzled, and I sighed, not wanting to explain.

A sharp rap at the door, followed by Frank's deep voice, turned Jake Jensen, who had started to look human, back into stone. One part of me wanted to pull him aside and explain, make excuses, keep him trying, while the rational part of me knew I didn't even understand it myself.

Jake Jensen was the epitome of everything I'd always looked for in a man. But that was the other me, the damaged, fragile daughter looking for acceptance. Somehow, this ordeal had made me stronger. It made me want to fight to live life my way. It made me want a future outside of steamy sex and an endless parade of empty, handsome faces.

It didn't make a lot of sense. I only knew it was the truth.

Twenty-nine

While Frank was trying to get through red tape with the phone company, I drove out to see Corrie at her apartment in Farmington. She needed to know Mark had contacted me. I needed to know she was safe.

I walked up the creaky steps and rapped lightly on the door. When she didn't answer, I tested the doorknob and found it unlocked. Frightened, I pushed through, grabbing a vase from the kitchen as I searched her house.

I found Corrie in her darkened bedroom, still in her nightclothes, though it was now eleven A.M. She didn't respond to me, couldn't hear me, didn't move.

Oh, God, no, not Corrie.

I leaned my ear close to her mouth and nose, kneeling on some papers she'd dropped on the floor. Her gentle breaths reassured me she wasn't dead, and I looked frantically around trying to understand why she wouldn't wake up. I could see no pills, nothing indicating she had tried suicide.

"Allison."

I jumped as she spoke and redirected my scattershot gaze to her face. Her eyes were now open, red-rimmed, the sorrow erased by sleep flowing back into her face.

"Corrie! You scared me. What's wrong? Why are you sleeping so heavily? Did you take something?"

With a swipe of her hand, she shook her head and sat up. "I just fell asleep, that's all. I cried all night."

"Corrie, I thought you were dead."

"I want to be dead."

I picked up the phone and tried to dial, intending to call Sandra Castle to talk to my sister. There was no dial tone. I clicked the receiver impatiently, but still couldn't get any response.

"I pulled it out of the wall."

"Why?"

"Because Mark called. Because I found those . . . those disgusting letters. I found a letter from his mission president, too. It was all a lie, Alli, all a lie and I believed him. I let him take me to the temple. I pledged to obey him for time and all eternity."

I looked down at the papers I knelt on and pulled one from under my right knee. Corrie reached over and flipped on the bedside lamp, then flopped back into bed with what seemed to be her last bit of energy.

Dear Mark, read the first letter, scrawled in childish handwriting. *My frend Katy is maling this for me. My dad said if you ever stepped foot back in town he wood kill you. The bishop says its my falt, because I shud no better. He keeps calling me in his offus and asking me to tell agin what we done together. Im saving my muny and Im bying a bus tiket to Salt Lake. You said you loved me. I dint tell no one about the baby, and they havent guessed yet becuz my close hide my tummy. Please right back. Send it to Katy Jones, P.O. Box 654, Bald Frog, Arkansas, 70696.*

I love you.
Sami.

P.S. My birthday is tomorra. Ill be 13. Will you think of me?

"Dear God in Heaven," I said, disbelief and anger roaring up inside me.

"Read the one from the mission president."

I sorted through the dozens of letters, most covered in the same childish script as the first one, until I found an official typewritten letter with "The Church of Jesus Christ of Latter-day Saints" scrolled across the letterhead.

"Read it aloud."

"Oh, Corrie, I don't want to torment you."

"Please?" Her eyes were open wide, staring at the ceiling but seeing nothing, except perhaps all her dashed dreams and expectations.

Dear Elder Peterson,
This letter is the official notification to inform you that you have been disfellowshipped from the Church of Jesus Christ of Latter-day Saints, for conduct contrary to the laws and order of the Church. Accordingly, you are to return home and meet with your bishop and stake president, so that you can fully repent and return to the Church as a member in good standing.

We encourage you to embrace the words of your leaders and repent for the sins that have caused you to be disfellowshipped, so you can return and fully enjoy the blessings of the Gospel.

It is an awesome responsibility to be called to serve a mission for God's true Church, and I sincerely hope that you will spend time considering the consequences of your actions.

Your parents have been notified of your arrival date in Salt Lake City, along with your ward bishop. I strongly urge you to spend many hours in prayer and

*repent your sins to the bishop, so that you can again
enjoy the fullness of all of God's blessings.*
> *Sincerely,*
> *B. Maxwell Wilson, President*
> *Arkansas Mission East*
> *Grace Hills, Arkansas.*

"He was sent home, and he never told me," Corrie said,
her voice full of unspent agony. "How long was he disfellowshipped? He sat beside me in church every Sunday before we got married, but always found some excuse to
leave just before the sacrament. I never even thought about
it. How stupid could I be? And why didn't the bishop tell
me when he gave us our temple recommends? Why did
they even *give* him a recommend? Why?"

"He got a twelve-year-old girl pregnant? Why wasn't
this in the news? Why wasn't he charged?"

"They covered it up."

"Who's 'they,' Corrie?"

"The church. His bishop. I called him when I found the
letters. He was confused, thought I was talking about something else. Corrie, Mark did it before, to someone else.
Someone even younger. And they never reported it. And
everybody knew he'd been sent home from his mission but
me. Everyone. The bishop said he'd been forgiven by the
time we got married, and it wasn't my concern what had happened in the past. He did it *before*, Alli, to a little girl!"

"This is sick. Do you know who?"

"No, the bishop wouldn't tell me when he realized what
he'd let slip. Just some girl. Seven, he said."

I sat down hard with a thump. A seven-year-old girl. I
was twenty-two, sexually experienced, and I'd been destroyed by the rape. What must it have done to a child?

I ran to Corrie's bathroom and heaved up the breakfast
Frank Kinderson had made me eat. The bile in my throat

matched the acid in my heart, and I wanted to buy a gun and kill Mark; hunt him down like the animal he was.

Corrie forced herself from the bed and came to my side, gently stroking my hair as I struggled with my retching. Finally, I sat back, and she handed me a wet towel. I washed my face and mouth, pressing the warm, wet rag to my tongue, trying to remove the taste.

"How did the letters get here without you seeing them? Didn't you wonder?"

"Mark got the mail every day. He was working nights, and I was working at the market during the day."

"Get your things, Corrie. You're coming with me."

She shook her head, but I was determined to remove her from this place where Mark once lived, to keep her from sleeping in the bed where he once slept.

"You're coming with me. You need me. And I need you, too."

Finally, she agreed, and we gathered up her things in a small overnight case. She was lethargic on the drive to Salt Lake City and even more so when I helped her into my bed.

I called Sandra and made Corrie an appointment for two o'clock, and then I called my boss. There was a story here, and it needed to be told.

Mark wasn't in this alone. He'd been aided by the men we'd been told our whole lives were responsible for our salvation. No one had punished him. I knew the problem was not the men themselves, but the system through which they operated. I intended to change that.

Thirty

I called Jack at the magazine and told him I wanted to write about my experience. I also gave him a brief summary of what had happened so far.

"Go for it. I'm glad you're doing something productive. How are you feeling, Alli?"

"Stronger. And, Jack?"

"Yeah?"

"Thanks for calling Detective Kinderson. He's been great."

"You're welcome."

I sat down and pulled out the *South Davis County Directory* from under the end table. I quickly discovered Mark had grown up on the street next to my high school friend Annette Tidwell. I knew Annette had married Charlie Parker while we were still in high school and they now had three or four children. I also knew Annette was a talker.

I found the phone number and dialed.

"Hello?" Her voice was the same, high and chipper. She reminded me of a squirrel on helium.

"Annette? This is Alli. Allison Jensen."

The scream almost pierced my eardrum, and I winced as I held the phone away from my ear.

"Allison, how are you? It's so good to hear from you! Why in the world are you calling me after all this time?"

I smiled. We'd only graduated four years before, but I had to agree—it seemed like an eternity.

"I wanted to get together. Are you free for lunch?"

"Today? Well, let's see, I drop Matty off at kindergarten at twelve-thirty, and I could meet you somewhere. But I'd have the twins and baby Jess. I don't think I could find a sitter on this short notice."

"That's fine. I'd love to see your kids."

We arranged to meet at a McDonald's in Bountiful after Annette murmured something about their budget and how little money she had to spend.

"And it will keep the kids busy. They can destroy Playland while we visit."

I placed a quick call to Frank, was told he wasn't at his desk, and walked into my bedroom to check on Corrie. She was asleep again, the heavy slumber of the severely depressed; and I studied her face. It was tight and drawn, her lips pursed as she mumbled unintelligible words.

She wasn't at peace. I hoped someday that would be different.

Annette hadn't changed much in the last four years, although she had a toddler clinging to each leg and a baby cinched in a carrier she clutched with her right hand. She kept bumping the child on the right with the baby carrier, and he looked up at her and whined his disapproval.

"Hurry up, Chaz," she prodded him.

She squealed her delight at seeing me, and we embraced. Her blond hair pulled back in a tight ponytail, she wore no makeup but had a clear complexion and dark blue eyes. Unlike the last time I'd seen her, though, those eyes were red-rimmed and hollow, dark circles pronounced above her cheekbones. Her figure was still petite; I assumed that was from constantly chasing kids.

She ordered two Happy Meals and a Diet Coke. I ordered two combination meals, complete with a cheeseburger and fries, and she gave me a funny look as we walked to our table.

We sat and her twin boys shot off for the play area, ignoring her pleas for them to eat first. They dived for a spot in a sea of toddlers, first one then the other disappearing in the ball pit.

"I wonder if a child has ever gone under all those plastic balls and never been seen again?" I mused.

"Oh, those two will come back. Believe me, they always do. Guess they'll eat when they get hungry."

She put the infant carrier on the top of the table. I knew by the pink blankets and outfit it was a little girl, and she had Annette's same blue eyes, although her sparse hair was darker. She sucked on a pacifier and fought to stay awake, a battle she would soon lose, judging by the heaviness of her eyes.

"Cute baby."

"Thanks. Her name's Jess. She has colic, cries all night. Really wears me out. Chuck has to work early at the Church Office Building, so I have to get up with her all the time."

Jess looked content to me, sucking on a pacifier and looking around the room with solemn eyes.

I set one of the cheeseburgers and an order of fries, complete with fry sauce, on Annette's side of the table. She looked at me in surprise.

"I invited you to lunch. This isn't La Caille, but I'm still treating."

She laughed and pushed a long strand of blond hair that had escaped the ponytail out of her face.

"Thanks, Alli."

She finished the cheeseburger and most of the fries before I was on my third bite.

"You know, I heard no one outside of Utah knows what fry sauce is. Weird, huh? I can't imagine eating these without it." She waved one of her two remaining fries toward me as she spoke.

"There are a lot of things about Utah that no one outside of the state understands," I responded.

She just smiled and laughed, ignoring my gentle jibe at the state's idiosyncrasies.

"Wow, you're still eating. I scarfed that down, didn't I? With a baby, especially a colicky one, you learn to eat fast while she's not screaming. That window of opportunity is very small."

She looked at the empty containers of food, picking up the fry package and examining it closely to make sure she hadn't missed something, then swept the empty packages to the side of the table with her arm.

"So," she said, sipping at her straw. "What have you been up to?"

"Oh, I'm working for *Salt Lake Magazine*."

"Wow, that must be glamorous. A real journalist. I always wanted to go to school, but . . ."

Annette knew she didn't have to finish her sentence. She had been one of the three cheerleaders who got pregnant our senior year in high school. She married Chuck in a dismal ceremony in the cultural hall, presided over by a bishop, and graduated in the Young Mothers program at the alternative high school. She wasn't even allowed to walk down the aisle with our class at graduation.

"So, how's Chuck? You said he works for the church?"

"Yeah, his dad got him on. It's better than the job he had working construction, and the benefits are good. With the four kids, though, and rent and the car payments . . . well, there's not much left."

"So you guys got married in the temple?" I knew only temple recommend holders could work in the tallest building in Salt Lake City that served as headquarters for the LDS Church.

"Yeah, about a year after Matty was born. It was pretty weird, but everybody was pressing us to do it. I was scared, but it wasn't that bad. Better than my civil ceremony, I guess, where my dad glared at Chuck the whole time and my mother-in-law sobbed through the entire thing. This time they were all happy."

"Well, I hope *you're* happy."

A sudden sorrow flooded her face, and she turned away. I decided to change the subject.

"Hey, what do you know about Mark Peterson? I heard some stuff about him."

Her eyes lit up. Annette lived for gossip. She always had.

"Oh, he was in my ward. What a freak. When he was thirteen, he did something to one of the little girls in the ward. I don't know what, I only heard what I did by listening to my parents talk when they thought I wasn't paying attention."

She leaned forward and her voice dropped to a whisper, even though it was impossible for anyone not sitting at our table to hear us, with the deafening roar from Playland.

"They said he made her put *it* in her mouth. 'Course I didn't hear that from my parents. I heard that from Tracy Kelly—remember her? She had really long black hair and—"

I interrupted her, wanting to know more about Mark. "Who was the girl?"

"Um, the Perkins family, I think. They had nine or ten

kids, all of them with red hair. I never knew which one was which. But look at me, here I am with four already!"

"Did they report it to the police?"

Annette sat straight up, her spine rigid, her mouth tightly closed. I imagined her as a small poodle scenting danger on the wind, ears pricked for the slightest sound, nose twitching.

"Allison, why are you asking about this? You're not going to write about it, are you?"

"He married my sister, Annette."

"Oh, God, no. I heard she was a *lesbian*." She emphasized the word with disdain.

"No, not my sister Christy. He married Corrie."

"Oh, how horrible. Well, maybe he's repented. You know, God gives us all a chance to be forgiven—"

I shut her down quickly. "He got a twelve-year-old girl pregnant on his mission. He raped me. He hasn't repented. And he needs to be punished."

She sat in shock, her mouth open wide, and stared at me. The shock quickly turned to alarm. "Oh, you're not going to quote me, are you, Allison? Man, Chuck would kill me. My dad would kill me. He's the bishop of their ward now, and they won't forgive me if I get quoted in some article about anti-Mormon stuff."

"Anti-Mormon stuff? Don't you get it, Annette? This man is a sexual predator, and by the church's hushing it up and not reporting it to the police, he's been given free rein to offend over and over again."

"Allison, please," she begged. "Keep my name out of it. I never should have come. I heard you left the church and were doing bad things, but . . . Oh, please, leave me out of it."

I stood up and shook my head. "I won't use your name, but I am going to the cops with this. And I'm going to write about it. It has to stop somewhere. Someone has to make it stop."

I walked out without looking back, leaving Annette with her little family among all the other young Mormon mothers, who all looked as weary as she did. I had the information I needed. I was going to find the Perkins family.

Thirty-one

Corrie's appointment with Sandra, however, came before my search for the abused Perkins daughter. I returned to my apartment and rousted her out of bed, forcing her to shower and dress and practically dragging her to my car.

"Allison, I don't want to do this. I don't want to talk to anyone. I'll be fine. I'm just tired."

I ignored her. We pulled into the parking lot of Sandra's office building with five minutes to spare, and I hustled her out of the car and inside. The air was stifling, as the balmy spring temperatures had given way to summer with little notice. Corrie fanned herself with a *Good Housekeeping* magazine while I signed her in.

Sandra came out and chatted with us both briefly, then asked Corrie to come back with her. I left my sister in the therapist's capable hands and drove to the police station to meet with Frank. He wasn't in his office—the secretary said he was out on assignment—so I wrote him a quick note explaining what I had discovered, folded it in two, and left it with her.

I had taken my phone directory with me to meet Annette, and it was still in my car, I sat in the parking lot with the windows rolled down and thumbed through it, looking for a listing for the Perkins family in Farmington. I found twelve.

"Damn!"

"Boy, you're never happy to see me."

I let out a little squeal of surprise at being caught so engrossed and silently cursed myself as I stared into the face of Jake Jensen, bent over and looking into my open window.

"You scared me."

"Sorry. Meeting Frank?"

"Not meeting him. I came to give him some information."

"Oh? News in your case?"

"Yeah, kind of. What are you doing here? Don't you work the graveyard shift?"

"Shift change. We alternate. Just went to swing."

"Oh, I see." I silently prayed he'd end the conversation so I could leave.

"So, Allison, you going to give me another chance? Or are you and Frank exclusive, now?"

"I'm not dating Frank! I'm not dating anyone right now, *Officer Jensen*."

"Don't get worked up," he said, chuckling. I got the distinct impression he liked me worked up. "I've got tickets to the Jazz game on Sunday. Care to join me?"

"Jazz?"

"Jazz, you know. Utah Jazz? NBA Basketball?"

"Shouldn't you be at church on Sunday?"

"Don't go to church. The NBA is my religion."

"Look, Jake, I'm really not in the best shape for dating right now, and—"

"Then let's go as friends. I promise to leave Rake home."

I gave him a grudging smile.

"Fine. What time?"

"I'll pick you up at noon. We'll go for lunch first. Game's at two-thirty."

"I guess you know where I live."

"Yep, even been inside now. See you Sunday."

I felt weak, unable to say no, to stand up for myself. I also was strangely intrigued. Surely my shallow self wasn't making a comeback? I shrugged it off.

There was plenty of time to learn to say no.

I collected a subdued Corrie from Sandra's office. she didn't speak on the way home and pushed a small piece of paper into my hand before she headed back into the bedroom and shut the door. I glanced at it and saw a prescription for Prozac signed by the psychiatrist Sandra worked with. I wasn't sure if she wanted me to fill it or throw it away, but I trusted Sandra, and Corrie was going to take them if I had to hold her nose and stroke her throat, like I'd seen them do to dogs.

Knowing it was unlikely she'd go anywhere, I left to fill the prescription and make another trip to Farmington to find the Perkinses. I'd narrowed it down to three families who lived in the vicinity of Annette's old home and was determined to visit each one. I had no idea what I'd say.

I drove up to the first house and parked out front. It was a tiny, ramshackle, cinder block house with old chairs and a washing machine on the north side and junk cluttering up a yard overgrown with weeds. A pink sheet covered half of a dirty front window, the other half hanging loose to expose the inside of the home to anyone who might want to peek in. I knocked on the front door, and the churning in my stomach told me how unprepared I was.

A tall, gangly woman with red hair, white skin, and freckles stood in front of me when the shabby, wooden door opened. She wore a blank stare and a weary demeanor, and the many wrinkles and crevices on her face told me she'd lived a rough life. I didn't know if she was forty or sixty.

"Who're you? If you're one of those Jay-Dubs, I already told you people we're Mormons. We have God's true church. Don't have time for none of your nonsense."

"Jay-Dubs?"

"Hmmph. Jehovah's Witnesses."

"Oh, no, I'm not a missionary."

"Well, you're not a Mormon," she countered, staring with undisguised contempt at my short-sleeved shirt and denim shorts that couldn't possibly hide garments.

"How do you know? I could be a Mormon and just not have been through the temple," I countered, then cursed myself. I couldn't afford to antagonize this unlikable woman. I needed information.

"None of my kids never dressed like that. They were good and modest."

"I'm a reporter. I'm doing a story on . . . on . . ."

Think, Allison!

"I'm doing a story for *Salt Lake Magazine* on Mormon missionaries, and how it changes their lives to go on missions for *the* church." I emphasized *the* in hopes she'd take my inference I was friend, not foe. "I'm really impressed with what I've learned so far. Quite a fascinating people you Mormons are."

The last part was pure genius. Now she would invite me in and tell me about her religion. They all did.

"Well, I don't know what you want with me. I'm busy."

Damn. Count on me to find the one Mormon who wasn't anxious to baptize the world.

"I'm sorry, Mrs. . . . . ?"

"Perkins."

"Mrs. Perkins. A friend from out this way told me your family would be a good one to talk to about this issue."

"What friend?"

"Jake Jensen," I said quickly, mentioning the first name that popped into my mind.

"Oh, Jake did, did he? Well, you tell that dirty rotten nephew of mine he better not be sending no more reporters to my door. And, furthermore, you tell him to get his skinny backside back to church where it belongs!"

With that, she slammed the door, leaving me stunned.

It couldn't be. Jensen was a common name, as was Jacob, a good Bible name. Could there possibly be a tie between Jake Jensen and Mark Peterson? They were about the same age. Did he grow up on this street? Had they been friends?

I ran to my car and sped away, stunned by suspicion and growing horror. The worst fear of all was not knowing if I would ever look at a person again and not wonder if evil lurked inside.

Thirty-two

I canceled my therapy appointment the next morning and sat at the breakfast table to watch my listless sister dutifully swallow the antidepressant capsule.

"You know, the Relief Society president told me just two weeks ago that all I needed was a prescription for Prozac and everything would be fine. That was after I confided in her my fears about Mark's problems."

"You told her about the pictures and . . . ?"

"No, I'm not stupid. It would have been all over the ward. I just told her Mark had some trouble telling the truth. That's when she told me I needed Prozac. Told me more than half the ladies in the ward are on it."

"Shit, Corrie, doesn't that tell you something? If all of this is so wonderful, why are they all so fucking unhappy?"

"Don't swear, Alli. It makes you sound so hard." She attempted to smile, then drifted off into languor again, nibbling at the toast and eggs I made her. After only a few bites, she shuffled off to my room, shutting the door and trying to shut out her misery. I knew it wouldn't work. I also knew I had to get to the bottom of this, to find Mark, to reveal the truth, before Corrie could begin to heal.

I called Detective Kinderson, who was once again un-
available, and my frustration mounted. Why hadn't he
called me? Was anything happening in my case? I forced
myself to get back in my car and drive to Farmington. I had
two more Perkins families to visit.

The tall, gaunt, unpleasant woman, with her harsh
words and stunning secrets, flew through my mind.

Please, make this time easier.

As I took the Farmington exit off I-15, I found myself
tensing. The nearer I came to the neighborhood, the more
anxious I became. I forced myself to take deep breaths, and
when I pulled up at the second address on my list I was
slightly mollified to see an old but neat and well-maintained
redbrick home. A large willow tree graced the front yard,
offering shade and a swing made out of an old tire.

I walked to the door and rang the bell, the familiar nau-
sea churning in my stomach. A tall, redheaded woman
opened it, and I nearly fainted. It was her!

"Yes?" she asked politely. Her manner and demeanor
were totally different from the other woman's, and I realized I was staring at an identical twin, although the years
had been kinder to this one.

"Um, yes, um, I'm Allison Jensen. I'm from *Salt Lake
Magazine* and I'm doing a story on missionaries . . ."

Her face hardened, and my stomach clenched in response. I wondered how I'd managed to twice trigger hos-
tile reactions in a sea of Mormons eager to spread the word
of their Gospel to the world.

"I don't go to church, thank you very much. I have nothing good to say about missionaries, or the Mormon men
that send them out there!"

I abandoned my pretense on a hunch.

"Look, Ms. Perkins. I wasn't being totally honest. My
name *is* Allison Jensen, and I *am* doing a story, but there's

more to it. I'm trying to find a young girl who was molested years ago by a man . . . well, I guess he was a boy then. A teenager. But she was only seven."

"What reason do you have for asking these questions?" Her hard glare turned to a pained expression. I knew my hunch had paid off.

"Because he raped me. And he got another girl pregnant, only twelve years old. Got sent home from his mission for it, but they never reported him, never. Now he's on the loose and stalking me. It's got to stop."

Her composure crumpled and tears fell down her face; she swiped them away with the back of her hand and opened her screen door, motioning me inside.

I followed her to the living room, where she sat on a La-Z-Boy recliner.

"Please, sit," she said, sniffling, and pulled a tissue from a doily-covered box on the side table next to her.

I sat without speaking and gave her a moment to recover.

"It was my daughter, Jenny. That's her," she said, pointing to a picture of a freckle-faced girl with her mother's hair and coloring, looking to be around six. "That was taken just before it happened. Now she's dyed her hair black and wears white makeup and black lipstick. She has piercings all over her face and body, and she goes for days without speaking. She dropped out of school last year. I haven't seen her for two weeks. I don't even know if she's still alive! He did this. Mark Peterson did this to my baby."

The tears started again, and I stood and walked over to her, putting my hand on her shoulder. She sobbed and gasped for breath, wiping her nose with the tissues until it looked red and sore.

With a final sigh, she shuddered, and a semblance of control returned.

"I didn't know what to do, so I did what they told me, and look what happened. Now other girls have been hurt."

Not wanting her to dissolve in sobs again, I quickly spoke. "Can you tell me what happened?"

"Please, sit back down. I'm sorry to be such a poor hostess. Would you like a drink of water? Or some Coke? I have Coke now, you know. After it happened and no one would do anything, I went out and bought beer and Coke and cigarettes, just to spite the church and the bishop who let my daughter be violated. Didn't ever use them, just bought them. Paraded up and down the aisles of the Farmington Mart just willing some of my neighbors to walk by and see me. No one did. Sounds stupid, I guess."

"No, sounds pretty much like something I'd do," I admitted. "Is it too hard for you to talk about?"

"I'm not sure I want a story done on it, Allison. That is your name, right? Allison?"

"Yes, but call me Alli, Mrs. Perkins. You don't want it to happen again, do you, with some other predator? Some other rapist or abuser?"

Her face hardened again. "Do you know what he did, Alli? He stuck his *dick* in her mouth. Seven years old, she was, just a baby, and he made her suck his dick!" She blanched as she said the hateful word, and my heart bottomed out with compassion.

"He's sick. I thought what he did to me was bad, but to do that to an innocent child . . . I hate him. He hurt my sister, too."

"What did he do to your sister?" she asked, alarm causing her voice to rise.

"He married her."

Karen, as she told me to call her, fixed us both a glass of Coke and ice, and said, "Let's sit in the backyard. There's a cool breeze that comes from Farmington Creek, and it's a beautiful day."

I followed her outside, unsure of how to phrase my next question.

"Karen, do you know Jake Jensen?"

"Jake? Of course. He's my nephew. Well, nephew on my husband's side, I should say. His father married my husband's only sister. My husband died about six years ago— I think it was what happened to Jenny that did it. Jake's father died the next year. Bad heart. You know Jake?"

"I'm not sure. Where is he now?"

"He's in Salt Lake City, working for the police department. Has a fine job. Takes extra pride in bringing down child molesters. Beat the tar out of Mark Peterson, him and my son Willie did. After it happened."

Was that why Jake took a special interest in me? Had his hard-nosed, bad guy persona been an act to impress me, so he could finally make Mark Peterson pay?

"I talked to your sister," I admitted with a shamed grin. "She practically threw me out on my ear. But she said Jake was her nephew, too."

"Oh, that one. Sheesh. She's a piece of work, huh? I fall away from church teachings and she just gets more fanatical. Downright ugly now, with her stupid husband cheating on her and boozing all the time. We married twin brothers. I got the good end of that deal. My husband was one of seven boys, and not all of them turned out well. But me and my sister, we used to be so close. Then . . . well, what can I say? Life happened. She puts on her best dress and goes to church like a pious soul. Told me it was Jenny's fault, that somehow she asked for it. Seven years old! What kind of crap is that from a grown woman?"

"Do you have other kids besides Jenny and Willie?"

"Nope, just the two. Never saw any need to populate the earth. Thought I'd let the other Mormons do it. Now my sister Kathy, she has ten kids. Ten! All of them rotten to the core. Go to church every Sunday and the rest of the week they steal and cheat their way through life. My hypocritical sister refuses to see it. We live on the same street but haven't spoken in seven years."

Annette had been wrong about which Perkins family had the molested child, but this spoke even louder. This caring mother would not have missed the signs of abuse.

"You went to the bishop?"

"Yes, Carlton, my late husband, talked me into it. I wanted to call the police, but he said, 'No, let's call Bishop Hansen.' They called the boy in, questioned him, he lied, and they let him off the hook. Said it was possible Jenny made it up. A seven-year-old girl? Where the hell did she get that idea?"

"Oh, I'm so sorry, Karen."

"Oh, it gets better. Carlton persuaded me, in all his Priesthood glory, to abide by the bishop's ruling. When they announced that pervert was going on a mission, I walked out of church. I called the bishop and met with him. I told him I was going to press charges and have Mark arrested. He convinced me it wouldn't be right. That if . . . it . . . had happened, Mark had repented and was now willing to serve the Lord. And now this."

"It's not too late. I'm not sure you could still press charges, but you could sue the bishop. And the church."

"Sue the church? Are you nuts? They have so much money, they're richer than God himself."

"Yes, but the publicity alone might be enough to change public opinion and make them revamp their policies."

"Maybe. Or it could just dredge up all the old bad feelings. Jenny's messed up enough as it is. My husband never forgave himself. Convinced himself it was his fault, especially since he urged me to follow the bishop's advice. Then, when Jenny started having problems, well . . . we both stopped going to church. And Jenny . . . oh, my poor Jenny. She screamed for two years afterward when any man tried to touch her. Then she just quit talking."

"I'm going to find him, Mrs. Perkins—Karen. I'm going to find him and make him pay."

She patted my hand gently and said, "You do that, Alli. You do that."

Thirty-three

I now had a new ghost in my life, only this one haunted me during the bright daylight hours—a specter of the person my sister used to be. She drifted silently between the bathroom and bedroom, coming to eat only at my prodding, nibbling at food, and returning to her self-imposed prison. Alarmed, I called Sandra.

"She's been through a lot, Allison. I have another appointment with her tomorrow. She did tell you, didn't she?"

"No."

"Well, it's tomorrow at one. If you think I should see her sooner—she's not showing signs of being suicidal, is she?"

"No, she's not suicidal. She's already dead."

"Give her time, Allison. Make sure she comes. She's taking the antidepressant?"

"Yes."

"Good. They take about six weeks to start working, unfortunately. When am I going to see *you*?"

I hastily explained what I was doing, and there was a moment of silence on the other end of the line. When she spoke, her quiet voice resonated through my psyche.

"Allison, please be careful. I hope you know that no one

is going to take care of you but you. Please call me if you need anything."

I ended the call and hung up. *Be careful.* I'd been careful up until the time I left my father's house. I never stepped on the cracks in the sidewalk, wanting to avoid breaking my mother's back. She'd died anyway. I never killed the rolypoly bugs on the sidewalk, instead guiding them to safety in the grass, when other kids teased them and played marbles with their little rolled-up bodies before squishing them with their shoes. Instead of treating me with kindness for seeing to his creatures, God saw fit to let a man treat me like a bug he could squash at random.

Being careful had never served me well before. I doubted it would do much good now. I intended to bring Mark Peterson to justice. I only hoped I didn't die in the process.

Thirty-four

"Allison?"

"Yes?"

"It's Russell. Russell Free."

"You're the only Russell I know. I guess you've forgiven me."

"I heard about Corrie's baby."

"Yeah?"

"I heard about Mark, too. How he's missing. How's Corrie?"

"She's okay, I guess. No, she's not. She's like a ghost. Everything she used to be, even as shy as she was, is missing."

"Are you scared?"

"For her?"

"For both of you."

"Yes, I'm scared."

"You want me to come stay at your place? I'm on days right now."

I hesitated, and I could hear the embarrassment creep into his voice with his next words.

"I mean on the floor or the couch, Allison."

"Russell, that's sweet, but we'll be okay."

"All right. Well, I'll drop by, okay?"

"Okay. Probably better call first."

"You that busy?"

"I'm working a story right now, Russell. Corrie will be here, if you can get her out of bed to answer the door."

"Allison. I want to be there for you. Even if it's just as a friend."

"I know, Russell. I appreciate it. And I'm sorry for what I said at the hospital. I really am."

"I know."

"Russell?"

"Yeah?"

"Can you get me a gun?"

Thirty-five

I'd called my father's house several times a day for the past week, and no one ever answered. I watched closely but saw no more signs he was anywhere in the vicinity of my apartment.

Frank Kinderson finally called me back after two days.

"Allison? Frank."

"Why haven't you called me? Where have you been?" I stopped, embarrassed. "Oh, man, I'm sorry. I sound like a harping wife. I didn't mean it that way. I've just found out a lot of stuff and I wanted to tell you about it."

He chuckled with good nature, and the throaty sound made me smile. It also made me remember that in a short amount of time I'd gathered a bevy of cops who appeared to have a personal interest in not only my case but me.

I frowned as I thought of Jake Jensen. I no longer knew what his interest was.

"Allison, I've been out on a lead. Went up to the Peterson property in Wyoming. Pretty big ranch up there, with a cabin. Cabin, hell, it's a nice place. Running water. Hot tub. We're pretty sure Mark was holed up there for a while. Signs that someone had been there recently were found, some opened cans and food and the like. Family denied it.

Tried to say they had a caretaker, but we asked around, and the neighbors said no one ever goes up there except the family, four or five times a year."

"But he wasn't there?"

"Nope, he wasn't there. Maybe saw the deputies driving by and ran."

"You got my note?"

"Yes, and I've touched base with the sheriff's office back in Arkansas. They're following up on that lead but meeting with dead ends. Seems no one wants to talk about it."

"No surprise. No one except a scared, pregnant teenager. The baby must have been born by now. Can you check the hospital records for babies born to young teen mothers?"

"You have a reporter's instinct, Allison. Yes, they're checking all of those things. But if the family or the girl isn't willing to talk, well, there's not much we can do."

"Oh, I am so stupid. I have her name. And the name and address of her friend. I'll drop the letter by your office. That'll make it easier. I can't believe I didn't think of that. I also found the girl he molested. The seven-year-old. I found her mother, anyway."

"You did? Man, you've been busy. Would she be willing to talk to me?"

I gave him Karen Perkins's name and number and assured him I believed she would talk.

"Let me take you to dinner tonight."

"I don't know if I should leave Corrie. She's . . . she's not well, and with Mark out there, I don't dare leave her."

"Okay, well, think about it and get back to me. I'll talk to you—"

"Wait!" I practically screamed it into the phone, and my colorful imagination pictured him wincing. "Sorry, sorry, I didn't mean to scream, but I need to ask you something. It's about Jake. Jake Jensen."

"Yeah?" Frank's voice took on a cautious edge.

"Has he been asking you about the case?"

"Yeah, well, he found you, so I figure he has a vested interest in the outcome."

"More than you might think. I just found out he's the cousin of the girl Mark molested. At the time, he and her brother beat Mark up pretty bad."

There was silence.

"Frank?" I prodded him.

"I know about it, Allison. He asked me not to tell you."

"I don't understand."

"Allison, I can't—"

"What the hell is going on?"

"Look, I'll send a car up to watch your apartment. We need to talk, but it has to be off the record. Totally off the record. You have to promise me."

"Fine. Off the record. I can give you the girl's name and address."

"I'll pick you up—"

"I'll meet you there. What time and where?"

We arranged to meet at Coopers at six o'clock, and he promised me a police car would be positioned in front of my apartment building. I didn't want him picking me up. I didn't know what he'd been hiding from me, but when I found out, I intended to be free to walk away.

I was tired of secrets and lies, and things I couldn't hear or know about because I was on the wrong side of the fence. I wanted the real truth, and amazingly, I felt strong enough to handle it.

I left my house only after a white police cruiser was parked on the side of the road directly in front of my building. The officer inside watched me leave, and I waved at him, acknowledging his presence.

At Coopers, I saw Frank seated in a booth at the back. He

204 NATALIE R. COLLINS

wore a dark-blue shirt that emphasized his eyes, and a chagrined look. He stood up and smiled when he spotted me, but I saw only guilt; I wondered what I was about to hear.

"Allison," he said, nodding his head slightly. The noise of his chair scraping the tile floor as he sat down and scooted it toward the table set my nerves on edge and made me wince. "You okay?"

"I'm fine." I pushed the letter with the information about the pregnant teenager in it toward him on the table. He picked it up and perused it.

"Heya, Frankie, how you doing?" Brenda, our waitress, greeted him. I was surprised, as I was a regular here, drinking away my evenings, and I'd never seen him here before—at least that I remembered.

"Whatcha gonna have?" she asked him, a coy smile fluttering across her lips.

"Coors."

"Shoulda known." She smiled widely at him, not bothering to write it down. She turned her look to me, her flirtatious manner completely gone. "And you?"

She'd served me gin and tonics many times, and I found myself irritated with her and, irrationally, Frank.

"Gin and tonic."

"Right." She wrote my order down, threw another soulful look at Frank, and left.

"You know her?"

"She used to work at Juniors. We dated for a while."

"Man, you cops get around."

Frank laughed unabashedly and again the sound warmed my soul, despite the niggling thoughts in my brain. One was telling me Frank was probably a ladies' man. The other reminded me he was about to tell me something I might not want to hear. He went back to reading the letter, and I saw the consternation in his face as his thick eyebrows tightened up, moving closer together to make almost one long unit.

"This is horrible."

"It is. It makes me so sick my skin crawls. So, tell me what's going on with Jake. I want to know the truth."

"Shouldn't we order dinner first?"

"Frank . . ."

"Hey, I'm hungry. Let's order and then I'll talk while we're waiting for the food, okay? It's not what you think, Allison."

"That's what they all say."

Brenda returned with our drinks, and we ordered the salmon special, complete with fresh-baked sourdough bread, broiled red baby potatoes with parsley, and a side of asparagus. We'd only just begun to talk when the food arrived. What we ordered sounded good on the menu, but when it was sitting in front of me, I found my appetite had once again fled.

As if reading my mind, when Brenda left to refresh our drinks, he said, "I swear, you look even skinnier than you did just a few days ago. Are you eating?"

"I try."

"Allison, I'm so sorry this happened to you. I really am."

"Jake."

"Sheesh, you can be pushy. Okay, well, Jake's been tailing Mark Peterson on his own time since the perv came home from his mission. He wants revenge for his cousin. Can't say I blame him, but basically what he's doing isn't exactly on the up-and-up, so he didn't feel like he could tell Castleton. He was on duty the night of the rape, so he didn't see Mark then—he has no proof. But he'd followed him there every night for weeks. Mark sat outside your apartment and watched it. Jake wasn't sure who he was watching, but he knew something was up. Then, when you were raped, he put two and two together. After I picked up the case from Castleton, Jake came to me and filled me in."

"I didn't think you two were close."

"I may not respect everything he does, but he's a good cop, Allison."

"So, basically, he's trying to get close to me to catch Mark. And is that why you're taking me so seriously? Did you even believe me when I came to you?"

"Whoa, you're going off on a tangent there, Alli. Of course I believed you. I just have more information now that adds to the severity of the situation."

The color drained from my face as what he told me sank in. "He was watching me?"

"No, he was watching Mark. He didn't—"

"No. I mean Mark. He'd been outside my apartment every night for weeks?" A shiver started at the base of my spine and traveled upward; goose bumps popped up on my arms and legs and the room chilled ten degrees. "He was watching me. Oh, God. Oh, my God."

"Yes, he was. He was stalking you, Allison. The rape would have happened sooner or later, although if Jake hadn't been on duty that night, it might not have happened at all."

All my anger at Jake and Frank for keeping me in the dark dissipated, and my composure fell in a puddle to the floor.

"I can't believe it. He could have . . . this could have happened anytime." I'd been in danger for weeks without the slightest inkling. "How fucking warped is this? What the fuck did I ever do to deserve this? If there is a God, he sure as hell hates me."

Frank scooted his chair toward mine, and that scraping sound made me want to burst into tears. He put his arm around my shoulders and pulled me toward him, nestling my head against his chest.

Do not cry. You will not cry.

Brenda showed up with our drinks, minus her smile, and

with a jealous look on her pretty features. I didn't care. I was beyond caring about anything at all. I felt like one of my ghosts.

"I'm going to get him."

"We'll get him," Frank said, stroking my hair. "We'll get him. I promise."

Thirty-six

Frank offered to follow me home and see me safely inside, but I declined. The closer I came to my apartment building, however, the more I suffered regret at saying no. My stomach started to churn, and I felt the hair rise on my arms and legs. Perspiration beaded on my forehead, and I wiped it away with the back of my hand.

I pulled into the parking lot with a full-blown case of paranoia, and I sat in my car for a moment, unable to move. Night had advanced into the valley and clouds blocked whatever light the sliver of moon might have supplied. Everywhere I looked I saw shadows and menace, and I grew dizzy with fear.

I could see no police car as I scanned both directions, and anger and confusion clouded my thought processes. They had been there when I left to meet Frank. Where were they now?

"Stop it! Just stop it, Allison Marie Jensen. Get a grip."

I forced myself to calm down, grabbed my purse, and opened my car door, determined to walk calmly across the parking lot and into my apartment building. A slight wind whispered down from the Wasatch Mountains, and I heard a scrambling noise in the bushes as I reached my door. A premonition someone was watching me heated up my face, and I ran the last few steps to the apartment door, no longer concerned with walking slowly.

The hand that grabbed me frightened me so badly I screamed as loud as I possibly could, and another one clamped down over my mouth.

"Shhh. Allison, it's me, Jake."

As soon as Jake was assured I wouldn't scream again he let me go; I turned and pummeled him with my fists, hitting him as hard as I could, tears flowing down my face.

"You stupid son of a bitch. What are you doing? You scared me to death, you stupid . . ."

"Whoa, slow down, Alli. I'm sorry I scared you."

He grabbed my wrists and held them tight to keep me from assaulting him any further. I collapsed against him and sobbed. The tears I'd refused to release for the past few days had backed up, and now poured from my eyes in relentless streams.

After a few minutes, I calmed down and backed away from him.

"I'm sorry, Allison. I should have known better than to approach you like that, without warning. It *was* stupid."

"What are you doing here, Jake? Where's the police car?" I wiped away the last of the tears, picked up the purse I had dropped when he grabbed me, and searched through the jumbled contents for a tissue.

"I was watching your house, that's all. They got called out on a murder/suicide, and I was close so I said I'd stay. I'm off tonight, and I was worried he'd come back."

"I know."

"You know?"

"I know who you are, and what Mark did to your cousin.

I know you've been watching me for weeks. I understand now why you've been trying to get close to me. You can drop the charade."

"I wasn't watching you, Allison. I was watching Mark. I didn't even know who you were until the rape. I guess Frank told you?"

"Only after I did some discovering on my own. I met your Aunt Karen and her sister Kathy."

"How?"

"Corrie found letters. Look, this is ridiculous. I need to check on Corrie, and being out in the open gives me the creeps. Let's go inside."

Jake followed me up to my apartment and leaned against the doorjamb while I unlocked the door. I pushed it open only to find it secured by the chain lock.

"Corrie? Corrie?" I yelled.

There was no answer.

"Corrie!" My voice became sharp and high-pitched with concern, and I pounded on the door heavily, even though it was now past ten.

Jake motioned me aside and had put his shoulder to the door, prepared to break the lock, when we both saw my ghost sister look through the crack. Her red-rimmed eyes were swollen and teary, her face pale and contorted in agony; she said nothing as she shut the door and undid the lock. When she reopened the door, I raced inside.

"Corrie, what's wrong?"

"She died."

Thirty-seven

"Who died?" I asked, my mind racing with possible victims.

"My baby died."

"Your baby died? Oh, I know that, Corrie. Come sit down." I guided her to the couch, wondering if perhaps she had suffered a mental breakdown. With everything that had happened to us over the past few weeks, it was understandable.

"I hate him, Allison. It's his fault. It's his fault my baby died. I've never wanted to hurt somebody so badly before. God will never forgive me for the feelings I'm having right now. I'd like to torture him."

"Corrie, God will forgive you. The God I know isn't vindictive, or mean," Jake said, and Corrie jerked her head toward him, watching his face as he spoke. "I went through some of this when my cousin was molested by Mark."

Corrie's mouth dropped open.

"Jake is the seven-year-old's cousin, you know, the one in Mark's ward?" I told her. "He'd been watching Mark before all this happened."

"Watching Mark?"

"Waiting for him to slip up," Jake explained. "I knew he'd

do it again. His timing was just better than mine. The night he raped Allison I was on duty, so I couldn't follow him."

Corrie collapsed onto the sofa, as if all her bones had turned to liquid. "I don't understand all of this. All I ever wanted was to do the right thing, to do what God wanted. Now everything's a mess."

She had thus far avoided her grief by sleeping and denial. Now she confronted it head-on. I was no therapist, but I knew this was good.

"Who are you, anyway?" she asked Jake.

"I'm Jake Jensen. I'm a cop, and I've been waiting a long time to see Mark Peterson brought to justice. I'm only sorry you have to go through this humiliation. He's a master manipulator. You can't blame yourself, okay?"

Corrie looked back at me for reassurance. I nodded, wondering if I gave her permission to trust Jake because she no longer had any faith in herself.

I was confused myself, the line between good men and bad men blurred and out of focus. I still had concerns about Jake's lack of honesty with me, but we had the same goal. We both wanted to see Mark Peterson stopped. That alone united us the way nothing else ever could. It was stronger than a bond of love, marriage, or family.

I wondered if Jake wanted to kill him, too.

Russell showed up at my apartment the next morning and said, "Come on, let's go."

"Huh? Where're we going?"

"To the shooting range."

"Russell, I haven't even—"

"Alli, I have to be at work at one. I need to show you how to use a gun."

"I'm surprised you agreed to get me one."

"I didn't get you one. I'm letting you use one of mine—actually, it was my dad's—but you have to know what you're doing first. And you can't carry it with you. You need a permit to carry a concealed weapon. This is just for your apartment. I wish you'd just let me come stay."

"Are you going to quit your job to baby-sit me, Russell? You and I both know that's not logical or feasible."

He grunted.

At the shooting range, he was terse and silent, only speaking when he admonished me for my style or closing my eyes as I fired. After shooting several rounds, I envisioned the paper target, an outline of a man's upper torso, as Mark Peterson, and I fired the automatic weapon seven times. I missed the target entirely, instead putting every shot in the area where the crotch of the outlined man would have been, had it not been chopped off below the waist.

Russell finally smiled, a small grudging grin that tugged at the side of his mouth. "Remind me not to piss you off, okay?"

I smiled back and handed him the weapon. He showed me the safety and how to load and unload it, and tucked it in the shoulder holster he'd been wearing.

"I thought you were going to let me use it."

"I'm keeping it until I drop you off. You can't carry it, remember. This is my gun, registered to me. You have to think of that, okay? It's against the law to carry a concealed weapon without a permit."

"Does that mean if I just walk around with it in my hand that I can carry it? As long as it's not hidden—"

"Allison!"

"Russell, I don't intend to use it. Unless I have to."

"And what circumstances would cause you to have to use it?"

"Mark's been stalking me. He watched my house for weeks before the rape. He knows where I live. If he breaks into my house, he intends to kill me. He called me and told me so. I don't intend to be his victim for the second time. If

Mark Peterson tries to touch me, or my sister, again he's going to die."

Russell made me promise six more times not to leave the apartment with the gun. I'd always hated firearms, but I felt a kinship with this one for some reason. The shiny metal spoke to me, whispered confident secrets into my ear, asked for my trust. I willingly gave it.

I tucked it under the couch cushion and felt a strong sense of relief knowing it was there.

Corrie was showering when I returned home from the shooting range, and I silently thanked Jake Jensen. She was finding her way back, tougher than I thought. I would drop her off at Sandra's office for her appointment, then do some more investigating.

"Corrie, hurry, okay?" I knocked on the bathroom door. "I need to shower, too."

There was no answer.

I waited at the door for a moment, then knocked again. "Corrie? Are you okay?"

"Allison, can you come in here?" Her voice sounded thin and scared. I pushed the door open to find the bathroom full of steam, great clouds of it rising and fogging the mirror. Corrie was in the shower, naked, the water pelting her thin chest and arms, running down her round stomach, which hadn't quite recovered from pregnancy. The shower curtain was only halfway closed, and I could see her red and raw-looking skin. I reached into the shower and cupped my hand upward, the steaming water stinging my skin.

"Corrie, this is way too hot. You're going to burn yourself!" I reached down and turned the water off, but she didn't move, just stared at something on the mirror. I followed her gaze and gasped.

BITCHES. WHORES. PREPARE TO DIE. It was scrawled on the mirror, written in my best plum lipstick. I froze for a moment, then chastised myself, trying to hear my own voice of reason above the roar of fear.

"I didn't lock the door when I left. I must not have. How did he get in? How could . . . ?"

She finally spoke as I handed her a towel, the shock of the message wearing off. "It wasn't you. It was me. The missionaries knocked at the door, and I answered. I thought of Kevin, and they looked so young I had to talk to them. After they left, I just forgot. But I don't know when he came in."

"Oh, why did I leave you? Russell came up, and I was only gone for an hour. But I shouldn't have . . . oh, damn him! He's an idiot. Lipstick on the mirror? That is so used. He's not even an original criminal. He's just plain stupid. I need to call the cops."

Corrie looked pitifully thin, shaking from the change of temperature from hot water to cold air. "Allison, I'm sorry I wasn't more careful."

"There's been a lot of things happening, Corrie. Did you hear him? Hear the door? Have any idea he was in here?"

"No, I didn't hear anything. I didn't hear—Allison! What if he's still here?"

My heart seemed to stop; I moved to the door as fast as I could, running for the phone in the living room, motioning Corrie to stay in the bathroom. I looked around briefly, but saw nothing. Still, I relaxed a little, because the apartment was so small there weren't many places he could hide.

When the door to my utility closet—located between the kitchen and the living room—burst open, it caught me by surprise. He moved so quickly toward me that he ripped out the phone cord before I could even react.

Thirty-eight

"Who's the idiot now?" Mark taunted. His hiding place was one I often overlooked. I used it to store my winter coats and items I rarely needed. He was even thinner and more gaunt than I remembered. "Corrie? Get in here! Before I shoot your darling sister."

He was holding a handgun in his right hand and had used the left to rip the cord out of the wall, rendering my phone useless.

The phone in the bedroom. Please, Corrie, be in the bedroom and call 911.

Corrie didn't respond, and I didn't hear any noise from the bedroom or bathroom. The shiny silver of Russell's gun called to me from its place under the couch cushion, just a foot from where I stood. I moved sideways one step and froze as Mark's eyes hardened and his grip on his weapon tightened.

"Don't. Don't move one step. You're trash, Allison, it wouldn't bother me at all to shoot you. Not at all. Corrie! Get in here!"

I didn't dare move my eyes away from him, but I heard a shuffle signifying Corrie had joined us. "You two are coming with me. Don't try anything, Allison. Don't even think about it, because you won't get away with it. Call me an idiot, you stupid bitch! Know how I got in here? Met the missionaries on the street, down by the homeless shelter. Told them I knew someone who would love to hear about the Gospel. I knew Corrie wouldn't remember to lock the door. I knew she was here. I'm not pathetic!"

Sweat beaded on his forehead, and his T-shirt was stained under the arms. He looked tired and dirty, with dark circles around his frantic eyes, which darted from place to place in little jerks. His hair was lank and stood up on end in some places, and he smelled like a junior high school boys' locker room.

He grabbed me by the arm and spun me around, sticking the gun in my back, prodding me toward the door.

"Move, Corrie, get in front of us."

She finally walked into my line of vision, a tiny forlorn figure in her big white bathrobe, and my heart sank when I saw she wasn't dressed. She hadn't made it to the bedroom. No one knew Mark was here, with a gun. We were his victims once again.

Anger rose in me, filling my chest, and I could hold back no longer. I screamed my outrage, and with all my strength I used my elbow to hit Mark's arm. The gun skittered to the floor and settled four feet away from him, and the sudden fear in his eyes gave me hope. I raced back to the couch and grabbed Russell's gun, turning and aiming at him. He ran out the door, his weapon left lying on the floor.

I hid Russell's gun back under the couch cushion. I left Mark's weapon where it was. I knew Frank, Jake, or any officer wouldn't approve of me being armed. I also knew that even though Russell gave it to me, he didn't approve, either.

"He's falling apart," I told Frank, who showed up shortly after the uniformed officers. "He looked like he'd been sleeping in the dirt. He's desperate. He must really be mentally ill. Why else would he be so stupid?"

"Despite what you see in movies, most criminals are not the smartest fellows on the block. I'm sure you're right he's falling apart, but it worries me he keeps returning, that he's so close. He's obsessed. You aren't safe here, Alli. I think you and Corrie should come stay at my house."

"Frank, I cannot let this man chase me out of my home. I can't."

"You're being stubborn and stupid. You need to face up to the fact you can't rationally talk yourself out of a dangerous situation with this man."

"Frank, if I leave here, what happens? At least, if I'm here, there's a possibility he'll come back again. You can step up patrol, watch it closer, set a trap, and catch him."

"Then I'm staying here. And when I'm not here, an officer will be."

"And if he's watching the place, he'll know," I pointed out.

Frank sighed, exasperation tinged with a hint of irritation. "Allison, I've let this go too far. He never should have gotten inside your apartment. Never. I'm responsible, and I'm not going to make that mistake again."

"Fine, pack your bags. You can sleep on the floor. I'm already on the couch."

I didn't intend to leave my apartment. I wanted Mark caught.

"Allison?" Corrie's voice sounded tiny, interrupting my spirited and loud discussion with Frank. "I think I need to leave. I'm going to San Francisco. Christy has a spare bedroom. I need to get away from all of this."

"Corrie, I can't let you go anywhere. What if he follows you? What if he—"

Frank's hand moved to my shoulder, and he squeezed gently.

"Let her talk," he urged me.

"Allison, it's not me he wants. It's you. We both know that. I think you should come, too, but I know you won't. And he might look for you there, so neither of us would be safe. I think I should go, but I think you have to stay. Let Detective Kinderson stay here, please?"

"You can't take care of everyone, Alli," Frank added. "You need to worry about yourself. You're in danger here."

I didn't want Corrie to leave, and I struggled to put words to my feelings. *Frightened* and *disconnected* came to mind, along with the word *LOST,* all in capital letters. The last few days I'd survived by putting all my energy into taking care of her. If she was gone, I'd have time to dwell on the trauma I'd endured.

I was still running from my past, my heritage, my birthright. If I ever wanted to feel safe again, I had to face it.

"Okay. Maybe you should go."

"Allison, you'll be okay. And so will I. You'll see." Corrie's assertion was firm, stronger than I'd ever seen her be.

If only I'd been as convinced as she was.

Thirty-nine

The funeral home obligingly moved up the baby's funeral service by a day, and only Corrie and I attended, with Frank standing respectfully behind us. I was surprised no other member of my family was there, but Corrie told me she didn't tell anyone else the time and date had changed.

"I don't trust Dad not to tell Mark's family. They might tell Mark," she said.

We both sobbed helplessly as the funeral home director gave a small eulogy over the tiny pink casket, there in the Farmington Cemetery surrounded by headstones and wilting flowers. Across the way another funeral was being held, and several hundred people crowded around. It must have been for a military veteran or police officer because at the end, the mournful sound of a bugle playing taps gave me shivers and made Corrie sob even harder. I held her as tightly as I could.

We went to her apartment after the service, and I helped her pack while Frank paced nervously. We drove her straight to Salt Lake City International Airport and loaded her on a plane to San Francisco. Frank pulled some strings with the airline and got her a ticket on a sold-out flight. I hugged her tightly as we stood in the terminal.

"It will work out, you'll see," I told her.

"Allison, things will never be the same. You know that and so do I. It isn't going to work out, not the way I planned."

"Corrie, different isn't always bad."

She just shook her head sadly. I watched her walk away through the gate. She didn't turn or wave, and soon she disappeared from my sight. Frank stood behind me, not interfering, trying to allow us time together. It didn't make a difference.

I stood staring long after they had closed the doors and the plane began to taxi away. Guilt flooded my heart. Growing up, I always stood up to our father. I caused his anger, and everyone suffered because of it. If I had been meek and mild, like Corrie, perhaps our childhood would have been easier. I knew Corrie had always believed that—she'd told me so. Now, Mark Peterson was wedged tightly between my younger sister and me, and even though she said she didn't blame me, I knew a part of her did. Inadvertently, I'd caused great disaster in my sister's life.

I was responsible for her heartbreak, and we would never get past that.

Frank took me to his house in the Avenues, and I waited while he packed his things. I wandered through his living room, smiling at the whimsy of his decor. His home was one of the older ones, a two-story house with charm, history, and high ceilings. Ivy wound its way around a trellis on the outside, giving the tan brick color and life. The inside was nicely decorated, with sturdy wood furniture, masculine pictures of wildlife scenes, and polished wood floors.

"Nice place. Pretty ritzy. They must pay cops better than they used to."

"Inherited it from my grandma. My mom grew up here. Since she and my dad are in St. George, I got this house."

I picked up the pictures of his daughter that graced the

fireplace mantel and all the tables and surveyed them closely. She'd been a beautiful black-haired baby, with Frank's startling blue eyes. Her toddler years showed her happy and smiling on her tricycle, with a proud and younger Frank in the background, smiling broadly. One showed her standing next to her mother in a kitchen, both of them covered head to toe with flour.

I surveyed the woman closely, poring over the small details the picture offered, clues to Frank's former life. She was thin and blond, with an engaging grin and a freckled nose. She looked energetic, happy, and quite pretty, even covered in flour.

I remembered how every Christmas we made cookies with my mother, a chore with five young children; Mom inevitably collapsed into bed at the end of the day, tired from all the baking, cooking, and cleaning.

Frank came into the living room carrying a small duffel bag. "She's a beauty, huh? Of course, I'm prejudiced," he said when he saw the picture I held.

I thought for a minute he meant his ex-wife, but he picked up a picture of his daughter at around age five and offered it to me.

"This was her fifth birthday. She was born on July fourth, so we always told her the fireworks were for her birthday. She loved that day."

The little girl was smiling in all the pictures, radiant and beaming.

Frank stood next to me as I watched his daughter grow up in the pictures on the mantel.

"She is beautiful," I said. "She looks happy."

"We've had our bad times. Missy didn't handle the divorce well. Went through periods where she blamed her mother. Then she'd switch to me. But it's evening out now. Sometimes."

"How often do you see her?"

"As often as I want. Used to be more, when she was little. Now she's a teenager, though, she's more worried about friends, boys, and clothes. Dad kind of takes a backseat."

I smiled and turned. "Ready?"

"Yes, let's go."

We traveled the short distance from his house to my apartment in companionable silence. My father's truck was parked in front of my building when we pulled up.

Frank stopped his car and looked at me.

"Stay here," I said, "Okay? Just for a minute."

"Allison, you haven't talked a lot about your family, but what you have said . . . are you sure you're okay with him alone?"

"Yes, I am."

He nodded; I exited the car, walking quickly to my father's truck and opening the door on the driver's side. He was watching the apartment and didn't see me coming. The shock on his face turned to annoyance.

"Allison, you startled me. What are you doing?"

"What am I doing? Try what are you doing? Why are you sitting in front of my apartment? And why were you here the other night? Why are you watching me? Looking for more evidence to hold against me?"

He was silent as he pondered my questions, and he seemed unsure of himself. "Look, I'm just watching out for you and Corrie, okay? Just making sure Mark doesn't come back."

"You're watching out for me and Corrie? You're too late. I've already been raped by the man you clutched to your bosom as a surrogate son. Corrie has lost a baby, a marriage, and her own self-esteem. What could you possibly do sitting here?"

"Allison, I'm the head of your family. I'm responsible—"

"You aren't responsible for me anymore. Erase that off your to-do list, okay? It's too late."

"Too late?"

"Yes, too late for 'I'm sorry,' and too late for 'I was just trying to do the right thing.'"

"What would I have to be sorry for?" he asked.

"Never mind. Just leave."

"Allison, where's Corrie?"

"Gone. She left town. It wasn't safe here."

"Gone where?"

"Gone. If she wants you to know, she'll tell you."

"You are my daughter, as is Corrie, and you are my responsibility."

"Yeah? Guess what? Christy's your daughter, too, but that didn't stop you from beating her, or from telling her to never set foot near you again, just because she's a lesbian."

He put on a pained expression and stared straight ahead, the heat of the day causing a tiny drop of sweat to balance on the tip of his large nose.

"God offers freedom of choice for all, Allison. I could only teach you girls the truth and point you in the right direction. The decisions you made from there, and the consequences, were yours."

"Talking to you is like talking to a tape recorder, one that can't be used again, or the message changed. I try to reason, and you spout out the same old rhetoric, unable to say anything new or different. Just repeating the messages told to you by the leaders of the church."

I turned to walk away, and he jumped out of the truck, grabbing me by the arm roughly and pulling me around to face him.

"For once in your life can you please show me the respect I deserve?"

Frank was at my side before I knew he'd even moved.

"Take your hands off her, please." His voice was stern and carried a warning, although his words were polite.

My father glanced over at him with a superior look crossing his face. "Who are you? Another of her many boyfriends? Another dog sniffing around my promiscuous daughter? You look old enough to know better!"

Frank took a step forward, and I held up my free arm and stopped him.

"You aren't worth it," I said to my father, contempt in my voice. "You've never been worth it. I would have saved myself a lot of pain and agony if I'd realized that years ago."

My words were arrows dipped in poison, meant to harm; they bounced off him like Tinkertoys, falling to the ground in a discarded heap.

"Allison," he said, tightening his grip on my arm until I wanted to scream. "I need to at least know where Corrie is!"

"I told you to take your hands off her!" Frank said, all attempts at politeness abandoned. "I'm a detective with the Salt Lake City Police Department. Unless you want to find yourself in jail for domestic violence, I suggest you listen."

At the mention of the police, my father let go, and I staggered backward, rubbing my arm where a bruise already showed signs of appearing.

"Does your department know what you're doing?" my father asked.

"Do you know what I'm doing, Mr. Jensen? I don't think you do. Your daughter is being stalked by your son-in-law. He's threatened to kill her and your other daughter Corrie, broken into Allison's apartment with a gun, and escaped."

My father aged ten years in a matter of seconds. The stomach and chest he'd puffed out with male pride caved in, and his shoulders drooped and rounded. His face slackened and his eyes registered confusion.

"I guess you didn't. Please leave, and don't come back, unless you're invited by Allison." Frank turned to leave, his hand cupping my elbow gently.

"I'm not sure . . ." my father said. "Are you sure she's telling the truth? Mark's a good boy—I mean, he's had some troubles, but he's never done anything—"

"You are such an idiot!" I screamed, clenching my teeth, trying not to attack him, to beat him, hurt him, make him listen.

"Allison, don't," Frank said, pulling me back. "Don't let him do this."

I took deep breaths, trying to calm down, and waited for the tide of red anger to leave. My father stared at me like the stranger I'd always been to him.

"He put his dick in a seven-year-old girl's mouth. He had sex with a twelve-year-old girl on his mission and left her pregnant. He raped me. He beat Corrie. He threatened to kill both of us, and you can stand there and try to defend him?"

My father's mouth dropped open, and he looked stupid, lost, and very old. Frank urged me to stop, but I wasn't done yet.

"You can take your church, and your temple, and all your blessings and endowments and shove them up your ass. I never want to see you again."

Forty

The confrontation with my father left me bruised physically and mentally. I didn't look back as I walked up the stairs to my apartment, and Frank didn't say much as he stuffed his small duffel bag into my closet.

I plopped down on the couch and covered my face with my hands, stunned by the confrontation and my reaction.

"Are you okay?"

"You probably think I'm horrible, talking to him that way."

"No, I didn't know it was that bad. You tried to tell me, but I never even imagined a father could act like that."

I moved my hands and turned to him, sitting next to me on the couch. "After my mother died, and he remarried, I set out on a mission to hurt him. I drank. I did drugs. I had sex with lots of different men. Anything to make me feel good. And it was all to hurt him. Just now, I had this vision, I guess. This understanding. I never hurt him at all. I couldn't. The only person I hurt was me."

Frank pulled me into his arms, and I relaxed in the comfort and safety he offered. We didn't speak; he didn't try to say the right words, as if understanding there were none.

"Wow, self therapy," I mused, my voice muffled by his embrace. Sandra would be so proud.

I looked up at him, and he smiled, leaning down and tipping my chin upward, moving his head to feather a soft kiss on my lips. It felt nice, but I tensed up, waiting for the fear to return.

He kissed me again, without insistence; and I returned the kiss, stopping him after a minute.

"Frank . . ."

"Don't talk. There's no pressure here, Alli. I know what you've been through. You're recovering from a rape. I'm not going to expect anything from you. Just know I'm there."

"Isn't it dangerous to get involved with the people you're trying to protect?"

"Physically or mentally?"

"Both."

"Yeah, it is, but from the moment I saw you, I knew you were something different. Something special."

"I'm not special."

"Yeah, you are. You just haven't realized it yet."

"Frank, tell me you haven't done this before."

"Done what? Kissed someone? Afraid I have."

"No!" I pushed him away. "I mean become involved with someone like me, someone who . . ."

"You're wondering if I have a thing for victims?"

"Yes, I guess I am."

"No. Never before have I considered dating a rape victim. Dated a few women I picked up for speeding when I was younger and on patrol, but, hey, there have to be a few perks to the job!"

"I'm not ready."

"You're right. You're not. But when you are, I'll be here."

• • •

Frank insisted on making me lunch, and he rummaged through my kitchen trying to find something to cook.

"Unless you have a magic wand, good luck. I haven't been to the store in weeks."

He emerged from my cupboards with a can of string beans in one hand and a package of instant noodles in the other. He surveyed both, looking from hand to hand, and set them on the counter.

"Where's your phone book? We'll order pizza."

"Aren't you supposed to be working?"

"You're my assignment today. I have to go in tomorrow, though, and do paperwork. So I'll have to assign someone—"

"God, Frank, please. I can't stand much more of this."

"Allison . . ."

"Okay, okay. How did this ever happen to me?"

"You're beautiful, and sexy, and Mark's a pervert."

"Oh, get real."

"You don't think that's true?"

"I believe Mark is a pervert."

Frank walked over to the couch, pulled me out of my seat, and walked me into the bathroom. He stood behind me and squared my shoulders so I faced forward, looking directly in the mirror.

"Tell me what you see."

"I see a skinny blond girl with no chest, freckles beyond belief, tired, washed-out blue eyes, and a silly yet handsome man standing behind her."

"Must be looking in a different mirror."

"Why? What do you see?"

"I see a beautiful, smart young woman with kissable lips, cornflower blue eyes, long sun-kissed blond hair, and a very sexy body. And when she smiles, I go weak in the knees."

"You need your eyes checked."

"No, she's there. You just aren't looking hard enough. See, these are the lips I'm talking about." He ran his index finger gently across the span of my upper lip, then brought it back around and circled the lower one. My stomach did a funny little jump.

"And these are eyes that can see into a person's soul."

"Frank, you've gone off the deep end."

He ignored me, caressing my hair with both hands, and I watched my reflection as the flush I had felt kindling in my chest showed in my neck and spread to my face.

My V-neck tee was tight, and he moved downward from my hair, caressing lightly over my arms and just grazing my small breasts before moving down to my hips. I had no doubt who was holding me and touching me. I could see him in the mirror, could watch as he stood behind me and his eyes met mine in our reflection.

"Maybe I'll be all right."

"You'll be all right."

"You want to make love to me?"

"No. Not now. It's not time. I just want you to see what I see."

"Frank?"

"Mmm-hmm?" He was busy raining the back of my neck with gentle kisses, my long hair held aside with his left hand.

"You're a nice guy."

"Yeah?"

"I don't do nice guys."

"You're gonna do this one."

I thought he was probably right.

Forty-one

"Did I ever tell you about Cindy?"

We were on the couch, watching the news, waiting for Mark's picture to flash on the screen as it had many times in the past few days. Every time I saw the celluloid image, a cold chill rippled down my spine, and a hot burn started in my stomach and moved up to my chest. Holding Frank's hand as a vision of the weak-chinned, spineless predator flashed across my television helped me to maintain a balance I felt would be impossible otherwise. I still wanted to kill him; I just didn't intend to do it right then.

"No. Is this another sister? How many of you *are* there?"

"I have three sisters. But Cindy, she was my childhood friend. She disappeared and they never found her. A man held us at gunpoint, and we ran, but I tripped over a root and fell, and when I woke up she was gone. He didn't want me. Just her."

"He held you at gunpoint?"

"And told us to strip. I was six."

"Holy shit, Allison. You've been through so much. I bet your parents just avoided that, too, right? Refused to ever deal with it, just acted like it never happened?"

I nodded slowly, digesting his compassion and understanding for what I'd dealt with alone for so many years. No one in my family ever seemed to "get" me, and my past male companions had been more interested in what they could get. In the short time I'd known him, this older man had cut through the many layers I'd hidden under for years and found the vulnerable, lonely Allison without stamping DAMAGED GOODS on my forehead and running in fear.

"I see that so often with rape victims, especially young ones," he said. "It seems to be epidemic in this society. Mormons don't like confrontation. Avoidance is better."

"That's not always true. My father is very confrontational."

"Yeah, but that's only when he thinks you're straying from the church, right? That's avoidance. He doesn't want to think there's any other possibility, or that you might be right about anything."

"There's only one truth to the man who used to be my father. It's always been that way. I used to think it was the church, but it's more complicated than that. The only truth to my father is what *he* believes. Nothing else registers."

Frank clicked the remote control and turned the television off.

"Hey, I thought we were looking to see if they reported anything about Mark."

"Allison, I'm the detective in the case. I already know the details."

"Oooh, cocky."

"I like it when you talk dirty."

He pulled me down beside him and covered my body with his, letting me know about his desire by the pressure of his body.

The phone rang, dispelling the sexual tension. Frank had bought a new cord, and it was functional again.

"Hello?" I said, a little breathless.

"Alli, it's me, Christy. Just wanted to let you know Corrie arrived safely."

"Thanks. Is she doing okay?"

"As well as can be expected. We've set her up in her own room and she's resting. She cries a lot. For the baby, I think."

"For everything, Christy. She's crying for it all. She blames me a little, you know? She doesn't want to, but she does."

"No, I don't think she does."

"Well, anyway, take good care of her. She needs it."

"I'm concerned about you. Corrie said you aren't working. Why don't you fly down, too? We'll make room. As long as Mark is on the loose, you're not safe. Here, Mo wants to talk to you."

My sister's partner got on the line, her deep voice resonating through the phone. "Alli, we want you to come. This guy's a prick. He's going to try to hurt you."

"Mo, you guys are sweet, but I need to stay here. I guess Mark's obsessed with me, though I don't know why, and he might come back. But if I come there, well, he might follow me. I want him in prison."

"But you're not safe."

"Actually, I now have around-the-clock police protection. After he broke in, they decided it was serious."

"Okay, well, you call us every night."

"Mo, that will cost a fortune."

"I don't care. You do it. Call collect."

Frank watched me closely as I hung up. "Lesbians," I said with a giggle. "They're so motherly and loving."

"You were talking to a lesbian?"

"My sister Christy and her partner, Mo, the ones Corrie went to stay with."

"I know. I'm just teasing you."

"I have an aunt who's a lesbian, too. Her partner Sandra is my therapist. They're the only members of my family I even talk to anymore."

"Well, I ought to fit right in with them. I love women."

"You're such a man."

"You keep reminding me."

"Huh?"

He pushed up close toward me, and I could feel his erection straining at the denim shorts he was wearing. I reached down and rubbed him gently, and he groaned.

"Don't. I'm trying to be good, and you touching me like that is not going to help my intentions."

"It's not bothering me. I'll let you know if I need to stop."

"No, you're not ready. I know you're not. I've dealt with enough of these cases." He sat up and pushed me away, then pulled me back to kiss me again. "Let's order pizza."

In the past, my memories had always existed in small clusters of vivid images, a series of screen shots that played at random moments with no order or reason. After I was raped it was as if my life slowed down, and I remembered almost every conversation, every scent, every image of each day that passed as if they were still photographs I could savor for hours.

In these moments with Frank Kinderson, seventeen years my senior, I wanted to hit the pause button and make time stand still. He dialed the pizza delivery phone number with strong, sturdy fingers. I turned the sound off in my head and watched his mouth move, his head tilt, saw his Adam's apple jiggle as he laughed.

It was a picture I would never forget.

Forty-two

I heard a noise and sat upright, wide awake and alert, my heart beating rapidly. Someone was in my apartment.

Frank. It's Frank.

The roar in my ears faded as I remembered making up the sofa bed for him, bending over for a gentle kiss, walking to my room with reluctance. Part of me wanted to climb under the covers with him, allowing him full access to my body; the other part worried I might scream when he touched me.

I had nodded off to sleep with the sound of his gentle snoring in the background, wondering why men found it so easy to immediately fall asleep. As a police officer, he'd seen many awful things, yet ghosts didn't seem to haunt him.

A rustling in the other room alerted me to his movement, and I heard the front door quietly shut.

"Frank? Where are you going? Frank?" I whispered. There was no answer.

I glanced at the clock on the bedside table. The digital numbers flashed 2:00. Where could he be going?

I left my bed and ran into the living room, seeing no sign of him save for the rumpled bedcovers and his shirt and shoes. His denim shorts were gone. His shoulder holster, draped across one of my chairs, was empty.

He left my apartment wearing nothing but his shorts?

Puzzled, I crossed to the window and watched as a dark figure moved quickly across the parking stalls under the carport, hiding in shadows, not wanting to be seen. Was it Frank?

Mark! Oh, my God, it had to be Mark. Frank went out there alone.

I ran for the gun I'd hidden in the cushion before remembering I'd moved it to the back of one of my bare cupboards, a place I knew Frank wouldn't look because he already knew I had no food. It took me only seconds to change direction and grab the gun, and I hurried out, running down the stairs dressed only in an oversized T-shirt.

Once outside I searched to see where he'd gone. I saw the dark figure moving purposefully away from the apartment building, caught a glimpse of a bare chest and shorts, saw his familiar profile, and knew it was Frank. I almost yelled his name.

No. Don't yell. Don't give him away.

I followed him, trailing behind as he made his way toward a blue car parked on the opposite side of the road, and watched as he hid in the shadows of one of the large weeping willows that lined my street. Careful to stay out of sight, I saw the outline of his face, staring purposefully forward, watching the car.

Mark. It must be Mark.

A light came on in the car, and Frank made his move so suddenly I had no warning. No time to yell. No time to tell him to stop. He raced across the road to the car and yelled *"Get out! Out of the car, hands up!"*

I heard another car approaching but couldn't take my eyes off Frank.

The roar of a shotgun blast took my breath away. In

slow motion I watched Frank crumple to the ground, watched as first one police car then another pulled up to the blue vehicle. I heard shouts as the officers surrounded the car, and I dropped the gun on the sidewalk and ran.

Frank lay on his back in the middle of the street. Blood. So much blood, seeping out from a place just below his heart. His eyes were open, staring, unseeing.

More police cars pulled in, their sirens filling the night. I covered the spot where he was bleeding with both my hands, put pressure on it, tried to remember the ins and outs of CPR. An officer tried to pull me away; Jake appeared, in uniform, bending down and listening, putting his ear next to Frank's mouth. The other officer tugged on me insistently.

"No! Leave me alone. Frank. God, no, Frank, can you hear me?"

All around me the once-still night bustled with activity. Out of the corner of my eye I glimpsed two officers pull the shooter from the car and throw him roughly to the ground, rolling him over and slapping handcuffs on him, tightening them with no mercy. I heard the roar of sirens breaking through the noise of crickets; I heard the words, "Officer down. Officer down." The radios squawked with activity, and I watched Jake perform CPR on Frank while I kept pressure on the wound, praying frantically in my head, asking for help from any unseen source.

Frank never said another word. Never acknowledged I was there. Never even blinked.

I knew he was gone, and I screamed, hysterical sobs escaping from my throat. My hands were covered with blood, too much blood. I couldn't stop it. He wouldn't stop bleeding.

"Please, Frank. Please, hold on. Please."

The paramedics rushed up, and Jake pulled me away, both of us covered in Frank's blood. He held me against him as they frantically worked on the body. It was a body. No more Frank.

"He's dead," I whispered to Jake.

He looked at me, tears running down his face, and nodded.

"Was it Mark?" I asked in a harsh whisper, the words barely escaping through my tight throat. I glanced over at the car and saw the two officers roughly shoving the shooter into the back of a vehicle.

Jake shook his head.

The blue car was an Oldsmobile, ancient and battered, covered with dents, dings, and rust, and so familiar. I remembered this car. I'd been in it many times.

This car belonged to my stepmother.

The light flashed on in the back of the police car, and I saw not the gaunt figure of Mark Peterson but the bulky body and age-lined face of my father.

Forty-three

"You son of a bitch! You stupid asshole! You shot him! You killed him!" I screamed profanities through the window of the car. Jake held my arms, tried to pull me away. My father's head turned, and he stared at me, a blank look on his face. I fought against Jake's grip as he pulled me ruthlessly back.

"Allison, stop it!"

Another officer walked toward us, intending to help Jake restrain me. I heard a shout from across the street. "Hey, what the—there's a gun over here."

Russell's gun lay where I had dropped it. The realization hit me like a fist in the stomach—I could have stopped it. I'd had a gun in my hands, and I had thought it was Mark. I should have shot at the shadowy shape in the car. I could have stopped Frank's murder.

I collapsed onto Jake's chest, and the sudden release of tension caused us to stumble backward and fall. Several officers came running up and offered a hand to Jake, but he shook them off and stood, picking me up like a small child and carrying me to the second ambulance that arrived on the scene.

The first one wailed off into the night, piercing the darkness with flashes of red and white, and that ungodly pitch a siren makes.

My elbows were skinned and bleeding, my blood mixing with Frank's. It was as close as I ever got to him again, and I willed my heart to stop.

I wanted out of this nightmare. I didn't want to be Allison Marie Jensen anymore. I wanted no part of the man who used to be my father.

"She's in shock."

"Morris, pass that blanket."

". . . about the other gun?"

"Who's notifying the family?"

"Allison, can you move over here, please?"

"Jensen, did you ask her about . . ."

"Somebody bag that . . ."

". . . her father? Why was he . . . ?"

"Allison, please lie down, okay? We're taking you to the hospital."

"Morris, start the IV."

"Allison, I'm sorry. Do you know why your father was outside your house?"

"Not right now, okay? She's in shock. We need to transport . . ."

". . . notify the family. Yeah, he has a daughter . . ."

"We're putting this belt on you for the trip to the hospital. Don't be afraid."

"Okay, Morris, we're ready here."

"Can I ride along?"

"Yeah, Jensen."

"Chief? Yeah, they just called. He didn't make it . . ."

"Allison, it's going to be okay."

"No. It's not. It will never be okay again."

Forty-four

"Did they give her something for the shock?"

"I think so."

I opened my eyes to find myself looking at the compassionate brown eyes of Sandra Castle. Behind her stood my Aunt Carol and sister Cathy.

"Hey, you're awake. How do you feel?"

"Dead."

"Well, you're not dead," Cathy said. "Thanks to Heavenly Father, you're alive. Allison, why did you have a gun? The police have been asking about it. They traced the registration to Russell Free. You didn't steal it, did you?"

I turned my head away from the question, closing my eyes. Thanks to Heavenly Father? What did I have to say thanks about? The only decent man I'd ever known had been shot down by my father, the man who had a knack for destroying lives with little effort.

"Cathy, maybe you should go check on your stepmother. You said she was hysterical . . ."

"Why? What did I say?"

"Where is he?" I asked.

"Dad?"

"No, I have no dad. Where is Frank? Where's his body?"

"Aren't you even worried about Dad, Allison? He was just trying to protect you. He thought Mark might be trying to get you, and . . ."

"Did you know about this?"

Cathy stepped back and was silent for a moment. "Yes, I knew he was watching your apartment, but he was just trying to keep you safe."

"It's a lie."

"What?"

"He wasn't trying to keep me safe. He didn't even believe Mark really did it. Not the golden boy returned missionary."

"Allison, it's not the church's fault. It's not the religion that's bad, just some people."

"Really? Tell that to the little pregnant girl back in Arkansas that Mark left behind. Tell that to the seven-year-old girl who is now a woman who won't let anyone touch her."

"This isn't a good time for this," Sandra interjected and gave Aunt Carol a look. My aunt escorted Cathy from the room, protesting the entire time, and Sandra shut the big hospital door and pulled a chair up to the bed.

"Well, we meet again in the hospital."

"He shot Frank. He sat outside my apartment waiting for the opportunity to destroy my life, and he shot Frank."

"Alli, I'm going to tell you what your father told the police. I don't want you to think I'm taking a side here, but you need to know. He told the police he was watching your house to protect you from Mark. He said he nodded off in the car and woke up to shouting and he fired reflexively. He said he didn't know it was Frank."

"It doesn't matter what excuses he's made. He killed Frank. He destroyed my life. Now I'll never know . . ." The tears rolled down my cheeks as I mourned for lost opportunities. I had never made love to Frank Kinderson. I would never hear his laugh again. It was all gone in an instant. Taken away from me by the callous father who'd let my mother die and beaten us all relentlessly.

"There's no good in him. None. I hope they execute him."

"Allison, you have a right to all these feelings."

"I hate him."

"I'm sure right now you do."

Sandra let me cry out my miseries, putting her arms around me tightly and holding me. I wanted to sleep, without dreams, for awake I saw the horror movie play over and over again, watched Frank crumple to the ground.

He'd been a good man. Perhaps that was why it happened. I didn't deserve any good in my life.

Sandra and Aunt Carol took me to their cottage when I was released from the hospital. I wanted to go home.

"No, it wouldn't be good. I'll go pick up your things. Just tell me what you need," Aunt Carol insisted.

I looked to Sandra for reinforcement, but she appeared to be in agreement with my headstrong aunt, and so I acquiesced to their wishes, too drained to fight.

They settled me in their spare room, and I took one of the Valium pills they gave me at the hospital, willing myself to nod off and sleep without dreaming. The world blurred as the medicine took effect, and I felt lightheaded and distant. I drifted off to the now-familiar woods, where I always searched for, and sometimes found, Cindy.

"Allison?"

I was jerked back to the bedroom of my aunt's cottage.

"Frank?"

"I'm here."

"You're not dead."

He laughed his familiar throaty chuckle, warming me. "Of course I'm not dead."

I tried to sit up but was unable to move, held by invisible bonds. My tongue thickened and I lost my ability to talk. I wanted to reach out and touch him, to hold him, and I couldn't move, the Valium holding me prisoner.

"I don't want you to worry, okay? I'll be fine. I'll take care of Kevin and Cindy for you. They're safe with me."

I wanted to scream but couldn't.

"I have to go now. You're special, please remember that. I knew from the moment I saw you that you were special. Oh, and, Allison? Your mother said to tell you she's sorry she left you alone. She never would have left if she'd had a choice. She loves you—she loves you for what you are."

Frank dissolved, and my invisible bonds loosened. I sat up in the bed and looked around wildly, searching for some sign I hadn't just dreamed his presence next to me, but there was none. I'd spent my whole life running from my father's staunch belief in the Mormon teachings of life after death, along with the other tenets, and I found it hard to believe the apparition of Frank had been anything but a Valium-induced dream. Yet it was one that felt so real I could still smell him: strong, masculine, a mixture of deodorant and testosterone.

Could he really have been there? My mother was sorry, and loved me for what I was? For the first time in a long while I felt loved, warm inside, almost calm. Those emotions fought with the terrible sadness I felt deep in the pit of my stomach. It was too much to handle, at least for me right now.

If Frank really was in some kind of Heaven, perhaps he would now become my guardian angel. I had a feeling I would need one in the weeks to follow.

Forty-five

My father was being held in the Salt Lake County jail, according to Cathy, who persisted in calling every half-hour or so to provide an update.

"Allison, please, he wants to see you. He needs to explain."

"No."

"Allison, he didn't mean to shoot Frank. He's beside himself. I'm worried he's going to have a heart attack."

I sighed deeply. "I can't. I can't forgive him, and I can't go see him."

Sandra and Aunt Carol exchanged knowing glances I saw from the corner of my eye, and irritation sharpened in me like a needle, puncturing the balloon of protection the pills offered me. I hung up the phone and walked into the bedroom, picking up the prescription bottle and walking to the bathroom. I heard the padding of feet behind me and knew I was being watched, but I didn't turn back. I dumped the entire contents of the bottle into the toilet and flushed, watching the pills swirl and bob before disappearing.

"Allison, why did you do that?" Aunt Carol placed a strong hand on my shoulder.

"I need to feel this. I need to grieve, to mourn. I've been covering up my feelings one way or another all my life. It's time to stop."

"Come sit down with us. I'll make tea."

I followed her back into the living room and sat on the comfortable sofa, tucking my bare feet up under me. I was still in a nightshirt, and it was already three P.M., just one day after Frank died. One day.

"Can I talk about him?"

"Of course," Sandra said as Aunt Carol scurried into the kitchen to set the teakettle to boil.

"I think I might have been falling in love with him. He was so different from any man I've ever met. He took care of me. He made me feel safe. He was a nice guy. I didn't even have time to tell him that. He never knew."

"Did he feel the same?"

"He told me I was special. Said he knew it from the first time he saw me, but he didn't push me. I was willing . . . I mean, I was willing to try to make love to him, but he wouldn't. He just said I wasn't ready and let it go. He didn't push at all."

"He was right. You weren't ready."

"Yeah? Well, now I'll never know what it feels like to make love with someone good, with someone who really cares. I'll never know. If there is a God, I must have done something horrible, because He sure does hate me."

"Allison, life has handed you a lot of ugliness. I believe, though, that you can handle it. I believe it's because you're strong."

"I don't feel strong. I feel like a baby kitten, abandoned and alone."

"I know you do. This will take time to heal from, but you will heal. I hope you can trust me."

"Does Corrie know?"

Sandra nodded. "Carol called her. She wanted to come

back, but Carol convinced her to stay, since Mark hasn't been found. There's nothing she can do here now, anyway."

"What's going to happen to him?"

"Mark?"

"No, my . . . Frank's killer."

"I'm not sure. Your stepmother has hired an attorney. They're petitioning for bail right now. The police want to interview you, but Jake's kept them away. We can't do it for much longer, though."

"I'll talk to them."

"Allison . . ."

"I'm sick of lies, Sandra. My whole life's been a lie. The church is a lie. The bishops lied to protect Mark. And I lied to myself. I told myself this would all work out. I'm tired of lies. Time to face up to the truth."

Sandra studied me closely, sorrow in her eyes. "I know this hurts, Alli. It hurts bad right now. But it will get easier. You'll heal. Every day you'll be one step closer to feeling better."

I nodded my head in agreement, mostly to make her feel like she was helping me. I didn't believe I would ever feel better.

The doorbell rang two hours later, and Sandra opened the door to Jake Jensen and two detectives from the Salt Lake City Police Department. I'd dressed in some jeans and a T-shirt Aunt Carol brought from my apartment.

Jake came in and the two detectives followed. He introduced them as Detective Carter and Detective Frederickson.

"Allison, they need to ask you some questions. I know this is hard, but we need some answers."

"I know." I was a little surprised to see the deference with which they treated Jake, since he was a uniformed officer and they were higher ranking.

"Thanks, Jensen," Detective Carter said.

"Please, sit down," Sandra instructed the men. "Can I offer you something to drink?"

"No, thank you," both men said, and she walked into the kitchen, catching my eye to let me know she was close.

Jake sat next to me on the couch, and Detective Carter took the chair Sandra had just left. Detective Frederickson moved across the room to another chair.

"Allison, we know this is a rough time for you, but we have to ask you some questions about Frank's death."

"I understand."

"Okay, good. First of all, we need to know why he left your apartment in the middle of the night like that. Do you know?"

"No, I was asleep. I woke up when the door shut. I suspect he saw the car and wanted to get closer and make sure it wasn't Mark Peterson."

"And when you heard the door shut, you followed him?"

"Yes, but I saw he took his gun, and so I grabbed the gun that . . ."

"Trooper Free's gun?"

"Yes, the gun he loaned me. He told me not to take it out of the house, but I was scared and worried about Frank. I didn't think it through, I just grabbed it."

Detective Carter nodded and took notes as I talked. Detective Fredrickson just watched me.

"And you dropped the gun when the shot was fired."

"When I ran to him. When I saw Frank lying there . . ." I still couldn't talk about it without crying.

"Why do you think Frank charged the car instead of waiting for backup?"

"How could she know that?" Aunt Carol yelled from the kitchen, making all three men jump. "She's not a police officer." I heard Sandra hushing her.

Detective Carter shot an irritated look at the kitchen and then looked back at me.

"Did he call for backup?" I asked, knowing he would have.

"Yes, he called dispatch and gave them a brief message requesting assistance. But we're a little surprised he charged the car and didn't wait. I'm just asking for your impression, Allison, since you were there. Frank's always been top-notch, never making mistakes like that."

"He saw him."

"What?"

"The light went on in the car, and Frank saw who it was. I couldn't tell from where I stood, but he was just across the street. He'd caught my father watching me before, so he knew him. They had a . . . a confrontation about it just that day, when my father grabbed me and bruised my arm." I held out my arm and pointed out the vivid green-and-blue bruise—five small bruises, actually, each shaped like a fingertip.

"Are you sure a light went on in the car? Your father claims he nodded off and was startled into reacting when he heard the shouts."

"The light came on."

Forty-six

Jake showed up on Sandra and Aunt Carol's doorstep the next day, a grim look making his boyish face years older. My eyes were red, swollen, and sore from crying my way through what seemed an eternal night.

"You look horrible."

"Thanks. What's wrong now?"

"Can I come in?"

I stood back and motioned him inside. Sandra had clients scheduled and was at her office, and Aunt Carol was working in her vegetable garden, getting ready to plant.

"Allison, the D.A. is going to charge your father with first-degree murder. Based on what you told the detectives, and the fact he'd threatened you and Frank before, they think they'll get a conviction."

"Good."

He silently surveyed me for a long moment before he spoke again. "Do you really think he meant to kill Frank?"

"He's always wanted to control every aspect of our lives. If we didn't do things his way, or follow his lead, he banished us."

"Yeah, but to shoot a police officer . . ."

I sighed heavily.

"I can't change the truth, Jake. Do you want me to lie to protect the man who's destroyed every aspect of my life? I finally met someone . . . I mean . . ."

Just then I recalled my father's ability to nod off anytime. I remembered his failing eyesight and the bifocals he was forced to wear to see.

"But he wasn't asleep, Jake. The light went on just before Frank charged toward the car."

"He's probably scared and lied."

Aunt Carol came into the house through the side door, her gardening gloves heavy with moist dirt. She stopped and said, "I didn't know anyone was here."

Large clumps of soil fell from her gloves to the wood floor, and she noticed it and grimaced. "Sandra's gonna kill me. She calls me Messy Marvin as it is. I need to get these outside. You okay?"

I nodded my head. "They're going to charge my father with first-degree murder."

"What?"

"Because of what I told them."

"Oh, Lord. This is horrible. I mean, I can't stand the man, you know that, and I'm hardly his biggest fan, but first-degree murder?" She walked into the living room and sat in the chair next to the sofa, oblivious to the dirt falling to the pristine wood floor. She stared at me with solemn eyes, and I turned to Jake, who watched me with a similar expression.

"What do you want me to do? Lie for him? Say I made it up? Say the light didn't go on? And you!" I pointed to Jake. "He killed your fellow police officer. Don't you want him to pay for that?"

"Allison, I'm thinking of you. I don't care what happens to your father. Can you live with yourself if he's found guilty?"

"Will they execute him?"

"No. It's not premeditated. He couldn't have known Frank would confront him."

"Then I can live with it."

"Allison, how are you coping with all of this?"

Sandra and I sat in her office the next day, where she preferred to talk to me even though I was living in her house.

"I'm okay. No, I'm not okay. I'm dead inside. I cry all the time. I wake up sweating and shaking. And I dream about him constantly."

"Allison, I'm going to make a suggestion. I think I've become too close to this situation. I'm going to refer you to a colleague of mine. He's had experience in dealing with former Mormons, and he's also dealt with other cults . . ."

"Cults?"

"Well, okay, I'm sure you don't think of Mormonism as a cult, but there is a certain amount of mind control that comes from being raised Mormon."

"Sheep."

"I'm sorry?"

"They wanted us to be sheep. To do as they said, and not ask questions."

"Yes, that's one way to put it. His name's Brian Ferry, and he's a great—"

"I don't want to."

"Why not?"

"I don't want to talk to someone else about all this . . . this sick, twisted stuff. I just want it to go away."

"It won't."

"I'll make it."

"You can't. Allison, I've become too close to you. I love you like a daughter. It has become impossible for me to effectively counsel you without impressing my opinions on you. If I were to be totally honest, the truth is I should never have been counseling you or Corrie in the first place.

I only did it because Carol and I didn't think you'd see or talk to anyone else."

"You're right. I don't want to meet with someone new."

"Please."

I gave in at last, wondering if I could find some way out. Sandra called Brian Ferry while I fidgeted in the chair. She wrote down an address and time for me, then gathered me in for a big hug. She smelled clean and fresh, without a hint of perfume or artifice. I felt like I'd just cut my own life-line.

"Sandra, I can't talk to someone else about all of this. I just can't . . ."

She pulled back and looked at me closely. "Alli, you have to do this. You don't have a choice here. You have your whole life ahead of you. You're so young. You can't die with Frank, just like you couldn't die with your mother, or Cindy, or Kevin. You have to move on. You have to come to terms with it."

"It's too hard. I just want to pull the covers over my head and go to sleep. It's more than I can handle."

"You're strong, Alli. You can handle it."

"I'm tired of being strong. I want someone to hold me and tell me it's going to be all right. I want someone to take care of me and let me know I'm okay just the way I am. That I don't have to say silly words, or attend endless meetings, or give them my money."

"Parents are supposed to offer unconditional love, Allison," Sandra said, a grim expression on her face, "but that isn't always possible. For some people, there's no such thing. To them, all love has strings attached."

"Strings that tangle, and get twisted and warped, until they're wrapped tightly around your neck and you choke to death," I added.

She nodded.

Forty-seven

Brian Ferry was a large, bear-shaped man with a bald pate, large hazel eyes, and the most enormous ears I'd ever seen on a human being.

He caught me staring, and I blushed.

"I know, I know, call me Dumbo. I could fly with these things. Blame it on bad genetics. Generations of Mormons marrying relatives in polygamous situations meant the bad traits got replicated over and over. Thus, Gigantor ears."

"Polygamists marry their relatives?"

"Oh, the stories I could tell you. My mother came from the Jameson clan. I'm sure you've heard of them. They marry each other. Remember the girl that escaped from a polygamous marriage, and ran away? Her father beat her until she nearly died? Anyway, she escaped. Not many do. Her father is my cousin. There is never a lot of press on them, until something goes wrong, because they are so secretive. And Mormons are protective of them, because of the early belief in polygamy. Anyway, Sandra let me know a little of your history. I'm sorry for the pain you've suffered."

"Thanks."

"I know that doesn't help much. Would you like to tell me what you're feeling?"

"Not really. I'm tired of talking about it."

"Okay, well, let's talk about something else. You like basketball?"

"No. Listen, I'm wasting your time. I didn't want to come, but Sandra persuaded me . . ."

"Look, Allison, I know it's hard to open up when you've gone through so much trauma. I also know you have major issues with your Mormon background—"

"Sandra told you all that?"

"Yes, but more as a friend than your therapist. We're close. She's concerned about you."

"Yeah, me, too."

"Would you like to talk about it?" He sat back in his chair, and it creaked loudly.

"No."

"It will help to let your feelings out, Allison."

"I just can't. Not now."

"Are you sure?"

"Yes."

Brian Ferry sat for a moment, stroking his chin, and then spoke again. "I have an idea. I run a support group for former Mormons. We meet at the Unitarian Universalist Church up on Twelfth Avenue, and it happens the next meeting is tonight. Why don't you come? You don't have to talk, but I think it would be good for you."

"I don't know. My father would laugh at the idea that former Mormons need support. 'Get your ass back to church' would be his answer."

"There are a lot of issues here, Allison. Things you probably haven't even thought of before. Please tell me you'll come."

"Maybe."

"I guess I'll accept that answer."

. . .

The Unitarian Universalist church was a small building that used to be a grocery store. It resembled nothing churchly to me; it had none of the trappings my memory held forever in association with the Mormon Church. The chapel consisted of folding metal chairs set up neatly in rows with a small wooden podium in the front. There was no place for a choir, no endless rows of mahogany pews, no Mormon hymnals.

The chairs were filled with chatting people of all ages, sexes, and sizes. Some looked happy, while others appeared engaged in serious debate.

"No, no, there is absolutely no proof anything resembling that was found in the Americas during the time frame the *Book of Mormon* took place . . ."

". . . and he told her Christians didn't have the true religion, the Mormons did! Can you believe that? I called the school principal up and gave him a piece of my mind. But what do they expect? They teach their kids that in church, and think they're not going to repeat it out in public?"

"Remember when we were kids, Liddy? We thought we were special. If someone wasn't Mormon, we thought they were bad. You can't blame the kids . . ."

". . . three versions of the First Vision. Joseph Smith couldn't make up his mind. Kept rewriting it. Can't believe people don't see through that. First he said he saw God, then God the Father and his son Jesus Christ. Or wait, was it the angels he saw first?"

Brian Ferry moved to the front of the room from a side office. "Okay, everybody, quiet down. Let's get started."

I quickly sat in the back row, staying on the end in case I needed to escape. The chair next to me scooted back and Jake Jensen plopped down in it, dressed in shorts and a tank top. My eyes opened wide at the sight of him, and he shrugged his shoulders and leaned toward me, whispering,

"I've been coming here for two years. How'd you find out about it?"

I pointed to the front of the room at Brian. Jake just smiled and turned his attention forward.

As the room quieted, I dropped my head in automatic response for the prayer then jerked it up as I realized what I was doing. I looked around nervously, but no one seemed to notice.

"Welcome, everybody. Sounds like some lively discussions going on out there. Let's move these chairs around and make a circle."

The sound of scraping chairs on the wood floor filled the room for the next few minutes, and we formed a circle. There were approximately thirty people in the room, so it was a fairly large one. I scooted close to Jake, nervous, waiting to see what these people would say, and how they would act.

"Okay, first off, I want to welcome any new members here with us tonight. We're glad to have you. Also, Steve has asked me to announce that his most recent batch of home brew is ready for tasting, and he's having a barbecue at his house on Sunday. All he asks is that you bring the food."

A titter rippled through the circle as a dark-haired man with an infectious grin and a large beer belly shrugged his shoulders. "Hey, I can't do everything."

"All right, then. We left off last week with Annie, and I'm going to go back to her because I think she still has some things to discuss. Annie?"

"Well, I know I mentioned I stopped wearing my garments. My husband finally confronted me last week. And I told him I think it's all a crock. I thought he'd get all mad, but he broke down and cried. Said we weren't going to be a family anymore. That we wouldn't be together in the Celestial Kingdom. Then he threw in the kicker. 'Don't you want to be with me and the kids, Annie?'"

She choked up as she related the story, and the woman beside her grabbed her hand and squeezed.

"My divorce is final tomorrow," said another man from the circle. He looked sad, scared, and lonely. "I guess I can relate, Annie. My wife just couldn't handle the thought I was willing to screw up her eternal progression by leaving the church."

"You know, that fucking pisses me off!" said a fiery redhead sitting to the left of me. The freckles on her face glared like angry red missiles. "Why in the hell would what someone else does matter to *my* eternal progression? Just like women can't get into the Celestial Kingdom unless they're married to a good Mormon man. What a crock that is."

I'd never heard talk like this before, and I stared in amazement. These people were like me. They'd been raised with the same fervor, the same tyranny, the same rhetoric, and they didn't believe it, either.

The rest of the evening sped by as I heard person after person relate their experiences, some with anger, some with regret, most with sadness.

"Great meeting, folks. We'll see you all next week. Or, if you make it to Steve's . . ."

"Deviled eggs and potato salad. That's what I like, ladies."

Another mass giggle and the mingling began, more chair scraping and snippets of conversation filling my ears.

Jake grabbed me by the arm and guided me outside. "Let's walk."

"Where?"

"Park over here."

He pointed to a grassy knoll across the street, and we headed in that direction, crossing the tar-covered road into the park's boundaries. We found a bench and sat down. He pulled a pack of cigarettes out of his pocket, followed by a lighter, and offered one to me.

"I don't smoke."

"I shouldn't. Picked it up when I was watching Mark. Helped pass the time. Now I'm hooked." He lit the cigarette and tucked the lighter away. "So, what did you think?"

"Lots of angry people."

"Yeah, ex-Mormons are some of the angriest people I've ever met."

"I wonder why."

"Probably because they figured out the truth, figured out they'd been lied to all their lives. It just reaches a point where it boils over."

"Why did you end up here?"

"Long story."

"I'm in no hurry."

Jake sighed. "It was after Jenny got molested by that bastard. For weeks afterward she screamed whenever a man came near her. They tried to fix her with blessings, and meetings with the bishops, but my uncle refused to get her counseling. I found it all building up inside me. I'd already beat Mark up bad, and his family called the cops. Bishop got them to drop the charges."

"Bishops seem to do a lot of that."

"Yeah, well, he convinced them Mark could get charged with the abuse, so it was best not to report it. That made me even angrier."

"So you started coming here?"

"Not exactly."

"What?"

"I joined the force and started following Mark in my spare time. Just keeping tabs, making sure he didn't hurt someone else. Things got a little better for a while, when he went on his mission. Of course, now we know he was up to the same tricks out there.

"One day, we got a call. It was an abuse call. Teenage boy forced himself on a six-year-old. At church. Mother said the bishop told her to let them handle it, but she was too mad. She said he was just protecting the boy, because it was his son. We went to investigate the kid, the father tried to intervene, and it got a little rough."

"You hit him?"

"Scuffled with him. Went to hit him, partner held me back. I got temporary suspension and was ordered to counseling. Brian was my therapist, and he referred me here. It helps to hear other people in the same boat."

"Wow. I never knew there were so many people who felt the same way."

We were quiet for a minute, the smoke from Jake's cigarette wafting through the air. I could hear a bird singing in one of the trees, and a light breeze whispered through the balmy night.

"What about your family?" I asked him.

"What about them?"

"Did they accept your choices? Do they?"

"No."

"Do you still see them?"

"I go out on my mom's birthday and Mother's Day. Pay a brief visit on Christmas. It's strained. My mom cries a lot about it, so I figure it's just easier if she doesn't have to see me—for both of us. My dad died a few years back. Aunt Karen has me over on holidays."

"I can relate."

Jake blew out a smoke plume and sighed. "Funeral's tomorrow."

A sudden chill shot through my body.

"I know."

"You going?"

"I don't know. I hate funerals . . . Jake, what if his family blames me? It was my father. He wouldn't have been there if it wasn't for me. None of it would ever have happened. How can I go to the funeral and look them in the eyes and know I'm responsible?"

Jake threw his cigarette to the ground and squashed it out with his foot, then reached down and picked up the butt, popping it back into his package. I gave him a quizzical look and he smiled.

"I don't litter. I'll pick you up. You can go with me. I'll help you through it."

"Sandra and Aunt Carol are taking me. But I might need a lot of help."

"I know."

Forty-eight

The day we buried Frank was a scorcher, as my grandfather used to say.

Both of my grandparents had died three years before. Grandma passed away from breast cancer, and three months later Grandpa died of a broken heart. Without the "old woman" around to nag and bitch, he became incredibly lonely. The doctors said his heart just stopped beating.

Sandra and Carol were dressed and waiting in the kitchen drinking coffee, a third cup sitting at the table for me with a piece of toast and homemade strawberry jam sitting on the side. The coffee smelled delicious, but the thought of sweet jam made my already nervous stomach churn.

"I can't eat."

"Just a few bites," coaxed Aunt Carol, who was wearing a short-sleeved blouse and wraparound skirt, fitting for the day's promised temperatures. Sandra wore a handsome tailored summer suit, immaculately pressed. As usual, she wore no makeup, and her long brown hair was straight.

"Look at all of us, sitting here dressed up to celebrate someone's death." My morbid thoughts took hold, and I choked on the bite of toast I tried to swallow.

"We're paying respects, Allison. We're celebrating his

life, not his death. We'll be there for you," Sandra said quietly.

I nodded my appreciation and tears stung my eyes. Neither one had any obligation to go. They would be there to support me, because they were my family. Because they knew what Frank meant to me.

The funeral was held at the Rock Chapel on B Street, the Mormon church where Frank's grandmother and mother attended meetings. Although he had not been religious, it only made sense, as the chapel opened up into a cultural hall that could hold the enormous crowd expected. Cars were parked up and down the Avenues by the time we arrived, and we were forced to find a spot four blocks away. We were sweaty and hot by the time we walked through the doors of the church and into the chapel, which was already half-full, a sea of blue uniforms dotted with occasional blotches of other colors.

My stomach tightened with dread as the familiar surroundings closed in on me. As was customary at Mormon funerals, a viewing was held in the Relief Society room, where one by one mourners marched past the body and comforted the family. The line to the room reached out around the outside of the church, and I shook my head when Sandra gave me a questioning look. I didn't feel up to facing his family with his dead body lying right there.

We found a seat in the rear and waited more than an hour while all the mourners paid their respects. Finally, the chapel quieted down, the bishop and his counselors walked to the front of the church and into place behind the pulpit, and the music started. The pallbearers walked up the aisle bearing the casket that held the remains of Frank Kinderson.

The family followed behind, heads down, handkerchiefs in hand, filing one by one into the front rows of pews reserved for them. I recognized his ex-wife and daughter from the pictures I'd seen, as well as his mother and father. The rest of the family were complete strangers to me. I felt more alone than ever before.

I tried to swallow back the tears.

Don't cry, Allison. Don't cry.

The bishop stood and gave a brief introduction, announcing the opening song we would sing. "The song will be followed by two speakers, Detective Christopher Smart, who worked with Frank for more than twenty years, and James Kinderson, Frank's brother. Following that, Frank's nieces will sing 'I Am a Child of God.' The closing benediction will be given by Salt Lake City Police Department Chaplain Jerry Lake. Interment will be in the Avenues Cemetery immediately following the service."

A blur of singing, remembrances of Frank's years on the force, and the hushed sobs of the crowd rolled through my mind, creating snapshots for my patchwork memory. I held tight to my tears, not wanting to share them, afraid to let them go.

I caught my breath as four little blond girls wearing identical frilly lace dresses of white traipsed up from the family section of the pews and stood on the stage facing the audience. A woman knelt in front of them and hushed them with a finger in front of her mouth. She motioned to the pianist, and the chords of a familiar song filled the chapel. The girls fidgeted, and their eyes darted around the audience. One of them, the smallest, must have caught sight of her mother or father because she smiled broadly and waved. The others looked around with wide eyes and pursed lips, and I was reminded of myself and my sisters, forced to sing when it was our family's turn to give the program at Sacrament Meeting.

The music started.

I am a child of God,
And he has sent me here.
Has given me an earthly home,
With parents kind and dear.

The off-key voices, the flashbacks of memory, and my
own childhood spent in church all combined with the reality of Frank's death and hit me with maelstrom force. I
wept, heart-wrenching sobs, and Sandra and Carol comforted me. I tried to cry quietly, but it didn't work, and people turned and stared. I couldn't stop.

Lead me, guide me, walk beside me,
Help me find the way.
Teach me all that I must know,
To live with him someday.

Sandra led me sobbing from the chapel, and Aunt Carol
followed behind. They took me home, knowing I couldn't
watch his casket sit on a metal transom above a freshly dug
grave, prepared to drop into the ground, never to see light
again.

Why, Daddy? Why?

Forty-nine

My footsteps echoed loudly in the long hallway leading to the visiting room of the Salt Lake County jail. My demons had dragged me here, kicking and screaming all the way. An armed officer stood in front of the heavy door and unlocked it; it shut behind me with a resounding click.

Seated at a table in the bare room was my father, wearing orange coveralls emblazoned with SLCJ. He looked weary and old, and his hands were folded together and rested on the table in front of him.

I reluctantly sat down in the only other chair in the room. "Hello, Allison."

What should I say? Hello? I wanted to rip him to shreds, to make him scream, make him bleed the way Frank did, the way I felt I had every night since the incident.

"I guess you haven't forgiven me."

"You killed an innocent man. I told you to go away. I didn't want you watching me, like some pervert. Watching what I was doing."

"I was trying to protect you. Surely you know that by now."

"I told them the light went on, Dad. I told them the truth. You weren't asleep like you told them."

His silence frustrated me. I wanted answers. I wanted remorse.

He finally responded. "If I told you what happened, you wouldn't believe it. You're too caught up in your anger."

"How did I get this way, huh? When are *you* going to accept responsibility for all you did to us?"

"I thought it was Mark."

"Huh?"

"Allison, are you familiar with blood atonement?"

"Yeah, an eye for an eye, and all that stuff you shoved down our throats."

"Blood atonement was a principle taught by Brigham Young. There are certain sins that are only forgiven if the offender is punished by having his blood shed. Adultery, although people certainly ignore that nowadays. Murder. Rape. He killed my grandbaby, as surely as if he stood there in the hospital and shot her. He hurt his wife. He defiled an innocent child and made her pregnant. No one stopped him. I decided to stop him. It was God's will."

"You forgot me."

"What?"

"You forgot what he did to me, but I deserved it, in your eyes. I deserved all the pain and suffering."

"No, Allison, I didn't forget. Why do you think I waited outside your house so patiently? I waited for him to show up again. I knew he would."

"You didn't know anything. You welcomed him into our home and our family like the son you lost. You didn't see one bad thing about him even when I told you what he'd done."

"I am just a man, Allison. I make mistakes."

"Oh, believe me, I know."

"I've atoned to my God for my mistakes, and I believe He's forgiven me. I was trying to protect my family. God will forgive me for that."

"Dad. You didn't kill Mark. You killed Frank, an innocent man. You knew he was at my apartment. You were watching. You shot him when he confronted you."

"It was an accident."

"You even lie to yourself."

I walked out without another word.

Fifty

Jake pulled up in front of Sandra and Carol's house. He'd taken me down to the jail and visited with his buddies in Corrections while I listened to my father's denials, then respected my silence on the way back.

"I want to go home."

"To your apartment?"

"Yes."

"Not a good idea."

"I want to go home."

"Then I'll be staying with you."

"Hanging around me is dangerous. Or didn't you notice?"

"I'll take my chances."

Sandra and Aunt Carol waved good-bye from the front steps, frowns of concern creasing both their foreheads. They had argued against the decision, but I refused to change my mind.

Jake drove me to my apartment; as we reached the tree-lined street where Frank died, I felt my heart begin to race. A roaring in my ears overwhelmed me, and my stomach began to churn as my vision faded.

Jake reached over and pushed my head between my knees, and I slowly came back to reality. He parked the car and turned to me.

"Are you okay, now? You looked like you were going to pass out."

"Just a minute. I'll be okay." I sat up, shaky and nauseated. I had to look.

There was no sign of the violence that had taken place in this street just days ago. A light breeze tousled the tops of the willows, whispering words I couldn't comprehend, and the houses looked safe and comfortable. I stared, listening, as though I could gain some understanding of what had taken place if I just listened close enough.

"Let's go inside."

The red light on my answering machine flashed. I ignored it. Frank's shoes and shirt were still on the chair, his empty shoulder holster hanging over the back.

I half-collapsed, falling to my knees, and Jake led me to the sofa and guided me down, leaving for a minute to get me a glass of water from the kitchen.

"I'm so tired of crying. I'm going to dehydrate if I don't stop. I don't know how I can have this much moisture in me. I feel so empty." I took a sip of the water and choked and spluttered. My throat felt tight, as though no passageway was there anymore.

Jake didn't speak, just took the glass from me and set it on the end table, then put his arms around me and let me sob. When I was through, he stood up and collected the shirt, shoes, and holster and found a paper bag in the kitchen. He shoved them inside and asked me where I wanted them.

"I want to hold them."

He handed me the bag, and I clutched it to my chest, breathing heavily, trying not to let my despair overcome me.

The phone rang, its peals startling in the silence, and we both jumped. It rang three more times before the machine picked up, and I heard my voice say, "It's Alli. I'm out. Leave a message." After the extended beep, which told me quite a few callers wanted to talk to me, I heard Russell Free's voice.

"Allison, I've been trying to get ahold of you. I heard about what happened. I'm worried. Where are you? I can't find you. I can't find Corrie. Your stepmother isn't home. Dad says she packed up and went to visit her sister in Idaho. They called me and said they found my gun. Allison, I might be in trouble over this. I need . . ." The click told us his time had run out.

"Who's he?"

"An old friend of my brother's. He gave me the gun, just to keep here, for protection."

"Dumb move."

"He's a UHP trooper."

"Even dumber," Jake said. "He must be after you."

"Why would you say that?"

"'Cause guys don't think with the right head when they're hot for someone."

I laughed, the sound so foreign I was surprised it was me.

"I like your smile. It takes you from pretty to stunning."

"Are you hitting on me?"

"No, just commenting. Did you want me to hit on you?"

"No. Not right now."

"Okay," he said. "I'm not. Did you love Frank?"

I sat for a moment and thought about the fledgling romance that had been callously destroyed. "I don't know."

"Frank was a good guy. He would have treated you right."

"I know he was. One of the first I've ever met. It's my fault, I think. I realize now I always set myself up. It doesn't really seem fair I finally woke up to this fact, just to have it taken away from me so quickly.

"When it happens like that, I hear that little voice in my head, the one that says 'What if they're right? What if these things are happening because I left the Mormon Church, or because of the way I've lived my life?'"

"Allison?" Jake's expression was serious, and I worried about what he would say. "You know my little niece? She was only seven. Not even baptized. How could she have asked for what happened to her? I see babies die all the time. I see abuse. Nobody asks for these things. It's not a punishment. I think it just happens. Too many people spend too much time looking for reasons and answers when there aren't any."

I nodded my head in agreement and leaned back against the sofa, still clutching the paper bag holding the only remnants of Frank I still had in my life.

Sometimes, things just happened.

Fifty-one

Jake was off until the next evening, and he left me only long enough to gather some clothes and personal things. He wanted to call an officer, but I promised to jam the kitchen chair under the doorknob after I locked it with all three locks, and he finally left me for twenty minutes.

I took the time to find a special place to keep Frank's things. His family had pictures, his house, everything else that had been a part of him. Everything but him. I didn't think they'd miss a pair of shoes, a shirt, and a holster.

After I tucked them away in my cedar chest, I walked back into the living room and pressed the button on the answering machine. There were four increasingly frantic messages from Russell in addition to the one I'd heard before. Two messages were delivered in the icy tones of my stepmother, informing me she was leaving for Idaho and wouldn't be back until the trial. "It's too *embarrassing* for the kids."

The last one, before Russell's voice came on the line, caused the blood in my veins to turn to ice water.

"You're such bad luck, Allison, aren't you? Anyone who touches you ends up dead, hurt, or in jail. Don't bother trying to trace this call. I'm not that stupid. You'll be seeing me soon."

Click.

Before Russell's last message ran again, I grabbed the machine and hurled it through the kitchen window, screaming my rage.

The frantic pounding at my door told me Jake was back and had heard the crash.

"Just a minute, I'm okay. Just a minute."

I pulled the chair away and quickly undid the three locks, throwing open the door. Jake stood with his gun pulled, his eyes darting around.

"What the fuck was that?"

"Uh, I threw my answering machine out the window."

"You did *what*?"

"The asshole left a message on it. Said everybody around me dies, told me he'd be back."

Jake shook his head, reholstered his gun, and dropped a gym bag on the floor. He took the steps two at a time and disappeared out the front door of the apartment building, reappearing a few minutes later bearing my broken and twisted answering machine.

"This is evidence, Allison. What were you thinking?"

"I wasn't." I heard a door slam down the hall, and the super, a nice elderly gentleman whose wife always baked cookies and shared them with the neighbors, hobbled down to my apartment door.

"Oh, Allison, what now?"

They knew of my troubles, which began the night of the rape and exploded with Frank's murder.

"I'm sorry, Mr. Greenwood. I just . . ." I couldn't lie, because Jake stood there holding the mangled evidence in his hand. The super cast a suspicious eye on the gun resting on Jake's hip.

"She had an obscene phone call, and due to the stress of the past month, she just kind of freaked out. I'm Jake Jensen, SLCPD." He moved the answering machine to his left side, tucking it under his arm, and reached out with his right hand to shake Mr. Greenwood's outstretched palm.

"Oh, Allison. Now I'm going to have to call a window guy. I'm afraid you're going to have to pay for this. The owner is already putting up a fuss about the goings-on around here. Some of the neighbors have called and complained. Worried about their kids."

"Great, so now in addition to everything else, I'm going to get evicted."

"Maybe it would be better if you did move," Mr. Greenwood suggested, an embarrassed look on his tired old face. "You can't have good memories of this place."

"Are you kicking me out?"

"Well . . . I hate to call it that. You know I like you, Allison, but the neighbors . . . and Mrs. Greenwood's heart isn't good, you know. The murder of that fine officer just about caused it to stop."

Another rip formed in the patchwork quilt, the fabric of my life frayed and coming unwoven. Two men were responsible. One sat in the county jail for murder. The other was on the loose, calling and checking in, like a gracious child, letting me know he was all right.

I wanted him dead.

Mr. Greenwood gave me another miserable look and turned and shuffled back to his apartment.

"Gotta call KR Glass. They have twenty-four-hour service. It'll cost more. I'll give you two weeks, so you can find another place."

I seethed, and Jake must have sensed it, because he put a hand on me and steered me inside, shutting the door behind us.

"This is so fucked up. Now I'm being forced out of my

home. I'm like this miserable wretch of a human being who belongs nowhere. It makes me sick!"

"Calm down. In a way, the old fart is right. You need to leave this place."

"But if I do, they might never catch Mark."

"He's not that smart, Allison. Dumb luck and sheer desperation are all that's saving him right now. He's going to fuck up, and they're going to catch him."

"Do you know if they ever tracked the girl down, the one he got pregnant?"

"I'm not sure who picked up the case after Frank. I'll call and find out."

He walked over to the phone and picked it up. He put the receiver to his ear, knitted his eyebrows together in puzzlement, and clicked the lever on the base several times.

"Oh, shit, it was attached to the answering machine!" I said, slapping my forehead in disgust.

Jake put the receiver down and got on his hands and knees, pulling out the torn cord and inspecting the frayed wires.

"There's one in the bedroom," I said, as a flash of memory brought the image of Frank kneeling in that same position just days ago, checking the cord Mark had ripped out.

Jake gave me an amused grin and walked into my bedroom, where I heard him dialing. While he conducted his conversation, I checked my fridge for anything edible or drinkable. I found a box of wine and pulled it out. Anything in the fridge that once resembled food had taken on a life of its own. I shut the door and willed it all to go away.

I pulled down two wineglasses and filled them with zinfandel. He walked into the kitchen, eyed the wineglass and said, "Don't you have beer?"

"Nope."

"Okay." Jake took the glass, set it on the counter, and leaned back against the cupboards, his muscled arms bulging when he folded them together—his gun made him look serious and dangerous. I liked it.

"News isn't good. Castleton is back on it. He's a weenie. Frank liked him, but I think he's a moron."

I took a big swig of the wine, waiting for the familiar warmth to flood through my body. "He's one of them. The Priesthood-bearing pricks."

"So, basically, we're on our own," Jake said.

"Oh, this really sucks."

"Yep."

He picked up his wineglass and took a sip, grimaced, and set it back down. "I have an idea: I rent a house with a cop friend. There were three of us, but Allred got married and moved out two months ago. We have a spare bedroom. It's a bach pad, but we can use help with the rent, and you couldn't be much safer unless you moved into the department."

"You want me to live with you?"

"You're not living with me. Just sharing a house. It's about four blocks from here."

I considered my options. I would never return to my father's house. Sandra and Aunt Carol would welcome me, but there I felt like an intruder. I could leave the state, but still had issues here to resolve and a job to return to.

I was also so frightened whenever darkness fell, I felt like a child haunted by monsters in the closets and under the bed.

"Okay."

"We'll move your stuff tomorrow."

Fifty-two

Eyes open wide, I stared at the ceiling, my body weary, my mind active. I didn't want to sleep, scared of what horrors might await me in my unconscious mind, yet I was so tired my eyes felt like grains of sand were stuck under the lids.

Through the partially closed door I could hear the tossing and turning of Jake Jensen, my newest protector. A deep sigh told me he wasn't sleeping, either.

Somewhere, Mark Peterson was hiding, plotting against me, waiting to pull the final brick out of the pile that would make the whole lot come tumbling down to crush me.

The clock flashed the time, three A.M., over and over, and I started to see spots in front of my eyes from watching it. I rose from my bed and walked to the window, parting the curtains and looking out at a moonless sky. Clouds dotted it, and no stars could be seen. Dozens of moths batted against the porch light, the only illumination I could see aside from one streetlight at the very end of the road.

I stared at the spot where Frank died, and the picture played over and over again in my head. The light went on; Frank charged; the thunderous shot roared; sirens wailed.

"Allison?"

I jumped, so deep in my reverie I didn't hear Jake push

open the door. He walked over to stand by me, wearing only gym shorts. I was very aware of his body next to mine, could smell his aroma, perspiration mixed with something intangible; and I felt a quickening in my stomach, a little jump of arousal.

Guilt flooded me. How could I be attracted to Jake when Frank just died? Should I feel guilt? We had only kissed, never made promises, never took a next step together.

"Can't sleep?" Jake asked.

"No," I told him. "Can't, and I'm afraid to. Nightmares."

"Can I smoke?"

"Okay." I shoved open the window, letting in a cooler night breeze; he went back to the living room to get a cigarette and his lighter. The flame flickered red, blue-tinged on the outside, and the bright red circle of tobacco burned. He drew a deep breath, then blew the smoke out the window.

"I never should've started."

"I wonder where he is?"

"I wish I knew. I think he's stupid enough to stay close. We'll catch him. But this waiting is driving me fucking nuts."

I studied his profile as he stared out the window, his face dark and moody. Jake Jensen had jet-black hair, startling blue eyes, a perfectly shaped mouth, and strong chin. He was almost a pretty boy—would have been, in fact, except for a hardness to his features that made him look dangerous and volatile.

He caught me watching him, and said, "What?"

"Nothing. Sorry, I was just off in space somewhere."

"We need to get some sleep."

"I know."

He finished his cigarette and left for the bathroom, where I shortly heard running water and the flush of the toilet. He came back into my room and gently pulled me by the arm toward the bed.

"I'll lay with you. On top of your covers. Don't worry, I'm not going to try anything."

The phone rang at five a.m., startling us both awake. With him on top of the covers, and me below, we'd become entangled; I struggled free, trying to reach the phone.

"Hello?"

"Ms. Jensen?"

"Yes?"

"This is Frederickson, SLCPD."

"Oh, yes, Detective."

"Sorry to call so early. Jensen said he'd be there, protecting you. I need to speak to him. It's urgent."

I handed the phone to Jake. He conducted his conversation with a deep frown, his features seeming to turn to stone in the early pre-dawn half-light. When he hung up, he looked at me.

"You've got more bad news," I deduced, wondering what else could happen.

"The girl, the twelve-year-old? The one he got pregnant in Arkansas? They tracked her down. She hid her pregnancy the entire time and gave birth in her closet. She bled to death. When her parents found her body, she was lying on top of the baby. It happened about six months ago."

Fifty-three

Sami Marquette came from a poor farming family in rural Arkansas. Slender and tall for her age, she wore baggy shirts and managed to conceal her pregnancy from her parents, teachers, and fellow ward members. I learned this much from the detectives.

It wasn't enough.

"You can't go, Allison. You must be nuts," Jake said, anger darkening his features when I told him what I intended. "What if he follows you?"

"He has no money, Jake. If he has a car and can figure out where I'm going, by the time he gets there I'll be back."

"You don't know he has no money. His family could be supporting him and protecting him. They did it before."

"Be reasonable, Jake. This isn't a Movie-of-the-Week, and he's no criminal mastermind. I'll be careful."

When my plane touched down at the Arkansas International Airport, I had two addresses, one for the hospital where the baby was and the other for Sami Marquette's family. I doubted I'd be welcome at either one.

I'd called the family before I left Utah and explained I

was doing an article for my magazine. They hung up the phone. I didn't blame them, nor did it surprise me. As I'd walked through the Salt Lake City International Airport after Jake dropped me off, I noticed the uniformed officers who trailed behind me. One smiled and gave me a wave. I'd felt a warm rush knowing Jake had gone this far to protect me, even though he disagreed with my decision to travel to Arkansas.

On the plane, I closed my eyes and let my mind travel the distance of the past month. The picture of a young girl, scared and alone, in pain and bleeding, flashed through my mind. Poor Sami. I wanted to respect her family's grief, especially knowing how strong my own was; but this story was going to be told, with or without their permission.

The baby was still in the intensive care unit of the closest hospital, 120 miles from their town, breathing only with the help of a ventilator. I would start there.

The taxicab ride from the airport took forty long, humid minutes. I stepped out into the moisture-filled Arkansas heat and felt like I'd been slapped in the face with a hot washrag. I walked confidently into the hospital, ignoring my drooping hair and perspiring face, scanned the listings for the NICU, and continued to that floor.

A young nurse sat at the desk outside the unit, filling out charts.

"Hi. My name's Allison Jensen. I'm doing an article for the *Arkansas Star-Tribune* on babies born with health problems who need long-term care. I wondered if you could help me."

"Oh, anything like that has to go through the hospital public relations department. I can ring them for you."

"Sure, that would be great."

I held my breath as she picked up the phone, knowing whoever answered would most likely be aware there was no *Arkansas Star-Tribune*.

She set the phone down in its cradle. "Voice mail. She's gone to lunch. Here, I'll write the number down for you, and you can call her."

"I appreciate that."

I peered around her into the nursery, where babies in incubators under lights had wires, tubes, and monitors attached to every available inch of their tiny bodies. Most of these were newborns. Sami Marquette's baby was much older, and should have been starting to crawl, gumming crackers and cooing. Instead, it was here, somewhere, with these other babies, most born too early. I flashed back to little Elise Marie, and my heart skipped a beat. What a horrible thing to live with. It added to my determination never to have children.

"Here you go," the nurse said, handing me a slip of paper.

"Thanks. How long have you been doing this?"

"Oh, this is six years for me in NICU. I wouldn't work anywhere else."

"Isn't it hard, though? My niece just died, after she was born too early. That's part of the reason I'm doing the story."

"I'm sorry. We do see that, but we see more success stories, and that keeps me here."

"How about the babies in there now? Do you think most of them will make it?"

"I'm not a doctor, but, yes, I think most of them will. There's one or two that won't."

"I heard there was a baby found under its mother's dead body. Is that baby going to be okay? What a sad, sad story. After what I've been through with my niece, I can't even imagine that."

"You know, I really can't talk about this. You need to get permission from the PR office. Hospital policy."

"Okay, I will. I was just curious. It made me sad."

I turned to go, having learned nothing, and she looked at

me and whispered, "Look, you can't put this in the story, but
I have to say it. Nobody comes to see the poor little baby.
It's all alone. The mother was only thirteen, just barely thirteen, and she bled to death. The worst part is, the baby will
live, but it has brain damage. It's going to be a ward of the
state. Now, that's sad. How can the baby's grandparents do
that?"

"I'm amazed every day at what people will do."

"I just think someone should write about it, about how
they abandoned that poor baby. But you didn't hear it
from me."

I thanked her and walked away. Another damaged life,
ruined by secrets and lies and the protectors of the guilty.
My anger flared again, and I headed out the hospital doors
back into the blazing sun. I hailed a taxicab and had the
driver take me to the nearest rental car agency. Bald Frog,
Arkansas, was a three-hour drive. I intended to question
every member of that town until someone told me how this
happened, how a Mormon bishop allowed a family's
daughter—an entire family—to be destroyed and didn't report it.

Bald Frog, despite its unique name, had nothing particu-
larly interesting or defining about it. The town consisted of
a small gas station/grocery mart, and a smattering of
houses—maybe twenty or so—up and down the main road.
The homes were small but well tended, with long stretches
of fenced-off acreage on both sides. The smell of manure
filled the air, and the mooing of cows in the distance re-
peated every few seconds. Against the horizon I could see
the tips of the Ozark Mountains.

I stopped at the station and asked directions to the nearest Mormon wardhouse. The attendant, a friendly elderly
woman with blue-gray hair, stared at me as if I were insane.

"Lord, child, I don't think we have no Mormons 'round here. Everyone I know is Baptist."

"Do you have a phone book?"

"Sure. Where you from, anyhow? You sure talk funny."

I smiled as I scanned the Yellow Pages' church listings. I found one for an LDS chapel in Grace Hills.

"I'm from Utah."

"Oh, you lookin' for some o' your own kind?"

I giggled. "No, no, just doing a story for my magazine, and one of the leads brought me here."

"What kinda story?"

"A story about a poor Mormon child who bled to death after she had her baby. No one knew she was pregnant."

"Oh, you mean poor Tom Marquette's daughter, Sami. They Mormons? Lord, I had no idea. Seemed normal to me."

"You know them?" I was excited to have a lead.

"Look out them doors, girl. This look like a big place? Everybody knows everybody. Marquettes kept to themselves, of course. Now I know why. Live 'bout two miles yonder. Nice people, just not easy to get to know. Mormons. Lordy. No idea."

"Did you know the baby lived? It's still in the hospital."

"Heard that. My friend Ema lives on the farm next to 'em. She took 'em food and bread and such, for a while. Said they were grateful but didn't say much. Lots of people came out and visited, though. People in white shirts, and ties, but not the cops. Cars goin' up and down the road, kickin' up dust day and night. Ema said she couldn't put her laundry out on the line 'cause it got so dirty from the road."

"I guess the parents don't want anything to do with the baby."

"I 'spect that'll change. They're still grievin' right now.

Daughter was their only child. Mercy couldn't have no more, 'count of plumbin' troubles."

"Did you hear who the father was?"

"Nope, and that's right strange. 'Round here, nobody has secrets. But haven't heard a word."

"Well, thanks for the information." I wrote down the address of the Mormon church and slapped the phone book shut, handing it back to her. She gave me a funny look, glanced around the store, and lowered her head toward me, motioning me with her finger. I moved a little closer.

"You be careful now, missy. We've had those Mormon boys in here, the missionaries in the fancy shirts and ties and name tags? And they're right persuasive in getting you to listen to their nonsense." Her voice dropped even lower. "They offer to help you and all kinds o' stuff, but they have a reason, oh, yes, they do."

I laughed. "Don't you worry. Being from Utah, I've heard it all. My family's Mormon."

She straightened back up. "Oh, well, I didn't mean no offense."

"None taken."

The Grace Hills LDS chapel was a familiar landmark to me, even though I'd never been there before. It seemed the Mormon Church had one blueprint for chapels: a spired front with a steeple, red brick, generic windows with tinting, and a large parking lot. I saw several cars parked in the lot, and I stopped the rental, regretfully turning off the engine and air-conditioning. I felt the heat settle in before I even opened the door.

I walked around the grounds to the various doors, trying one after another. Unlike other denominations, Mormons locked their buildings when services or meetings were not being held, as they had no full-time caretakers.

On the side entrance near the parked cars I found the

door open, and I pushed into the air-conditioned building.
A sick feeling churned in my stomach, a combination of
the heat and memories of Kevin's missionary farewell and
Frank's funeral. The smell of polish and cleaning supplies,
along with leftover traces of stale perfume and baby pow-
der, lingered in the air, testifying to the families that piled
in here on Sundays for hours of meetings.

"Hello. Can I help you?"

A tall, balding man in his mid-forties stepped out of an
office marked BISHOP. He was wearing a short-sleeved shirt
and neatly pressed khaki pants.

"I'm looking for the bishop. Is that you?"

"Yes, I'm Bishop Jorgenson. Do I know you? You look
very familiar to me."

His Southern accent made the words sound warm and
inviting. I refused to be taken in.

"Were you the bishop who sent Mark Peterson home
from his mission? I mean, the bishop of the girl he got
pregnant?"

His features hardened slightly, and the honey-drenched
tones of his voice were now sharp. "I'm sorry, but that is
something I can't discuss with you. Who are you? Wait . . .
wait just a minute."

The look of dawning recognition on his face puzzled
me. I'd never seen this man before, nor had I ever been to
Arkansas.

"You're Allison. Mark Peterson's girlfriend. He attended the ward here and—"

"What? What the . . . ? Girlfriend? No, Mark was married to my sister, and—"

I stopped talking as all the implications hit me. This man
knew who I was, and believed me to be Mark's girlfriend.
But Mark had served his mission here before he met Corrie.

"I'm not his girlfriend," I finally said, the words feeling
heavy and thick. "How do you know me? How?"

"Well, Mark carried your picture around, of course. Had them all over his room, too. I always found it a little odd he only had one picture, just a lot of copies of it. But that's neither here nor there. He said you were waiting for him at home."

"I never met Mark Peterson until he married my sister."

"Oh, my. This is definitely odd. But at any rate, I can't discuss him with you. I'm sorry about what's happened, but this is church business, and—"

"You're guilty, you know. Almost as guilty as he."

"Guilty? Guilty of what? This is a mighty strange conversation we're having here."

"You're guilty of raping me. Sami Marquette's blood is on your hands. You might as well have stood there and handed him the tissues when he was done, because you are so fucking guilty it makes me sick."

"Look, young lady, this is a house of the Lord! We don't speak that way here, and I'm not sure what's up with you, but I'm going to have to call the cops if you don't leave. I'm sorry Mark got sent home, but he—"

"Why wasn't he charged? You protected him, just like his bishop back home protected him. All the bishops have just let him go and continue to destroy women. You're all responsible."

"Mark was disciplined—"

"Spare me your crap. Nobody ever stopped him. Nobody. Until now. I'm going to stop him."

I walked out of the church without looking back.

Fifty-four

The flight home to Salt Lake City passed in a blur as I struggled to reason through what I'd learned in Arkansas. I'd tried to visit the Marquette family, but an extremely large woman who identified herself as Sister Hurst was playing watchdog, and she wouldn't let me past the front door.

I checked into a hotel near the airport and booked a flight home for the next morning. On the plane I sat next to a friendly businessman who tried to start a conversation and finally gave up after I only answered him with single syllables.

Where did Mark get my picture? It couldn't have been from Corrie, because he had it on his mission. Since we both lived in Farmington and he was my age, it stood to reason we had attended school together, but I didn't remember him. With three hundred students, our class at Davis High School in Kaysville wasn't exactly large, but with the two towns combined, there were plenty of other people I didn't remember.

He stalked me. Long before he met Corrie, he was stalking me!

Did he somehow arrange to meet Corrie because of me? Did he only marry her as a substitute?

I groaned aloud, not liking the direction my thoughts took.

"Are you okay? Should I get the flight attendant?"

"No, no, I'm just thinking. Sorry."

"Must have been heavy-duty thinking," my seatmate said with a smile, encouraged by my five-word sentence.

I gave him a cursory grin and leaned back, closing my eyes to shut him out and end the conversation. The one in my head, though, I couldn't stop.

How long had Mark Peterson been obsessed with me?

A silent and brooding Jake picked me up at the airport, surprising me when I walked off the plane to find him standing there, dressed in his uniform.

"Aren't you supposed to be at work?"

"Yeah, I am, and let's hurry because I need to get back to it. Got special permission to pick you up."

We walked in silence to the baggage claim carousel, and I finally broke through the invisible wall standing between us.

"Look, I know you didn't want me to go, but I had to, Jake. I had to have answers. I got more than I bargained for."

"You could have gotten killed. That's no bargain."

"Oh, for Heaven's sake, stop acting like a big worry wart and listen to what I found out."

His glare told me my worry-wart comment had not gone over well.

"If I say I'm stubborn, and stupid, and I'm sorry, will you forgive me and listen?"

"It was more than stupid."

"Fine. It was more than stupid. But, Jake, Mark had my picture on his mission. The bishop of his ward there recognized me. All I can figure is he got it somehow when we were in high school. And he didn't have just one, he had a lot of them."

Jake stared at me for a minute, then turned and grabbed my small bag off the luggage carousel. "I talked to Castleton right after you left. He agreed it was stupid for you to go. He also told me something else. The bishop of Mark and Corrie's ward told him Mark seemed to have some problems, and that they stemmed back to you. He wouldn't be specific, said he couldn't, but he'd known for quite a while there were issues."

"Great. The conspiracy grows. I don't think anything else could surprise me."

"Maybe, maybe not."

"What? Do you know something else?"

"The bishop tried to warn your dad. Said he wouldn't listen."

Jake had been busy while I was in Arkansas, and he and several friends had moved all my possessions to his house.

"You packed my underwear?" I asked him, not sure if I was thrilled with his take-charge attitude.

"Yeah, I did. I packed everything. Didn't want to give you a reason to go back there. Look, Allison, you have too many bad memories there, and it's not safe."

"You're trying to control me, just like every other—"

"Don't start. Don't even. I'm trying to help you."

The garage of his three-bedroom house was filled with my belongings, except for my bed, which was set up in a small bedroom along with my dresser and night table.

"You can decide whether you want this stuff in our house or whether you want to store it. Most of it's nicer than anything we have."

I felt out-of-place and lonely as I wandered through Jake's—our—house. A short, chubby blond man with a baby face sat on the couch watching the Jazz game. It was Sunday.

"Hey, didn't you have tickets to that game? We were going to go. Good Lord, it feels like a year has passed since you asked me," I said to Jake.

"Yeah, well, I gave them to a friend. And I traded shifts so I could be here tonight with you."

I wandered into the kitchen and back out, aimlessly, trying to feel like I belonged.

"I need to get back to work, Allison. I'll be off at four. Pete's off today, so he's offered to stick around until I get back."

"I don't need a fucking baby-sitter!"

"Whoa, she's feisty. Don't worry, I don't bite," Pete said from the couch without pulling his eyes away from the action on the TV set. His gun was strapped to his side in a shoulder holster. It didn't make me feel safe.

Jake just shook his head and pointed a finger at me. "Don't leave. Not alone, anyway. I've already called Sandra and Carol and told them where to find you. They said they'll let your sisters know."

With that, he left; I wanted to yell at him to come back, to not leave me alone here with Basketball Pete and these unfamiliar surroundings.

"Stockton to Malone!" Basketball Pete shouted to no one. "Dugga! Two points."

I wandered into the bedroom and closed the door, lying down on the bed and trying to will myself to sleep. I hadn't rested much the night before, my dreams filled mostly with images of Mark Peterson watching me from every angle. I had cried out for Frank, but only Mark was there, his evil presence chasing off all of my more friendly ghosts. And he wasn't even dead.

I thought of him holding my picture, showing it to people, lovingly calling me his own, touching it with his fingers, and masturbating while my eyes watched unknowingly. Cold chills traveled up and down my spine. I had to stop him. It seemed no one else could. He was still out there looking for me: I could feel it. I held some attraction for him I couldn't begin to understand, but I knew he would be watching and waiting.

I sat up abruptly. I had to do something. I had to get Mark before he got me—or someone else.

I knew just what to do.

Fifty-five

I left my room and crept across the hall to the door I knew led to Jake's bachelor chambers. It was ajar, and I slipped inside, cringing as I listened for my bodyguard. I heard several shouts of "Yeah! That showed 'em!" and knew I was okay so far.

Jake's quarters were sparse, with an old waterbed covered with a brown masculine spread, a boxy dresser that was missing knobs, and some shelves made out of old orange crates. The only elaborate decoration in the bare room was an ornate mahogany gun cabinet, his pride and joy; he'd shown it to me on my brief tour of the house. I knew it was locked—Jake would never have been so careless as to leave it any other way—but I needed a weapon.

I went to it, trying not to set off the squeaky boards of the old wood floor, then stared at it, thinking. Looking around, I grabbed an old T-shirt that had been carelessly thrown on the floor and one of Jake's barbells. Wrapping the five-pound weight in the shirt, I struck lightly at the glass on the side of the cabinet. Nothing happened. I hit it slightly harder and heard a crack. One more light tap was all it took, and I was able to pry the pieces of glass out of the pane. Inside, within reaching distance, I saw Jake's favorite 9mm Glock. I knew it was a Glock because Russell had lent me the same kind of gun.

I set it on his dresser and dug through the top drawer until I came out with a box of bullets marked for the gun. I loaded it, pushed the safety on, and stuck it in the waistband of my jeans, pulling down my T-shirt to cover the bulge.

I made my way to the kitchen, and Basketball Pete nodded at me, watching for a minute as I passed through the living room. I opened the door of the refrigerator, scanned it swiftly, and grabbed a jar of pickles from the top shelf. With only a moment's hesitation, I dropped the jar on the floor and swore loudly as I stepped back so that only a small amount of pickle juice landed on my clothes.

Pete ran in from the other room, his gun drawn, and stopped short in the doorway when he saw the mess.

"I'm sorry. I made a *huge* mess. I'm just so rattled right now. I'll clean it up." I stood with my left side to him, facing the refrigerator, so he wouldn't notice the bulge on my right side.

"Okay. You sure? You need help?" he asked, glancing back to where the basketball game was still playing as he tucked his gun into his holster.

"Oh, yeah, go watch your game. This is going to take a while." I indicated the glass shards and sticky pickle juice that covered the kitchen floor.

"Okay, broom's in there," he said, indicating a closet. "Uh, mop's in there, too."

As soon as he left, I headed for the back door and opened it, hoping the creaking noise it made would be mistaken for the sound of the closet door. I took off running down the back alley behind the house, expecting to hear shouts at any moment, but my ruse had worked. Basketball Pete was there to protect me from Mark, not from myself. No one had ever been able to do that.

I easily ran the few blocks to my old apartment building, passing the street where I would normally turn and going one street farther. I knew my VW Bug still sat under the carport—Jake had assured Mr. Greenwood we would move it in the next few days. Since they didn't yet have a new tenant and the elderly superintendent felt guilty for asking me to move, he told us to take our time.

I always kept a spare car key in a magnetic box in the left front wheel well.

When I reached the halfway point between my block and the one above it, I turned down the narrow alleyway that ran between both streets and slipped into the building through a back entrance, never locked. The door led to the laundry room in the basement, and I ran up the stairs to the front door. Once there, I stopped, composed myself, then walked briskly out the front door and to my car.

I knew Mark was there, watching. I didn't dare scan the streets, not wanting to give myself away, but I could feel his presence.

When I got to my car, I looked down at my empty hands, as if surprised to find myself without my purse or keys, and then stamped the ground in faux frustration. Finally, I walked around to the driver's side and reached up under the fender, feeling around for a minute until I found the key. Once inside the car, I started it and drove out of the parking lot, pulling a pair of sunglasses out of the glove compartment. I hoped that, by wearing them, I could hide that I was looking in my rearview mirror.

I traveled away from the Avenues and downtown area, taking Fourth South up toward the East Side bench, the place I always went to think and stare out at the lights of the city. I watched the cars behind me carefully but could see no sign of a tail. Still, I knew he was there.

When I reached the bench I pulled onto the side of the road and waited. I pulled the gun out of my waistband, turned the safety off, and dropped my hand to the seat between my leg and the door. My heart pounded as I waited, but I could see no sign of anyone out there; and in time the pulsating rhythm slowed, the roar in my ears diminished. Every time a car came by, I flinched. This was a well-known make-out spot, so traffic was fairly consistent—cars filled with teenage lovers.

A vehicle pulled in next to me, about twenty feet away, and my heart began pounding again; but I looked over and could see two heads in the car. I purposely stared. The female looked in my direction, turned back to the driver, and they started up the car and pulled out, tires spinning on the loose gravel. I watched them, amused, a grin twitching at my strained lips as I imagined the conversation inside the car where the boy wanted to get lucky and the girl didn't want to get caught.

When my passenger-side window shattered and the door flew open, I was not prepared.

"Hello, Allison," Mark said as he slid into the seat and pointed a gun at my chest with one hand, shutting the door with the other.

"Hello yourself, prick," I replied, and pointed the Glock directly at his head.

Fifty-six

Mark Peterson stared at the gun in shock and disbelief. "You have a gun," he said.

"Give the man a medal, and tell him what he's won!"

"You knew I'd follow you. Are the cops here? I didn't see them. You bitch. You set me up." He strained his neck as he looked for the officers he thought were hidden all around us.

"Of course they are," I lied. "And now you are going down, you bastard."

"Wait a minute," he said, narrowing his eyes and then smiling at me in a cruel, mirthless fashion. "They wouldn't give you a gun. No way the cops would do that. There are no cops, are there, Alli? But you knew I'd be here. You came alone. Why?"

"So I could shoot you myself," I said, suddenly not at all sure why I had decided to set myself up as bait. I wanted him off the streets, but I knew Jake and the police would never have allowed this. I also knew that Mark would have seen through it if they *had* agreed to use me as bait. Now, there was no one but me to end this. In theory, I wanted to kill him, but holding a gun in my hand, I wasn't sure I could follow through.

"Doesn't matter," he said, still smiling that same cold

smirk. "I'll just shoot you. Even if you shoot back, I have nothing to lose now, nothing. You took it all away. Now I'm going to take everything away from you."

Anger spurted through my veins, sharp and bitter, along with fear; but oddly enough, the anger seemed to win in the fight for emotional control. I spoke acrid words.

"You already did."

Mark shook his head briskly. He was pale and thin, and sweating profusely. His clothes were stained and torn and looked as though he'd slept in them for more than a week. He had a peach-fuzz beard and a reeking body odor, and I felt dizzy and nauseated.

"You don't get it, do you?" he said.

"You can't do this," I answered, ignoring his question. "Please, Mark, stop this now. I know about Sami Marquette, and I know about Jenny Perkins. And me. I know about me! How could you? How could you marry my sister while you were . . ."

"You don't know anything. You don't even know the half of it!"

I stared at him, shocked and scared, wondering what he meant. I couldn't miss the pain and fear telegraphed on his face, and I wondered what caused him to feel that way. What right did *he* have to be hurt and scared, after what he had done to me and my family?

"Why don't you just shoot me now?" he asked, his tone slightly mocking. "Just get it over with. Then I'll shoot you, and we'll both have what we want."

"Because I want to know why."

"Why what?"

"Why did you rape me? Why did you molest those girls? Why? What gave you that right to take their innocence away? They were only children. What gave you that right?"

He ignored the question, dabbing at the perspiration on

his forehead with his forearm while keeping the gun trained on me. "You like it here, don't you? You always come here."

"You followed me here. That night. The night you raped me, didn't you?"

"You never even looked at me, you know. At school. Never even gave me the time of day."

"I don't remember you, Mark."

"Yeah, I know. You didn't even know who I was. You didn't know what I saw."

"What do you mean, what you saw?"

Shocked, I watched as tears flowed from his eyes. He hastily scrubbed at them to make them disappear.

"I was there. I watched him as he held the gun on you and her, and then I watched him, saw what he did to her, *saw* him kill her. I watched. I was only five."

"You saw— Are you talking about Cindy? Are you telling me you saw the man who held us at gunpoint? That you know who killed her? And you never told anybody?"

He heard the anger in my voice, the disgust, and his face hardened.

"You have no idea what it's like. I was only five. And he lived with us. He told me if I told anyone, *anyone,* he would tell them our secret. He would tell them that I touched him! It didn't start that way. It wasn't that way."

"Oh, dear God." I felt the blood rush from my face and my heart plummet as his meaning struck home. I almost dropped the gun but forced myself to keep it aimed at him. I didn't intend to be his victim again.

The tears continued to fall down his face, and he rubbed his nose fiercely. He still held the gun, but his hand shook so much I was afraid he was going to pull the trigger by accident.

"Who was he?" I asked, almost afraid to hear the answer.

Mark snorted, the look of derision on his face set off oddly by the tracks of his tears.

"My parents took him in. His wife died and he was alone. The bishop asked us to help him out because we had a spare room. He was a part of my family, and I could never tell them, *never,* because I knew they would believe him. They would never believe me."

A rush of sympathy flooded me, confused me. I knew that feeling. I had felt the same way. Never once, however, had I considered that someone else—someone like Mark, the man who raped me—would understand it.

My mind flashed back to the July 24 celebration when I was seven, the year after Cindy disappeared. The bearded man had stood there holding the hand of a young boy—a boy with large, sorrowful, bright-blue eyes. I realized it must have been Mark. With this knowledge came a rapid-fire slew of emotions—anger, more fear, shock, disgust, and worst of all, empathy for the child Mark had been.

"You have to tell them," I said. "You have to tell them what happened. And where Cindy is buried. You can barter your charges down in exchange for the information. It's a murder, Mark. There is no statute of limitations on murder. They'll find him and arrest him—"

"Oh, just shut up," he snapped, his voice hoarse and full, throaty. "You don't understand. The fucker is dead. He's dead. He died years ago, and left me holding all these stupid secrets. Left me with the memories. Left me alone. I just didn't want to be alone anymore. And, anyway, they knew, or at least suspected. After he died, the cops came and searched our house and took a bunch of stuff. My parents told me never to mention his name again. The bishop even called me in, ordered me to never speak about him to anyone."

"Why?"

He shrugged his shoulders. "Didn't want a mark on the church, I guess, since he was the one who asked my parents to take the bastard in. I don't know. I don't even know how much they knew. They damn sure didn't tell me."

"Mark, where is she? Where's Cindy? Where did he bury her?"

He just looked at me, a sad, withdrawn look with none of the hostility that had always been present between us. Then he dropped the gun to his side.

"I never would have shot you," he said. "I just wanted you to *see* me. I wanted you to know that I understood. We belonged together. We had a bond, one that couldn't be broken. But you wouldn't see me. You wouldn't even *look*. So I made you pay. But I'm sorry. I'm sorry."

"Mark, you owe it to Cindy's mother. She's been waiting for Cindy to come home for years. She needs to bury her daughter." I slowly lowered my own gun as he turned and sobbed into his hands.

When he hit me hard across the face, I fell back and moaned, stunned, but I pointed my gun at him again. My cheek felt raw and bruised, and I tasted blood in my mouth.

"Shoot me," he said, way too quietly. "Get it over with."

"What?"

This time, he screamed. "Shoot me! You hate me. Shoot me. Do it!"

"Mark, you need to tell Cindy's mother where she is. You can plead these charges down."

"You don't get it, Allison. You never have. I was only five. I can't remember where she is. I followed him there, and I tried to find it later, but I can't remember where she is."

"What was his name?"

He shook his head and reached into his back pocket to pull out a worn brown wallet. He threw it toward me. I reached down and picked it up, still keeping the gun trained on him.

I opened the wallet and almost dropped the gun as I saw *his* face. On top of all the pictures in Mark's wallet was one of the man with the beard. The man who haunted my nightmares. He'd been so close.

As I stared, Mark bent down and picked up his gun, aiming it at me again. "I am going to kill you, so you might as well shoot me first. *Shoot me!*"

I stared at him, appalled. "I can't. I can't shoot you."

I lowered the gun again, and the fury went out of his eyes, replaced by resignation and despair.

"Please shoot me," he pleaded in a whisper.

"I can't."

He turned the gun toward his head and fired as I screamed and leaned to grab it. The shot resounded loudly in the small car.

Mark slumped against the door, his shattered head resting on the blood-drenched window frame. I looked down at the picture, at my hands, at the car, all now covered with Mark's blood and bits of bone and brain matter and I screamed.

Once I started screaming, I couldn't stop.

I scrambled out of the car door and ran, still holding the blood-spattered wallet. A car stopped by the side of the road, followed closely by another one. A young man stuck his head out of the first car.

"Hey, you need a . . . ? Whoa! Are you okay? Were you in an accident?"

I stared at him, shaking, in shock, and he waved to the car behind him. The driver got out—another teenager— and he told him to go find a phone and call for help.

"I think she's been in an accident."

My whole life had been one big accident.

Fifty-seven

The police drove me back to Jake's house when they were done questioning me, and I found him waiting there, his face white and strained, guilt written on his features. He winced when he saw the blood and tissue in my hair and on my clothes.

Despite my appearance, he pulled me close. "I thought you'd be safe here . . . You weren't."

"I'm safe now," I replied, burying my face in his shirt, a cotton tee that carried his unique scent as well as the lingering aroma of fabric softener. I savored the feeling of relief I had experienced so rarely in my life.

It was over, at least the part where I was constantly looking over my shoulder, wondering where Mark was and when he would strike. I'd learned more than I ever thought I would. I knew who killed Cindy, although not his name. The only two people who could have rescued her remains and allowed her proper burial were now dead. Nonetheless, I had a phone call to make. Somebody had been waiting a very long time for her to come home. I needed to tell her mother that now was the time to turn the porch light off.

The intensity of my emotions made me dizzy, and I fell

back onto the couch Jake led me to, surprised to find tears coursing down my cheeks.

I cried for Corrie, for Frank, for Kevin. I cried for me, and the girl I had once been, and the one I would always be. I even cried tears for Mark Peterson. And most of all, I cried for Cindy. My life, traumatic though it had been, was still a life. I grew up, could still experience love, could still grow and mature. Hers had been cut short. She would never know any of these things.

I also felt an overwhelming sense of need, a longing for the one thing most profoundly missing from my life.

I wanted my mother.

Fifty-eight

"Please be seated," intoned the bailiff.

Judge Henry Carlson gravely studied the crowded courtroom, his eyes fixing on me for a minute, moving to Corrie, and finally back to the defendant's table where my father sat with his lawyer.

The jury of my father's peers, most of the twelve sporting the familiar lines of garments under their clothing, were stony-faced and somber. They had deliberated only four hours before returning with a verdict. If this had been a TV legal drama, right now his attorney would jump from his seat and unveil the real killer. But my father was the real killer.

The district attorney stood up. "Your Honor, the city has reached a plea agreement with the defendant. In exchange for a plea of guilt to second-degree manslaughter, with a sentence of five years to life, the defendant Richard Lamont Jensen has agreed to tell the court exactly what happened on the night Officer Frank Kinderson was shot."

The judge looked disappointed, as did part of the jury. My stepmother gasped and covered her mouth with her hands. I watched her for a moment, before turning back to the events unfolding before us.

I'd told my story on the stand without emotion, refusing

to alter any details despite the pleadings of my stepmother and sister Cathy. Corrie sat silent and hollow-eyed, seemingly devoid of any emotion. She'd testified in a manner just like mine. Had my eyes showed the same pain and fear I saw in hers?

We were both marked by the curse of our father and by an obsessed man. We could never escape it. When I'd told her Mark's story, her face remained stoic, unmoved. Perhaps one day she would feel sympathy for him, but now all she could feel was hurt and loss.

My father made his way to the witness stand. He looked old and frightened, and his formerly strong features now seemed weak and confused.

The bailiff swore him in, and the district attorney began to question him.

"Mr. Jensen, can you tell us exactly what happened on the night of May fifteenth, 1987?"

"I was sitting in my car, watching my daughter Allison's house. She was being stalked by Mark Peterson, my other daughter's husband, and he'd raped her. I felt responsible, because I knew something was wrong with him. His bishop approached me with concerns Mark was obsessed with Allison. I didn't believe him. I guess I blamed Allison, because she always wore immodest clothing and had a . . . a reputation for sleeping around."

My heart hardened as he told his story. Even in accepting blame, he found an excuse to turn responsibility back on me.

"And on this night?" the DA prompted him.

"I was watching her apartment, as usual, and I knew that cop, uh, Detective Kinderson, was there. I didn't think it was right for Allison to have him staying there, with no chaperone, but I didn't want to confront him. I didn't. I was just watching for Mark. I must have fallen asleep, because I woke up and realized I'd dropped my gun. I turned on the light to look at my watch and had just picked up the gun when I heard a man yell at me. It startled me and I thought it was Mark. I thought it . . . The gun just went off, and I heard the sirens and the . . . I didn't mean to kill anyone. Not even Mark. I mean, I thought I did, because he took so much from our family, but I . . ."

The tears began running down his face, more tears than he'd ever shed before in his life, at least that I knew about. The DA asked the judge for permission to stop a minute, and my father's attorney led him from the room for a fifteen-minute recess.

He was sorry, or at least as remorseful as he knew how to be. I didn't need to hear any more. I left the courtroom, feeling my stepmother's eyes bore into my back. Corrie followed closely behind me.

I knew that, even given his convictions, he would never have killed Mark—not for me, even though he believed in every tenet of the Mormon Faith. He even believed in the one called *blood atonement,* a principle only the most diligent and faithful Saints still practiced. Some sins could only be forgiven if the blood of the sinner was shed. Evidently, I wasn't worth it.

"Allison, I'm going back to San Francisco," Corrie said. "Christy and Mo want me to live there, and I found a singles ward I like."

"You're going back to the church?" I was astounded to hear she planned to return to the institution that had been the source for all the trials in our lives. I couldn't fathom stepping foot inside another Mormon chapel for the rest of my life. It hurt just to drive by one.

"It's our heritage. It's part of who we are. You can't run away from that. You might as well try to resign from being a Jew."

"But, Corrie, those bishops, those men, they have a responsibility here! They never stopped Mark. The patriarchy in this religion is so oppressive a woman can never function in it and still be a recognizable human being!"

"Get off your soapbox, Allison. The truth is I still see more good in it than I see bad. Do I believe it's the only true church? No. Not anymore. I used to, but my eyes have been opened. But it's the only familiar thing I have in my life now. It's a comfort, I guess. We're all just human. No different than anyone else. It's time to move on. Time to forgive. These men are just doing the best they know how."

I just shook my head. "And how are you going to explain your living arrangements to the ward members? Do you think they'll approve of our lesbian sister and her lover?"

"I don't care if they do or not. That's between me and God."

I knew I would never return to the chapels of my youth and pray to the same God as the men whose decisions had wreaked havoc on my life and the lives of those I loved. Would I ever lose this anger? Forever, I would remember my mother dying to have another baby to populate my father's kingdom in Heaven. I would remember Kevin, who died while trying to convert people to join a religion most of them had never heard of when he was still nothing more than a boy himself. Could I ever not blame the men? Maybe, but the system needed to change.

Even Mark Peterson was a victim. He'd been abused as a child by someone he was taught to respect, and lived the rest of his life hiding his pain. He also hid the fact he had witnessed a murder. I didn't exactly forgive him, but I understood, now, why it had happened.

He had lived every day with the guilt of his unhealthy longings; and when he finally went too far, he could no longer abide himself. Perhaps if someone had stopped him years ago he could have been helped. Perhaps.

"It's not the church that's bad, Allison. It's the people who make it that way. You have to remember that."

Corrie turned and walked away. In the parking lot of the courthouse, I watched as she drove off in her minivan, the one that would never transport the score of little Petersons she must have imagined when she bought it. The Mormon bumper sticker on the left side of her bumper read FAMILIES ARE FOREVER. Another sticker on the right proclaimed CTR, for "Choose the Right." And in the middle, torn and faded, were the words AS I HAVE LOVED YOU, LOVE ONE ANOTHER.

I drove out to Karen Perkins's house with the newly printed copy of *Salt Lake City Magazine*. She'd agreed to be quoted in the story I wrote about Mark and what had happened. Tomorrow, the story would hit newsstands, and my popularity among the Mormons, already shaky because my father's case had garnered negative national media attention, would plummet even further. I wondered how I would feel in the morning. Right now, I was numb.

I knocked on Karen's door, and when she opened it I handed her the magazine. She invited me in, and I saw her daughter, a wraith dressed in black, face ghostly white, hair of ebony, as she moved from the kitchen to another room down a hallway. She only stared at me, didn't speak, and I knew I'd just encountered another ghost, one that walked among the living but didn't really belong here.

I remembered Karen telling me how the little girl had screamed whenever a man came near her for the first two years after her attack. I wanted to help her but knew I couldn't.

Karen read the story through tears, her left hand holding the magazine, her right clenched over her mouth. She set it down when she finished and reached out to me. We hugged, and I let her cry a little more.

"I called a lawyer, Allison. I've decided to sue the

bishop and the church. I know I won't win. But like you said, maybe the publicity alone will be enough to stop this from happening again."

"I'll be right by your side," I assured her.

Fifty-nine

Basketball Pete moved out of the house three months after I moved in, right around the time Jake and I began sharing a bed. Jake had become an anchor, allowing me to rest with more peace than I could ever remember.

The first time we had sex I cried through the entire act. He kept trying to stop, but I wouldn't let him. Neither one of us gained any satisfaction from that endeavor, and it was two months before we tried again.

The next time was easier, more natural, and I didn't cry. I didn't feel any real pleasure, but I knew he did, and that was enough to start. My new therapist, Jennie Mitchford, assured me it was a step in the right direction. Brian had referred me to her when he learned all the details of my upbringing and subsequent rape.

"I want to be with him. He turns me on, really. But then when we actually get to that point, it's like somebody throws a switch and I freeze," I told her.

"Time, along with open communication, will fix that, Alli," she said. "Talk to Jake."

So I did, but Jake and I didn't talk of love, marriage, or babies. Perhaps that was part of the attraction he held for me, because I didn't want any of those things and neither did he. I supposed one day I might change my mind, because I was still young, but I believed I had time to wait for that day, if it ever came.

My brother's boyhood friend, Utah Highway Patrol Trooper Russell Free, tracked me down at the magazine after I went back to work and my father was sent to prison. I'd seen him at my father's trial, but I always avoided speaking with him. He stood in front of my desk, in uniform, and watched me with a look of consternation.

"Allison, why haven't you called me? I tried your number and it's been disconnected."

"I'm living with Jake."

Russell's face went white, his freckles standing out even more vividly than before; and he stared at me, speechless.

"Look, Russell, I'm sorry I didn't call you. And I'm sorry about the gun. I had Jake check and he said you just got a reprimand for loaning it to me, and I'm grateful for that."

His boyish face showed how hurt he was, and I felt like a callous woman.

"Russell, the truth is you're just too close to home for me, okay? Every time I look at your face I see Kevin, or my father. You remind me of everything I want to leave behind. It's not you, but the situation. I can't go back there now. I'm sorry."

He turned and left, still without speaking.

Three weeks later I received an envelope at the magazine marked PERSONAL. Inside was a card with a big smiley face on the cover.

> *Allison, I understand. It hurts, but I do. I wish you the best. You're a wonderful person. Don't ever forget that. Love, Russell.*

I'd been right. Russell was one of the good guys.

Sixty

Despite what I'd told my father, I had never requested my name be removed from the records of the Church of Jesus Christ of Latter-day Saints. I knew that would all be taken care of for me, once my story hit the streets of Salt Lake City.

One week after the article was published, my step-mother called me at the magazine, her familiar frosty tones grating on my nerves like nails on a blackboard.

"Allison, it's Eileen."

"What do you want?"

"You could at least be civil."

I sighed. "Look, Eileen, I'm working. What is it you need? And don't ask me to go visit my father."

"The bishop of your ward just called. They tried your number, but it was disconnected."

"And you're telling me this why? You and Dad are the ones who told them where I lived anyway. I never wanted any contact with them."

The church had an excellent tracking system. I'd joked with friends that they should market it and sell it to the FBI and CIA. In our Mormon community, there was always a friend or family member willing to turn your contact information over so you could be brought back into the fold.

"Allison, this is serious. He said you need to call him right away. They're convening a bishop's court. You're probably going to get excommunicated."

"Good," I said as I hung up.

That night the phone rang and Jake answered it with a surly, "Hello."

He didn't like the phone for some reason.

"Who the hell is this? Bishop who? Did she call you? How did you get this number?"

Almost feeling sorry for the hapless bishop, I pulled the receiver away from him. "This is Allison Jensen."

"Sister Jensen, this is Bishop Hansen of your ward."

"I'm not your sister and I don't have a ward." His tone and implied familiarity set my defenses on alert. I wished I'd let Jake handle the call. "How *did* you get this number?"

The man on the other end of the line sighed deeply, as though dealing with morons was more than he could handle, and slowly explained, "I'm the bishop of your ward in the Avenues. I know you didn't attend church here, but I'm still your bishop. I've been contacted by the leaders of the church and informed that I'm to schedule a Bishop's Court to discuss your membership."

"Take my name off."

"What?"

"I don't want to be a Mormon. It's all a load of crap."

"Sister Jensen—"

"I'm *not* your sister."

"Are you saying you don't wish to present a defense at the bishop's court? I'll be forced to excommunicate—"

"Listen carefully, Mr. Hansen. I want my *name* taken off your records, and I want it taken off yesterday! I'm not coming to any stupid Bishop's Court. And don't think you can just excommunicate me and not do as I ask, because I have rights, and I also have a lawyer. Do you know I work for *Salt Lake City Magazine*? I presume you know that, since that's the reason they're trying to excommunicate me! If you so much as put the letters E-X on my records, I'll sue the Mormon Church into next week!"

I finally ran out of steam, but the line was silent, as though Bishop Addle-head expected me to say more.

"Well?" I demanded. The answer was a dial tone.

I put the receiver back on the hook and turned to see Jake watching me with an amused smile.

"Wonder how they got the number."

"Cathy probably told my stepmother," I said, a knot of tension forming in my neck.

"You won't win against the church," he said, "but I'm sure as hell looking forward to seeing you try."

Sixty-one

I understand now why I can't leave Utah, although I will never be a genuine part of the masses. My ghosts are here, and I can't leave them behind. They are a part of me now, my friends, and I cannot betray their memory.

Once every six months, Corrie comes back to Utah, and we meet at the Farmington Cemetery, carrying fresh flowers in the spring and summer, and artificial ones in the winter. We don't talk much as we get out of our cars, nodding to each other and wending our way down the path to the graves we have come to visit.

We stop first at Elise Marie's, a small plot with a headstone engraved with a cherubic angel. ELISE MARIE PETERSON, BELOVED DAUGHTER OF CORRIE JENSEN PETERSON, BELOVED NIECE OF ALLISON MARIE JENSEN, BELOVED GRANDDAUGHTER OF ELISE SMITH JENSEN, DIED APRIL 30, 1987.

Corrie refused to sully the grave with any mention of Elise's father or grandfather. We had been raised by a religious tyrant, and he colored our choices in men terribly. Now we were left to pick up the pieces while he wasted away at the Utah State Prison, still cloaked in his self-deception. He would never waver from his belief he was living God's word.

Elise's tiny grave is directly across from my mother's larger one. We were lucky to be able to purchase the small plot from a family who had fallen on hard times and had to sell it quickly. So, this year again, after we laid the sunflowers in front of Elise's headstone, we crossed to Mom's grave. I'd been lucky to find some early blooming lilacs on one of my daily runs along the Avenues. Lilacs had been her favorite flower, both in color and aroma. She had planted bushes of them all around our yard at the Farmington house and clapped her hands in delight at the first sign of a tender bloom.

"I miss you, Mom," I whispered, as I knelt down and touched the headstone.

"Do you think she would have let Dad go as far as he did?" Corrie asked, breaking our customary silence.

I pondered the question. "I don't know, Corrie. She believed it, too, but never with the fervor he did. So, probably not. I think she would have wanted to protect us. At least, I like to think that."

As we walked to the last grave, we fell back into our companionable silence. This was a different site, one that had a fancy marble angel with beautiful snowy wings and a cherubic expression. This grave held no body, for there had been none to place here. The answers I'd searched for all my life would always lie hidden with Cindy's eight-year-old body.

This site had been built in her memory, and Nancy told me about it in one of her now-weekly phone calls. My eyes had widened with delight the first time I saw it. Mormon angels don't have wings, at least not in the pictures we'd seen in Primary and Sunday school, but this one sported a pair of beautiful, wide-spanned wings that would take her on glorious journeys.

I carefully placed the wreath of sunflowers around the

head of the angel and stood back. The bright yellow and rich-hued brown of the big flowers reflected nicely off the white stone, and I knew Cindy would be pleased.

Perhaps tonight in my dreams she would open her eyes and talk to me, smile at me, tell me how or where she was. I looked forward to it.

After we visited the graves, Corrie and I hugged briefly, and, as always, she got into her van and drove away. She'd probably stop at a motel in Wendover and spend the night before continuing her journey back to California. She never stayed in Utah. It was too painful for her.

I had another grave to visit, one located at the Avenues Cemetery. I visited once a week at least, and sometimes three or four times. I'd seen Frank's daughter and mother there on the last two visits.

The first time I was shocked, sure they must blame me for what happened. Frank's mother merely reached out a hand and squeezed my arm tightly, and her granddaughter watched me.

The second time they both just smiled at me. I'd seen them at the trial and wondered what they thought of me. I was too afraid of the answer to ask. Maybe someday I would.

Today, I walked across the lawn, carefully avoiding the flat tombstones that marked the last resting places of many Utahans; and when I arrived at Frank's gravesite, I sat on the grass next to it.

"Well, it's been almost a year since you died, Frank. Can you believe it? I brought you some lilacs. They were my mother's favorite. I don't know what kind of flowers you like. Last time I was here I saw some tulips. Was that your mother?"

I looked around the wide expanse of the cemetery, seeing a mother and young child holding each other and crying at the site of a fresh grave. All around me were the fresh-cut flowers of spring, decorating the landscape in bright floral patterns.

"Yes, it was me."

The woman's voice, rich in tone and almost regal, startled me. I scrambled to my feet, dusting off the seat of my pants, and I looked Frank's mother in the eyes. She was tall, and had white hair I knew had once carried the same black sheen his had. Her eyes were kind, and the fireworks in my stomach eased a little.

Frank's daughter was not with her today, and I felt some relief I wouldn't have to face her.

"I'm sorry I startled you," she said. "I see you here a lot. Frank told me about you, you know."

"He did?"

"Yes, he thought you were very special."

The thought of Frank speaking of me to his mother made me smile widely.

"That's what he really loved about you. Your smile. He said it lit up the entire room."

"I never got the chance to know him very well. I'll never forgive my father—"

"Allison, Frank would have wanted you to move on. It's over. Your father is serving out his sentence in Hell. I'm angry with him for what he did to Frank, and also for what he did to you. I heard things in that courtroom that made me very sad for you and your brother and sisters. But even though I'm angry with him, I'm not going to let it destroy me. You shouldn't, either. Frank wouldn't have wanted that."

"No, he wouldn't have."

We stood at the grave for a few more minutes, both of us silent; and then she knelt, touched the tips of her fingers to her mouth, kissed them, and laid her palm on the grave marker.

"Remember, Allison. Frank wanted you to be happy."

"I'm not sure I know how."

"You'll figure it out. And I think you'll always have Frank there as your guardian angel, watching over you."

The memory of Frank telling me everything would be okay was still strong in my mind, and I decided she was right. Maybe, with Frank watching over me, I would. If anyone could use a guardian angel, surely it was me, if for nothing more than to corral the ghosts that still haunted my nights. Perhaps tonight, I would finally sleep well.

Sandra told me I was strong, and I would survive all that happened for that reason. I still wasn't sure, but I knew I owed it to Frank, Kevin, my mother, and most of all to Cindy, to fully live the life I still had. I owed it to them to be happy.

Most of all, I owed it to myself.

Read on for an excerpt from

the next novel by Natalie R. Collins

Behind Closed Doors

Coming soon in hardcover from St. Martin's Press

PROLOGUE

I am Sarah.

At least, that is the new—and secret—name I was given by the temple worker during my endowments several months ago, shortly before I bailed on my wedding. I would not answer to this name if you hailed me with it on the street. In fact, I would probably not even realize you were talking to me.

I need this name so my husband can use it to recognize and acknowledge me and pull me through the veil—which separates this life from the Celestial Kingdom—into Heaven. Since I have no husband, and the only man who knows it is complete anathema to me, it seems a moot point. I don't consider myself Sarah. I am—as I have always been—Janica Emily Fox.

My best friend Melissa has been wild-eyed and slightly freaked out for the past few minutes, ever since the elderly female temple worker reached under the white vestment and blessed her various parts, washing and anointing her and providing her with the garment of the Holy Priesthood. After that, she put on all the temple garb—worn over her beautiful dress—before she was paraded through the various rooms and movies that make up the endowment ceremony. That's around the time she got her new secret name, too, and I wonder how that makes her feel. Was it as strange and unsettling to her as it had been to me?

I'm sure that the new name, along with trying to learn the secret handshakes and passwords that guarantee one's entry into Heaven, have really thrown her off on this day that is supposed to be the most special in a young Mormon girl's life. They don't call them handshakes, of course, or even handclasps, which is more representative of what they encompass. They are called tokens, and along with the signs, they come with an ominous overtone—penalties for revealing the sacred description of the rite. You don't tell people what goes on in the temple. Not without horrible consequences. The powers that be are vague about what those are, but they include the wrath of God, a threat that has left me terrified all of my life.

Knowing Melissa the way I do, having been her best friend for the past twenty years, I knew she wouldn't much like that part of the temple ceremony. The endowment was one of the most bizarre rituals I have ever endured, and my former fiancé swears it led me to bolt before our actual wedding ceremony took place.

He is only partly right. But today is not about me, or Brian Williams, who watches me now from the other side of the room, glowering slightly, as if to say, "This should be us. We should be kneeling before the altar."

This is Melissa's wedding day. The pallor from her slight state of shock has worn off, and she is radiant, beaming with her happiness, almost as though she has completely forgotten what came before. Only I know that's not true. Her arms by her sides, her fingers play a piano scale up and down her legs, always the telltale sign she is nervous. She doesn't show much outwardly. She never has. Melissa has confidence by the gallon jug, and doesn't allow many people to see through to the vulnerable person who exists inside all young women, brought on by the terrors and uncertainty of adolescence and the expectations of adulthood. But I know it's there because I know her. No one knows her like I do.

And no one really knows what to expect on their wedding day inside the temple of the Church of Jesus Christ of Latter-day Saints. These things are sacred, and only the most worthy enter here. You don't get much preparation. She begged me to tell her, but I wouldn't—I couldn't. Now, the worst part is over, and she is waiting for her husband to pull her through the veil which symbolizes the entrance to the Celestial Kingdom, so they can be sealed for time and all eternity.

She looks lovely. Even though I cannot see her modest white gown, which I helped her pick out, I know it features intricate beading, a tight bodice, and cap sleeves that will cover her garments—the Mormon underwear she will wear from this day forward. The reason I can't see her wedding finery is because she is wearing the Mormon temple garb over them—a green fig leaf apron over a bulky robe, one that fits over one shoulder and then is tied with a sash that must fit over the top part of the green apron, with the bow of the sash on the right hip. It's all part of the ritual.

All the dramas, including the fall of Adam and Eve from the Garden of Eden, have been acted out, played before us on a movie screen. All that is left is the sealing, and it is simple, and sweet, and nothing like the dramatic and terrifying endowments. At least, I found them terrifying; my mother always claims to have found them soothing. I spent the majority of the time worrying about how I was going to remember all those signs so my Father in Heaven would know to let me into His kingdom, and suffering an extreme form of claustrophobia that reached boiling point right as Brian was calling my new name to guide me through the veil.

I could not answer to Sarah.

Melissa's parents watch, smiling and nodding, happy and complete in their daughter's achievement—an eternal Temple marriage. Michael's parents, standing next to them, are beaming. My parents also watch Melissa, although my mother's face is easy to read. Why Pete and Angela's daughter? Why not hers? Why did *her* daughter turn tail and run, thrash her way out of the temple, and require paramedics to be called to calm her hysteria? The little old lady serving as a temple matron whom I had knocked down in my desperation to find an exit had also required medical attention. Three days later, I called my wedding off. Melissa begged me to tell her what had me so freaked out, but I couldn't. I took an oath.

So she bravely withstood her own endowment nightmare (she'd whispered to me afterward, "That was very weird"), but the slightly wild look in her eyes when we first entered this sealing room is gone; she now seems quite calm and serene.

The room itself is unremarkable, unlike other parts of the temple, which are elegantly and elaborately decorated. The walls are mirrored, and in the middle is an altar where Melissa kneels on one side and Michael on the other. They take each other's right hand in the "Patriarchal Grip," the Second Token of the Melchizedek Priesthood, also known as the Sure Sign of the Nail, thumbs and little fingers interlocked, and index fingers placed on the wrist just above the hand. Melissa fumbles around with it a bit, and blushes, as all around them stand the signs of achievement in Mormondom—worthy, temple-recommend-holding adults watching in benign love and grace as yet another young couple commits their lives to God and the Church. It is quiet and peaceful. There is no music. No flowers. No young children dressed in their Sunday fineries, playing tag around the feet of the adults. No celebration. It's . . . a little bland.

Michael looks proud, slightly arrogant (as he always has), but also a little humble (which he rarely is). His vanity and calm "take-charge" manner has always attracted Melissa. Her mother is a little flighty and given to nervous spells where she takes to bed, when she isn't ordering her family around; and her father is quiet, and meek, and unable to hold down a job for longer than a year at a time. I am sure Michael will always be strong and the leader of his family because that is what she has always wanted—a priesthood holder, a man to lead and support his family. I know Michael will always do that. He is—well, a take-charge kind of guy.

My Brian—my ex-Brian, I should say—has always tried to be the same way, but he paled in comparison to Michael. He is a "second-in-command" type, always waiting for Michael to lead the way. All through school, there was Michael and following behind, albeit closely, there was Brian. They looked enough alike they could be brothers, both tall with dark brown hair, broad shoulders, and strong, handsome, sturdy features. But whatever Brian did, Michael usually did it better. Brian got used to letting someone else lead, and so he looked to me to make all the decisions in our relationship, our upcoming nuptials, our marriage.

Poor Brian was always slightly outside, all throughout our childhood and growing up because his *parents* were outsiders. They were Gentiles—non-Mormons—who had allowed their only child to be baptized Mormon so he would fit into our predominantly Mormon community. Because he didn't have the parental backing we did, the family heraldry of Mormonism, he never pushed ahead to lead our group. There were only a few times where he had taken the lead, where he had pushed to be my patriarch, my Priesthood holder, and the results had been disastrous. So he backed off and let me lead—and I did. I made the decision that I would never again set foot inside this temple and endure something as creepy as the endowment ceremony.

Luckily for me, I had only bolted my marriage and sealing and had already endured the endowment, so I was able to see Melissa be married—I still had a valid temple recommend. Others were not so lucky, like our school friends who weren't yet married or hadn't gone on missions, or her younger brothers and sisters. It had taken all the strength I had—and some Xanax we stole from Melissa's mother—to get me back through these doors.

When the brief ceremony is over, everyone congratulates the couple as they stand together and smile. It is quiet, and we all hug them quickly, then shuffle out and down to the dressing rooms to change into our street clothes—or in my case, my sea-foam green bridesmaid's dress and dyed-to-match shoes—so we can stand in front of the Temple and on the grounds and have our pictures taken. There are no photos allowed inside the sacred temples of my birth religion.

Melissa holds Michael's hand tightly for one more minute, and then they separate, but not before sharing bright smiles. She follows me to the ladies' dressing room, although, as the bride, she has her own special room where only she and her mother can go. In that room, she will remove her temple wear and put on the beautiful veil that came with her gown in place of the simple veil worn for the ceremony.

"Well, Mrs. Melissa Holt, how do you feel?" I ask her.

"I'm so happy. I've been waiting for this all my life."

CHAPTER ONE

Five years later

I got the call that changed my life forever around ten A.M. on Tuesday, June 28.

The coffee I had poured thirty minutes before had gone cold as I stared into my computer screen and talked on the phone, arranging for a restraining order against the husband of one of my repeat clients. Debbie Talon floated in and out of our shelter every several months, convinced her husband Brandon was going to kill her. I was convinced, too, but it made no difference. Debbie always returned to him, and they always paid a reunion visit to their bishop, who praised their decision to keep the family unit together. In another couple of months, Debbie knocked on our door again, dragging with her a four-year-old son, eight-year-old daughter, and, once, a fetus that didn't live through the night, having been punched and kicked to death while still inside his mother's body.

The Salt Lake City Police Department had finally gotten involved after the last one, even though Debbie begged everyone, including me, not to tell them. She loved Brandon. He was her eternal companion.

Somehow, her eternal companion convinced them she was clumsy and fell down the stairs. No charges were filed, but they were watching him. Without Debbie's testimony, they could do little because there was no proof that anything except a terrible fall had happened. She backed up the "clumsy" story. They knew what I knew, even though they couldn't—and some wouldn't—move against a fellow priesthood holder without black-and-white proof—apparently, black-and-blue was not enough.

Yesterday, she had shown up with a new complaint—a multicolored patch on her daughter's back. This time, she swore she wouldn't return, wouldn't put up with this, wouldn't even call her bishop. I knew better, but maybe Brandon didn't. So for now, I would try to get her restraining order, even while knowing it was probably pointless.

I arranged the order and wrote down instructions for Debbie—which she would undoubtedly ignore. After I was done, I picked up the mug and took a sip of tepid coffee and almost spit it back out. Blah. Coffee was evil. I knew that. If anyone from my past life—the one I led before I first attended a session in the Mormon LDS Temple—saw me, they would be shocked.

I was not honest with those who knew me from before. It pained me, but it was necessary. I could not handle their pressure. It was just easier to pretend I still believed, that I attended church on a regular basis, that I never drank coffee or alcohol, or even thought about sex. Of course, the last was not true at all. I thought about it all the time. I just wasn't doing it.

I stood up to refresh my coffee, the phone rang, and I sighed. Some other disaster, some other abuser, some other horrible omen or event to attend to—maybe even Sunday dinner at my parents' house, where I would be grilled endlessly about the Singles Ward I told them I attended, and about any possible prospects for marriage, and—worst of all—whether or not I had considered going on a mission.

Since I wasn't married, and showed no signs of ever being so, that was expected of me. It was the fate of all old maids. Next month I would be twenty-six years old.

"Oh, Jannie," came my mother's voice over the line.

I'd been right. Somebody give me a quarter and call me Madame Zelda.

But I didn't correctly predict what she would say next.

"Jannie, something terrible has happened. Lissa is missing. She's been gone half the day. She never showed up for work, and, Jannie? Jannie, are you listening?"

My mother needed constant reinforcement that everyone within miles was attuned to the sound of her voice. The scary part was they usually were.

"I'm listening, Mom. I'm just in shock."

Melissa, my long-time friend, had been missing for six hours and everyone was getting frantic. Steady, dependable Melissa, who always reined her emotions in, would not just up and disappear. She would never just *not* show up to work, or fail to call in, so we all knew that something was wrong.

"Please come," my mother said, her words compact and tight, her unusual brevity a sign that things were horribly out of kilter.

I left my desk at the YWCA Women's Shelter, hurried down the long hallway to my boss's office, and popped my head in the door, quickly explaining that I needed to leave, to join the search party combing the canyons behind Michael and Melissa's apartment. Millicent Stone, a fifty-year-old former Catholic nun who had saved more women from monsters than any knight in shining armor could ever claim to have done, understood completely. Millie was small of frame and stature, with short, close-cropped grey hair, a heavily lined face, and eyes that expressed more than she could ever say in words. There was usually a touch of sorrow in those eyes. In our line of work, disaster is always little more than a phone call away. We've learned to adapt.

As I drove my Honda Civic toward the Canyon View Stake Center, where the command post for Melissa's search had been set up, fear raced through my mind. Surely Melissa had just lost track of time, or thought she had arranged for sick leave because she had a prior engagement.

But what if that wasn't that case? What if she had been kidnapped, taken by an unknown assailant for nefarious purposes? Although I knew the odds of that were slim, the case of Elizabeth Smart still loomed in my mind. *The obvious suspects are those closest to the victim. Stranger abduction is rare. Look first at the family.* As a domestic abuse counselor, these were my mantras.

But Michael and Melissa had a strong relationship. She laughed sometimes, and I frowned and fought to keep from speaking my mind because he always wanted to know where she was, who she was with, what she was doing. He bought her a cell phone and then had to up the minutes because he called her so often they were hit with huge overage charges. Sometimes, when we were together, she'd sigh when the phone would ring. No one else called her. It was always Michael.

But she loved him. And he adored her. I remember him serenading her, back when we were in high school, singing silly, sappy romantic tunes and then sulking when she laughed at him, even though she did it kindly.

They had problems, but who didn't? I couldn't even stay in a relationship for twenty minutes. Michael would never lay a hand on her. So who would hurt Melissa? Was she dead? *No, no, don't think that way. No! She's fine. She just got busy and forgot to go to work, and to call in and tell them, and to . . .*

Everyone loved her. She was the type of person who really listened, who met new people and immediately knew everything about them, all their secrets spilling out, and they walked away saying "What a nice person" without even realizing they knew absolutely nothing about her.

Melissa even knew *my* secret, one I had shared with no one else.

My cell phone rang, and I answered with a quick and breathless hello, praying it was someone calling to tell me that Melissa was fine.

"Jannie, it's Brian. Melissa is missing. Have you seen her?"

His voice sent a cold chill down my spine, and I felt the fear, the anger, and the claustrophobia return. God help me, I really hated him. It wasn't healthy. I kept my voice calm and modulated.

"No, Brian, but my mom called me. I'm on my way."

"Good. Michael needs support. Lissa's car has been found in the parking lot of the 7-Eleven close to their house. It doesn't look good."

I felt as though someone had punched me in the stomach. I didn't want to hear this.

"Why would she have gone there?" I asked, after a moment's silence.

"She went to buy milk. Mike says they were out of it, and she told him she was going to go get some, even woke him up, since he was sleeping. She left, he went back to sleep, and when he woke up again, it was ten A.M. He just figured she let him sleep and went to work. And you can find out more when you come here. You're great at supporting your friends. You've always been good at supporting everyone but me." He disconnected. I guess he hated me, too. I'd broken his heart. His lack of spirit and chivalry had broken mine. If only my relationship had been more like the one Mike and Melissa shared.

Melissa . . .

Flashes of the last time I'd seen her played through my mind. It had been an odd encounter. She'd shown up at my doorstep around seven-thirty one evening the week before. We hadn't seen each other in months and had only talked on the phone once or twice. So, to open the door and see her standing there was a bit of a shock.

Her long brown hair was swept back into a harsh ponytail, and her dark brown eyes seemed deeper-set than normal, surrounded by hollows that spoke of sleepless nights and stresses that I, in my single and unencumbered state, could not begin to imagine. I knew Michael and Lissa struggled for money—her job working as a secretary for an insurance company was not terribly high-paying, but she'd never gone to college, opting instead to marry young and support Michael while he attended first college and then medical school.

"Can you keep this for me?" she asked, without even a hello. She thrust a medium-size shoebox toward me, and I reached out and grabbed it, stumbling a bit from the force of her movement. I put my hand on the doorway to steady myself.

"Geez, Liss, what's up? You don't look great. Why don't you come in and I'll—"

"I can't stay. I need to get home. Mike will be home soon for dinner. Just keep it for me, okay? Someplace safe?"

"What is it?"

She tightened her lips and shook her head twice, standard Melissa posturing for things she did not wish to discuss. I was used to this type of behavior with her. Growing up, it had usually signaled one of her mother's bad spells. What that could possibly have to do with the box I held I didn't know, but I knew I wasn't going to get it out of her until she was ready. Eventually, she would tell me. She always did.

"Okay, it's not anything live, is it?" I asked jokingly, trying to coax a smile out of her. "Something that will smell my place up if I ignore it for too long?"

She finally smiled—not the full, open, wide-mouthed smile she usually displayed and for which she had received one of those silly Senior Spectacular awards at graduation—but a smile, nonetheless.

"Are you sure you don't want to talk?"

"Not today," she answered. "I have to go. Thanks, Jannie. I really appreciate it."

And she turned and left.

"Oh, my God. The box," I said with a gasp, as fear gripped me. Could the box she'd left with me be connected to this? Her behavior had been strange, her conversation terse, her smile forced. Now she was missing. What, if anything, did the box have to do with it?

Instead of heading straight up 400 East in downtown Salt Lake City, I flipped on my blinker and moved over to the right-turn lane and headed south on 700 East. I had a small apartment in Sugarhouse, and although it seemed a long shot, perhaps I would find the answers to Melissa's disappearance there.

I had to open that box and find out what was inside it.